IN THE

DEAD

OF THE

NIGHT

ERIN BOWMAN

Published by Bolt Books

Copyright © 2024 by Erin Bowman

This is a work of fiction. The names, characters, and events in this book
are products of the author's imagination or are used fictitiously. Any
similarity to real persons—living or dead—is coincidental.

ISBN (paperback): 979-8989707171
ISBN (e-book): 979-8989707188

Cover design by Erin Bowman
Cover photography by Paul Pastourmatzis, Ján Jakub Naništa, and
Kalen Emsley

First edition

For the scrappy girls with big dreams

CHAPTER
ONE

arrive at the lake house shortly after 2 a.m., cold and exhausted and dripping with rainwater.

I slip inside and silence the alarm. Drop my backpack and duffel unceremoniously in the entryway. It's dark—pitch black—but I don't reach for the lights. It's better this way. Helps me avoid the family portraits that line the walls, hanging happily in their frames, each one a lie.

I can picture the photo to my right, just beside the light switch. Eight-year-old me, springy and small and as buoyant as a red helium balloon. Mom and Dad are standing behind me, him with his hand on my shoulder. In the photo, he's smiling like he means it.

He's good at that, it turns out. Pretending.

I shed my waterlogged shoes and lightweight raincoat, and step deeper into the house, moving by memory. In the living room, with the threat of pictures behind me,

I finally turn on the lights, cringing in the sudden brightness.

Exposed beams stretch overhead, spanning the width of the A-frame ceiling. The great fireplace is empty, unused since the last time I was here—a weekend visit over the winter with Mom. A flat-screen is mounted above the chunky, cedar mantel. It's off and will stay that way. I have no intention of turning on the news.

I pull my phone from my back pocket. Service is non-existent here, but I use the Wi-Fi calling to phone Mom, ignoring the dozens of new text, email, and DM alerts that ping and chime in my ear once I'm connected to the internet. Mom picks up on the second ring.

"Eleanor, where *are* you?"

"I couldn't be there any anymore. I came up to Corwin early. I'm staying at Bradley House until camp starts."

"Jesus. You could have at least told me before you left. I've been worried sick."

"I'm sorry. I just wanted to be alone, and I was due to come later today. I figured arriving a few hours earlier wouldn't matter."

She makes a tiny noise, a *hmph* of annoyance.

I collapse onto the couch, put my feet on a coffee table Mom found at an estate sale a couple years back. Across the room is a wall of windows. It's too dark to see the lake beyond them, or even the deck that wraps around the house. Instead, only my reflection looks back at me. I'm wide-eyed, pale—like I've seen a ghost.

"I'll be back in August," I tell her. "Call the office if

you need me? There's never cell service at camp." I don't ask if she's coming to Bradley House the first week of July, when our family typically arrives every summer. She'll be preoccupied for a while. Dad made sure of that.

"How did you even get up there?" Mom's voice switches from curious to annoyed. "I saw you didn't take the car."

"Kylie drove me." It's easier than the truth, which is that I took the C to Penn Station and then a bus to Albany, where I hitchhiked the rest of the way. Camp Durant has a shuttle that transports staff from that bus stop to the campgrounds, but it won't run until 5 p.m. Saturday. It's currently the wee hours of Saturday morning, and when I left the city last night, even that short wait felt impossible. I just wanted to be alone—away from the public, my own friends, social media—as soon as humanly possible.

"Kylie drove you?" she repeats, sounding equal parts relieved and annoyed.

"Yeah."

She's too busy to confirm it with Kylie's parents. Even now, I picture her obsessively watching the news. Or maybe standing at the window of our eighth-floor apartment. That's where she'd been when I left. Staring down at the waterlogged sidewalks of East 75th and waiting for him to come home. As if returning could fix things.

It won't. That's why he ran.

"Okay. Well, I'm glad you're safe," she says. "Maybe I'll swing by in a few days. If things calm down a little."

I can hear the hope in her voice, but she was holding a

mug of coffee when the feds showed up at the apartment this morning, and she was still holding it when I left, the drink cold and untouched. I wouldn't be surprised if she's still holding it now.

"Mom?"

"Hmm?"

"Don't wait for him too long. He doesn't deserve it."

"We said vows, Eleanor. For better or worse. This is the *worse*. I can't bail just because it got hard."

But that's exactly what he did, I want to remind her. "Right," I say instead. "Okay. Love you, Mom."

"Love you, too."

I hang up, disconnect from the Wi-Fi, and toss my phone onto the coffee table. Then I lean back on the couch, wet clothes and all, and sleep like the dead.

CHAPTER
TWO

When Sunday morning dawns, I'm on edge and dreading the next twenty-four hours. They will undoubtably be the hardest. Potentially harder than the first twenty-four after the scandal broke. That awful period when my phone pinged nonstop with texts. When my DMs exploded with hate— some from strangers, most from people I had considered friends just days earlier.

My throat constricts. I exhale hard.

It's been better since I got up here, my phone falling silent with the lack of service. But today, I have to face people again. None of them my classmates of course, just the staff of Camp Durant for the summer season, but still.

My stomach is too uneasy for breakfast, so I gather my things. My white All Star sneakers are finally dry from Friday night's rain. I pull them on, grab my gear, and head downstairs.

The front door I used the other night leads to the driveway and the county road. But Bradley House is built into a hill, and the slider in the downstairs family room puts me at ground level facing the lake.

It's cool and damp outside, and the wrap-around deck overhead leaves me shivering in its shadow. Before me, a winding trail of stone steps carves down the steep terrain and ends where the dock extends into the water. A whirligig loon mounted to a post idly spins its black wings. Mom and I got it at an arts festival in Inlet last summer, when Dad had locked himself in his office, too busy working to see an ounce of sunlight, let alone his family.

God, I hate him. Him and this mess he left behind.

I descend the steps, careful to watch my footing on the moss-covered rocks. Mist rolls off the lake in twirling ribbons. It's thick enough that I can't see more than a stone's throw beyond the dock, but two miles north lies Camp Durant, where I'm due to check in for staff orientation by nine. It will be tight. I have to kayak. Because I'm car-less. And because the main road is far less direct than the water and will take me even longer to walk.

I wrestle the kayak out of the boathouse—it's still in storage from the winter, hanging from the rafters, and I nearly kill myself getting it down. By the time all my gear is loaded—duffel stuffed inside between my legs, backpack strapped to the front under the cargo elastics—it's almost eight.

The kayak cuts through the water like a knife in butter as I push off.

It's calm this morning. Still. Barely a breeze. And a good thing, too. Two miles paddling is no easy feat. Somewhere beyond the fog, a loon cries mournfully. The wail sends a shiver up my limbs, and I suddenly feel as though I'm being watched, as though a pair of eyes lurks deep within the fog, tracking my every move. I half expect a reporter to jump forward, microphone extended, or a classmate to appear, hurling insults. I even check my phone, but of course there's no service. Which is what I wanted.

I dip the paddle in, pull, lift, dip the opposite side, pull again. Over and over. My palms sting in protest. The more progress I make, the more the knot of nerves tightens in my chest.

This won't be like when I was a kid, heading to Camp Durant for the summer and reconnecting with friends from all over the northeast. It's been five years since I fit the age range to attend as a camper. Five years since Mom and Dad shelled out several thousand dollars for a full-summer, seven-week session of swimming and canoeing and campfires at one of the Adirondack's most prestigious summer camps.

After I turned thirteen, I spent the summers at Bradley House instead of camp. Mom filled her days drinking wine. Dad worked constantly. I sat on the docks, bored out of my mind for a variety of reasons, depending on the

7

year. The first summer, it was because I was missing my camp friends. The next because Kylie had to visit her grandparents on the Cape and couldn't spend the summer with me. Last summer, it was because Mom refused to let me have even a sip of her wine and wouldn't let me out of her sight either, because maybe then I might see other humans my own age and they might have alcohol of their own. "Kids get into trouble without supervision," she said.

Apparently, so do husbands.

This summer, Mom decided it was time I got a job and earned my own money. She said it would be good for me. I didn't disagree, but I'd wanted to spend summer in the city, working an internship at a magazine or photography studio, and enjoying the apartment while Mom and Dad came north. It would have been good experience, a line to include on my college applications and make me stand out from the others hoping to major in photojournalism.

But since Mom doesn't control enough of my life already, she had to pick my job, too. Back in April she called in a favor to one of her best friends—an old sorority sister—and two months later, here I am: Camp Durant's newest counselor, paddling up Corwin Lake to report to orientation.

I'd never admit it to Mom, but I'm glad to be up here now. I can't imagine being in the city, Dad's headshot flashing in every news report and our family name a permanent fixture on chyrons at the bottom of each screen. I bet cameras are still lining the block outside our apartment building.

He wasn't home when the cops first showed up. Mom and I thought he was at work, but they said he wasn't at the office either; they'd tried there first. He'd disappeared.

It's like he knew it was coming. Like he knew he stood no chance. No chance with the law, and no chance of mending the broken pieces of his family, either. If he reappeared tomorrow, I wouldn't have a thing to say to him. He better keep running because he's as good as dead to me.

I wonder, for the first time, what people back home will think of *my* running. When I left New York, everyone at school had turned on me and the media was already starting to speculate about our family. How much did Mom and I know? Were we in on it? Are we as heartless and greedy and cruel as him?

The answers are nothing, and no, and of course not. But those are boring answers, and people love a scandal. Perhaps the only thing they love more than a villain is *making* villains.

I don't know what I've missed on the news this weekend, and I'm not sure I want to find out.

———

My kayak hits bottom beside the swimming area at 9:07. I'm officially late.

I scramble out, ignoring the cold morning water that

bites at my shins, and tug the kayak farther onto the sand so it doesn't float away. Fog still hovers above the lake like a moth-eaten shawl, obscuring the opposite shoreline behind a hazy white. Glancing inland, things are clearer.

Camp Durant looks unaltered by the years that have passed since I last set foot here. Already, I can sense the dampness of the place down to my bones: a sluggish, heavy weight that makes me feel lonely. I curl my toes into the wet sand and fish my sneakers from the bottom of the kayak.

Beyond the beach, several worn walking paths cut through grass, climbing the rise toward the woods. There, the pines appear weary, limbs sagging with the weight of the recent rain. The paths disappear into the trees, leading toward the cabins. I've spent enough summers here to know exactly where they'll appear between tree trunks, dank and humid and smelling of moss. Each is named after one of the Adirondacks' Great Camps, houses and estates built by the rich, and now famous for their quintessential Adirondack architecture. So quintessential, that Mom had Bradley House fashioned to mimic the style, though I'm not sure the builders pulled it off.

West of all these paths, is a small clearing that's home to the Performing Arts Building, where orientation will be held, according to an email I received a week ago. I set off at a brisk pace, knowing I'll be a solid twenty minutes late by the time I arrive.

When I finally shove inside, things are already underway. The door screeches in protest, someone speaking near the front stage pauses, and dozens of faces swivel to greet me. Most of them are young. My age. Teens working as counselors for the summer.

"Is that her?" I hear someone whisper.

"Eleanor Bradley?"

"*The* Bradley? From the news?!"

"Yeah, that's the one."

I immediately question everything. They all hate me. They hate him too, which is justified, but the way their eyes are now widening into shock and gall, as if to say, *How dare she show her face here?* is too much.

But for all the people talking about me, I realize there are just as many who look confused, clueless. They haven't placed me yet, or maybe they haven't even heard the news. Perhaps coming a few hours north *was* enough to escape the worst of things.

Someone touches my arm. A willowy woman wearing a light-blue fleece pullover and a bit too much makeup. It takes me a moment to place her. Mrs. Goodwin—owner of the camp, Mom's BFF, and the reason I have this job. "Nell, darling," she says. "I'm so glad you could join us. I didn't know if you'd be coming, not with . . . Well, why don't you grab a seat?"

Everyone is still staring.

"Hi," I announce with a small wave. "I'm Nell."

"Thief," someone coughs out from the back of the room. A few teen staff members chuckle. The older staff members bristle uncomfortably.

"You know what? Let me just get this out of the way."

I roll my shoulders back, stand a bit straighter. "Yes, my father is Duncan Bradley. Yes, he's wanted for embezzling funds from his clients. No, I don't know where he is, and no, my mom and I weren't in on it."

There, I've said it. It's out.

And just like that, the room erupts in chaos.

CHAPTER
THREE

"All right, all right, that's quite enough. Settle down." Mrs. Goodwin flaps her arms like she can stuff the outburst below the floorboards at her feet. She races for a podium. "Please. Quiet now." Everyone ignores her effortlessly. She fiddles with the diamond pendant of her necklace while desperately eyeing the older staff standing along the side of the room.

A short woman in jeans and a navy blue Camp Durant hoodie sticks her thumb and forefinger into her mouth and whistles loudly. The shrill noise instantly kills the chatter.

"Thank you," Mrs. Goodwin says. She tucks her necklace away, smooths a bit of hair behind her ears. "As I was saying before our late arrival"—her eyes dart to me—"Mrs. Towers is the camp director this year and I'm going to let her take things from here. Mrs. Towers?" She holds a hand out, passing the metaphorical mic.

"Thank you, Laura." Mrs. Towers turns out to be Whistle Lady. She's middle-aged, with mousy brown hair and a tan that suggests she spends most of her time outdoors. Despite being a good six inches shorter than Mrs. Goodwin, her energy feels larger, her blunt, clipped voice giving off the impression that she shouldn't be tested.

As she launches into a speech about responsibility and the importance of role models, I move toward the back of the room, looking for somewhere to sit. It's impossible to ignore the eyes that follow me, counselors and staff incapable of not stealing a close-up glance. My eyes connect with a girl in the back. She's pale, built like a bird, and wearing a black, long-sleeve tee that says *F*ck the Patriarchy* on the front. Her dark hair is cut into a shoulder-length bob and the ends are dyed neon pink. She jerks her chin at the empty seat beside her, mouths, "Take it."

I slip into it soundlessly.

She plucks an AirPod from one of her ears and whispers, "Hey. I'm Vivian. Viv for short."

"Eleanor. Nell for short," I say back.

She digs around in a backpack at her feet, then yanks the multitool keychain attached to the zipper to close it. "Want a piece?" She holds out a stick of gum.

"Oh. No, thanks."

She shrugs, snaps her gum in response, and slips her AirPod back in. Then she's wrestling with the multitool-keychain-zipper thing again to stow away the unwanted stick of gum.

From the stage, Mrs. Towers is still droning on about how she expects us to act like the respectable young adults she knows we are. She says cabins will be checked weekly for drugs and alcohol. We shouldn't have any of it to begin with, but she'll still be checking. After taps, it's quiet hours for us as much as the kids. She doesn't want to hear about anyone sneaking out to meet up with other staff members. She expects us to do our jobs and do them while smiling. All the while, Mrs. Goodwin stands off to the side, looking us over like we're soldiers she plans to send into battle.

When Mrs. Tower's monotone starts to make me sleepy, I dare to glance around the room.

The bulk of the audience appears college-aged or late high school, although a few look like they're in their thirties or forties. If they aren't a counselor, they're either general staff (like maintenance workers), or they're a sports or activity leader. With the amount of money parents spend to send their kids here, Camp Durant has nothing but the best on staff. When I attended as a camper, some bow-and-arrow prodigy from Arizona State ran the archery program, swimming was taught by an Olympic-hungry twenty-one-year-old, and a Broadway-bound junior at Julliard spearheaded Performing Arts. I doubt much has changed in five years.

"That about does it," Mrs. Towers says approximately five hundred hours later.

"Excellent." Mrs. Goodwin claps her hands together. "Everyone, please form a line and collect your schedules from Mrs. Towers. Lunch is at noon and then you have about an hour before campers will begin getting dropped off. The welcome bonfire is tonight at nine and everyone is invited. We hit the ground running first thing tomorrow."

The room is again filled with commotion—squeaking shoes as people stand, chairs skidding, noisy chatter. Viv and I end up last in line because she says she needs another stick of gum and by the time she'd dug through her bag to find one, everyone else is ahead of us. I don't hate it. At least at the end of the line I can't hear what they're all saying about me. Better yet, they can't ask me any questions.

Finally, Viv and I are up. She's a counselor for the girls in Pine Knot and is given their activity schedules, and a list of their allergies, medications, emergency contacts, and so on. And I have . . . no one, apparently, because Mrs. Towers can't find my papers.

"I was supposed to be a counselor?" I prompt unhelpfully.

"Oh yes," Mrs. Goodwin rushes over to interject. "That was before . . ." She trails off. "Well, let's just say that wouldn't be great optics for us right now."

For a second, I'm not even mad. It's just hilarious. "No twelve-year old is going to recognize me. They probably don't even watch the news."

"It's just not worth the risk, Nell. I'm so sorry. I switched you to the kitchen staff, just to be safe." She fiddles with her necklace again.

Oh, it must be so hard for you, I want to say, *keeping up appearances. So much pressure and strain this must have put on you.*

"Maybe Nell can help me," Viv suggests. "She could be a support counselor or something. When she's not busy with kitchen stuff."

A heavy sigh. "That's probably not the best idea right now. I appreciate your understanding."

Mrs. Towers hands over my schedule, which says *Kitchen Staff* at the top instead of *Counselor* like Viv's.

"You're both in Staff Cabin Eight," Goodwin adds. "And lunch is at—"

"Noon," Viv interrupts. "We know."

She's glaring at Goodwin as though the woman just tried to slit my throat. I decide I like her quite a bit.

"God, what was *that* about?" Viv grumbles as we step into the mid-morning light.

It's muggy now, but I'm still cold. The fog has vanished and somewhere through the trees, far beyond my current line of sight, Corwin Lake will be reflecting a cloudless sky.

"Come on, let's drop our stuff at the cabin." Viv grabs my hand. "Jesus, you're like ice."

I squeeze my fingers into fists, blow on them. It's like I can't shake the chill I caught on the trip up here, not even forty-eight hours later. I hope I'm not getting sick.

"So what's your deal? Where are you from?"

It dawns on me that she doesn't know, that whatever she was listening to on her AirPods earlier was playing loudly enough that she didn't hear my announcement. She has no clue who I am. I know I can't avoid it forever, but I want just a few more minutes of this normalcy. I want her to keep looking at me like I'm not a villain.

"You first," I say as we start back through the trees. It's shadowy and cool beneath pine boughs, the floor a soft carpet of needles. The scent of wet dirt is pungent.

"Not much to tell. I'm from a small town outside Glens Falls, where nothing happens."

I have no clue where Glens Falls is, and my expression must communicate my confusion.

"It's about thirty minutes north of Albany," she explains. "I can't wait to get out. Just one more year and then college. I'll probably end up at one of the SUNY schools, so, not really escaping upstate altogether, but it's something."

"It's that bad, huh?"

"Ugh, it's insufferable. There's this kid Davie Prentiss in my class and he is literally Satan's walking incarnation. He's made my life a living hell since fourth grade. I can't wait to never have to see him anymore."

"Wow."

"Yeah. And it's like I can't escape him. He lives on my street. He was on the shuttle bus with me. I think I might be cursed."

"He works here?"

"At the boys' camp across the lake, thank God. But the shuttle was the same for both staff. For half the bus ride, I had to listen to him talk about some girl he banged on

18

prom night." She makes a gagging noise. "What about you?"

"I'm from the city, but I used to come here as a camper when I was younger."

"Ooh, rich kid," Viv says with a wink.

"Well, my mom knows the owner. They're old friends. Maybe she got a discount or something." I force a smile. It's not true, but I want her to think it could be. I don't want the one person who's tolerating me to think I'm some spoiled, out-of-touch, rich asshole—whose dad stole from people, no less. "That's actually the reason I have this job, too. She called in a favor."

"Connections," Viv says sagely. "It's all about who you know."

"I'm going to be a senior in the fall also. Vassar is high on my college list, so I won't be 'escaping' New York state either if that works out."

"Major?"

"I'm thinking about Photojournalism. You?"

"Social work."

I'm about to ask why she wants to get into that field—it's not one I've seen many of my peers gravitate toward—when the cabins appear up ahead. At first, they're only glimpses of worn wood siding, barely visible through the trees. But soon they come fully into view: a series of small, squat, unimpressive staff cabins scattered beneath the trees. Farther up the path are the larger cabins for campers, rectangular plaques above each door with a cabin name etched into the wood.

"Home sweet home," Viv says and yanks open the screen door of Staff Cabin #8.

I move to follow her, but I'm struck with a blow of coldness, like an ice pick to the heart. My hair on my arms stands on end.

I whirl around, almost expecting to spot a nosey counselor among the trees, watching, glaring, taking photos to send to the tabloids. But of course there's nothing, just a slight breeze rustling the pine boughs, their needles brushing together like nervous fingers.

CHAPTER
FOUR

The cabin is tiny and smells like mildew and damp earth.

It's essentially one cramped room of about twelve by twelve, with two bunks pushed against adjacent walls. The third wall has a doorway that leads to a small bathroom. (Another reason Durant is so expensive: running water in all cabins.) The fourth holds the entrance Viv and I have stepped through.

Two girls have already claimed the bunks on the far wall, leaving Viv and me the set closest to the main door. She throws her bag on the top bunk, and announces, "I'm Viv. This is Nell."

"Jocelyn," says a girl in the process of tacking up photos of her boyfriend against the dark, stained walls beside her bed. At least I assume he's her boyfriend. He's shirtless in half the pictures and has his arm slung around her in several others. She's beaming in every shot, a perfect pearl-white smile contrasting against her olive skin.

Jocelyn barely turns around to greet us, but when she steals a glance over her shoulder, her eyes linger on me a beat too long. With her lips pinched together, she looks different from the girl in the photos. Intimidating and not nearly as approachable. Her dark hair is pulled into a bun that makes her already impressive height seem even greater. She's wearing gym shorts and a plain white tee, but it somehow looks high fashion. I instantly want to impress her even though everything about her screams *I cannot be impressed.*

"I'm Gretta," the other girl says. She's closer to Viv's height, but not nearly as slight in build, with red hair that's plaited into two French braids and a spattering of freckles across her nose. "Are you guys counselors too?"

"I was supposed to be, but they switched me to the kitchen," I explain.

"No surprise, really," Jocelyn scoffs. "What else was Goodwin supposed to do? If I was a parent, I wouldn't want *my* kids being counseled by a criminal's daughter."

"Huh?" Viv looks confused.

Jocelyn rolls her eyes. "Have you been living under a rock the past two days? Her father's been all over the news. Duncan Bradley? Esteemed Wall Street banker? Suspected of embezzling funds from his clients and now on the run from the feds?"

Viv laughs sheepishly. "We don't really watch much TV."

"Do you not have a phone either? No internet access?"

Viv's face goes blank and I know instantly that Jocelyn's hit a nerve.

"I just don't live on my phone, okay?" Viv says evenly. "Nice meeting you guys. I'm hungry. Gonna head back to the mess. I'll catch you later."

The screen door thwacks shut behind her.

"Are you gonna go to the bonfire later?" Gretta asks me, as if nothing awkward has just transpired. "The welcome one?"

"Don't we have to attend?" I ask, shifting uncomfortably.

"I . . . I don't know, actually. Jocelyn?"

"Yes, Gretta, we have to."

Gretta turns back to me, awaiting a reply.

"Okay, then I'll be there." I eye the door. Viv hasn't made it far. "I'll be right back," I say and race after her. "Hey, you okay? I'm sorry about Jocelyn. She seems like an ass."

"Don't apologize for other people, Nell. It's hard enough to own your own shit."

She's got a point there. "Fair enough," I say.

It's quiet for a moment, then Viv launches into an explanation, even though I haven't asked for one.

"My mom stopped paying the cable bill months ago. There's no internet at the house anymore, and if I go over on data it's . . . bad. So I'm only really online when I'm at the library or a cafe or someplace with Wi-Fi, and then I'm not reading news. I'm catching up with friends and wasting my time on TikTok like a normal human." She glances at me out of the corner of her eye. "Was it true? What she said about your dad?"

"Yeah. I guess. It was news to me and my mom when the feds showed up at our apartment. That was Friday morning. As in two days ago. My dad had already bolted. He must have known it was coming."

"Do you think he's guilty?"

The question surprises me. I'd expected her to ice me out like everyone back home. I hesitate for a moment, not because I'm uncertain how to answer her, but because it's scary to say it out loud. "If he was innocent, he'd have called our lawyer, met with the authorities, and fought the thing. But he ran. He's in hiding. Maybe he's even left the country already."

"Jesus," Viv says.

"Yeah, well now you know. Just like the rest of the world." The weight of my phone in my rear pocket seems to triple, as if it can sense the overload of messages just waiting to come through.

"Still, it's shitty what Jocelyn said. And how Goodwin is trying to hide you in the kitchen or whatever. It's not like *you* stole people's money."

"That seems to be a hard concept for some people to grasp."

As we walk, Viv tells me about *her* dad. He's dead.

Overdosed. He got injured at work last winter, then hooked on the meds he'd had for pain management. Viv's mom emptied their savings to try to get him help. In the end, they lost him anyway, and now they're in serious debt. Hence the lack of cable.

"I wish I could see him again," she says, eyes glassy. "Just once. Just to have one more day."

It's such a foreign sentiment to me; Dad and I were never very close. If Mom hadn't demanded he start spending one-on-one time with me on Sundays when I was eight, who knows if we'd have ever actually interacted.

The outing was always the same: A quick walk through Central Park. Lunch for me on the terrace while Dad checked his emails. *Work never sleeps,* he was always saying. When he managed to put his phone down, I had to endure the same never-changing history lesson about how Bethesda Fountain was built to commemorate New York's first fresh-water system. "That lily she's holding?" Dad would say, pointing at the angel at the center of the fountain. "It symbolizes the water's purity. You can imagine how important clean water was to a city that suffered a cholera epidemic."

When these outings started, I could barely comprehend the concept of epidemics, and Covid wouldn't happen for a few more years. But I do remember when I started to see the irony of lily pads and algae growing in a fountain whose water was supposedly pure. The day I pointed it out, Dad scoffed. His fatherly duties only extended to a one-hour walk and a reoccurring history lesson, not thoughtful conversation.

"You think you'll see your dad again?" Viv asks.

"Not unless they catch him. My mom thinks he'll come back though. She's waiting. Like an idiot, she's waiting for him."

"Love's weird like that," Viv says with a shrug.

We've reached the mess hall. It's positioned in a perfect round clearing surrounded by trees—like a crop circle was made and the building plopped down in the middle of it.

I feel somewhat dizzy, like I've spent the day moving in circles.

"Hey, are you Eleanor Bradley?"

I glance up, bracing for whatever insult or attack is coming. The voice belongs to a boy standing on the path that leads around to the back of the mess hall. He's wearing a grease-stained apron over a plain white tee.

"Yeah?" I say, only it comes out as a question.

He plucks a toothpick from between his teeth, and I spot chipped black paint on his nails. "I was told to come find you. You're supposed to be prepping lunch with the rest of us."

"Right," I say uselessly. "Coming."

"Catch you later," Viv says, and bumps her shoulder into mine in parting.

I follow the kitchen boy around to the back of the mess hall, using a rusted metal door—once green, now half orange—to access the kitchen. The scents of grease, burnt food, and tomato sauce assault me as I step inside. Staff members are bustling about, prepping meals, opening and closing fridges, moving pans on the stovetop in a way that sends flames sparking up toward their eyebrows.

"Yo, Dolores! I found her," the boy says, signaling a burly woman wearing knee-high socks despite the summer weather. Her curly gray hair is trapped beneath a hair net and her eyes lock onto me as she glances up from the clipboard she's carrying.

"Thanks, Arlo. You can get back to it."

Arlo leaves, moving toward a sink overflowing with suds. The woman—Dolores—appraises me up and down, then says gruffly, "I don't care where you come from or what your history is or whether it's true what they say your Dad did. I care that you do a decent job in here, show up on time, and don't slack. I told Goodwin I'd take you, but that's only if you can pull your weight."

"I can pull my weight," I echo, only my voice sounds meek and not very convincing.

Dolores grunts. "Go help, Arlo. You guys are going to be cleaning buddies." Then she yells across the kitchen, "Arlo, you tell me if she's not pulling her weight."

I thread my way between the aproned staff and join Arlo near the sinks and dishwashers. "Hi again. I'm your new partner. What do you want me doing?"

"You can scrub." He nods at the first set of sinks.

"What about the dishwashers?" There's four of them, all industrial sized.

"Still gotta get all the baked-on crud off before we load 'em." He winks like this is a clever joke, then disappears, carrying a stack of yellow and coral melamine bowls into the front half of the kitchen.

I pull on a pair of rubber gloves, reach a hand into the suds, and go fishing. I catch a frying pan with God-knows-what caked onto the skillet. I fish around a bit more until I find a Brillo Pad, then start scrubbing.

An hour later, I'm still at it, my fingers pruned and pink and aching. Arlo bustles around me, loading and unloading the dishwashers, stacking plates, sorting utensils. He manages to do a bit of everything while I scrub and scrub and scrub, the pile of dirty cookware always growing beside me, cooks dropping off this and that. Pots, pans, cutting boards, knives, spatulas. It's endless.

The hum and chatter of folks eating out in the mess swells, then slowly fades, until finally, the dishes stop arriving.

"You want me to grab you something?" Arlo says. "It was sloppy joes and salads."

Sloppy joes. Guess that explains the crud stuck to half the pans. My stomach coils. "No thanks. I've kinda lost my appetite."

"That happens working back here," he says with a smirk. He lifts a hoodie from a hook beside the door and replaces it with his apron.

I'm thinking that despite the awful labor, it might be a blessing being tucked into the corner of the kitchen with Arlo, who doesn't seem to realize who I am, when he adds, "See you at dinner, Manhattan. Put some lotion on those baby-smooth fingers in the meantime. They're gonna be chapped."

He's gone, the metal door banging shut in his wake, before I can reply.

CHAPTER
FIVE

The campers arrive sporadically throughout the afternoon. Parents show up in everything from shiny Lexuses to chrome-rimmed Escapades to drop off their kids. A few even arrive by hired chauffeur. I can't decide what's worst: how much money the parents dropped to hire a private driver, or the fact that they're not even here at drop-off to say goodbye to their own offspring.

The kids are small and eager-looking, all limbs and wide, gleaming eyes. One particularly anxious girl hangs back, hesitant. The returning campers always run off to find their girlfriends, but this girl's new, I'd bet my paycheck on it. Her mother tells her to buck up and keep smiling, then leaves in a hurry.

"Sometimes it's hard to keep smiling," I tell the girl as she struggles to gather all her bags. "Sometimes it feels like it would be easier to just give up. But it will get better, I promise."

She looks at me like I'm crazy, then stalks toward the cabins. I think she could tell I was lying.

I hope she doesn't say anything to the staff. The last thing I need is Goodwin on my case, lecturing me about how I'm supposed to be hiding in the kitchen, out of sight, not interacting with the campers.

While Viv (and all the counselors) are off meeting their campers and running team-building exercises, I drift down to the beach.

The morning's fog is long gone, the sun high overhead. A late-afternoon stillness has spread across the lake, rendering the water a flawless mirror. If I stare at the opposite bank long enough, it's hard to see where the world ends and the reflection of shoreline begins.

I slink to the end of the longest dock and sit cross-legged, staring across the lake. On the opposite side, set into a small inlet, is the boys' camp, which, from this distance, looks like little more than a pale stretch of beach, and the docks extending into the water like tiny pieces of driftwood. To the right of the beach, there is nothing but pines. To the left, more pines, but also Windsor Camp, an estate set back among the trees. Overlooking Corwin from its perch on the rocky outcropping, the house appears shrouded in shadows, dark and dreary, but not entirely uninhabitable, even though it's been deserted as long as I can remember. Campers used to dare one another to sneak into it every year, but no one ever did. I've poked around in it only once, just last summer, when my boredom reached epic levels. I'd told Mom I was going kayaking and that *was* true, but I'd made a pit stop at the estate, traversed up the rocky hillside, and seen what all the fuss was about.

The place is creepy in a way I don't know how to explain. Empty, but full of something—a feeling, a lingering sense of dread.

Something pinches in my ribs. I shouldn't be here on the dock. I should be . . .

I'm not sure where.

Just not here.

The lake ripples as a mallard lands in the swimming area to my right. I shiver despite the sun's heat, pull my knees to my chest.

I check my watch. Dinner is in an hour. I head back to the kitchen.

———

After another long stretch of scrubbing, during which I ignore Arlo's cheerful humming and snarky remarks about my delicate hands, I head to the bonfire. It takes place on the commons, a stretch of open field near Goodwin's office that offers an impressive view of the lake— and Windsor Camp.

The campers are gathered together, chattering and giggling. There's an obvious divide between them and the staff on the other side of the fire pit.

I spot Viv from a distance, talking with Jocelyn and Gretta and a few other counselors I don't know. She's got her hair pulled back into a stubby tail, the pink ends standing out from the timid shades of blonde, brunette, and black surrounding her. I know joining everyone could result in unpleasant stares and uncomfortable questions. An evening breeze nudges at my back and I take it as a sign that it's worth the risk. I let myself be carried along the path and up to the bonfire like a skittish leaf.

"It's haunted, didn't you know?" Jocelyn's saying. She's twirling a section of her glossy black hair around her forefinger, her eyes locked on the house across the lake.

"Haunted," Viv says doubtfully.

"Tell her, Joce," Gretta nudges.

Jocelyn stands a bit straighter. "It burned down," she says dramatically, firelight playing over her features.

"And was rebuilt?" Viv's eyes drift back to the estate. In the fading daylight, it's barely visible.

"*Half* of it burned," Jocelyn corrects. "You can't see it from here, but the front of the house . . . the bit that faces the road? It's charred black. Kids sneak in and have campfires in the ruined ballroom, and sometimes squatters live there too. We snuck in last summer on a dare from the boys' camp. The county came and boarded the place up a couple years ago, but you can still get in if you're determined."

"My cousin broke in last fall," one of the girls I don't

know offers up. "He said he heard voices. And all the crosses are turned upside down on the walls."

"It burned but there's still crosses on the wall?" Viv asks.

"*Half* of it burned," Jocelyn snaps. "Gosh, why is this so hard for you to grasp? Go spend a night there and see for yourself. The place is creepy as fuck. And the cross thing makes sense. The place burned during an exorcism."

Viv's brows peak, finally intrigued.

"The Windsors had one daughter: Avery Jane," Jocelyn continues, a smile creeping over her face as Viv leans nearer. "Avery was a child pageant star down south. Her family came up here every summer from Georgia and one year, when Avery was like eleven or twelve, she refused to visit the lake. She spent every second in the ballroom, dancing the waltz with an invisible partner and muttering things in some made-up language. When her parents tried to drag her out of the ballroom, her eyes rolled back and she started screaming for them to let her go, only it wasn't her voice coming out, it was a someone else's."

Viv bristles. The other girls nod seriously.

"A bunch of doctors made house calls, only to be chased out by mysterious blasts of wind and threatening voices. Finally, the only person who agreed to see her was the local priest. He said Avery was possessed and the only option was to banish the demon living inside her. But I guess the demon had other plans, 'cus in the middle of the exorcism, Avery threw herself on the ground and started writhing and screaming that she was hot—burning up inside. Next thing the Windsors knew, the whole ballroom was engulfed in flames. By the time the fire department got there, half the house was gone, and they discovered that the ballroom doors had all be locked. Everyone inside was killed."

I can't take it anymore; the lies and exaggerations, the way that poor family's tragedy has been turned into entertainment. It all feels a little too close to home.

"I've been in that place before," I cut in. "It's not haunted, just creepy. The Windsors were super religious and I bet teens breaking in flipped the crosses. And I'm pretty sure I heard somewhere that the fire was an accident. The Windsors left candles burning or something. There wasn't an exorcism."

Everyone's head swivels around to face me.

"Hey, Nell, when'd you get here?" Viv asks.

Jocelyn doesn't even acknowledge my presence. "That place is seriously disturbing," she insists, staring at Viv. "You really don't believe me?"

"No, not really," Viv says with a shrug.

Rage flickers over Jocelyn's face—there and gone so quickly I wonder if perhaps it was a trick of firelight. Because now she's smiling and laughing and asking who wants to make s'mores. She grabs sticks and marshmallows and passes them out. When she reaches me, she happens to be one short. "Oh, sorry. Guess I didn't grab enough," she says in her sweetest voice.

"That's okay. I'll go steal one for myself."

"I bet you will. You're family's good at that."

I force a smile like it doesn't bother me, like it's only words. But when I get to the s'mores table, I'm practically shaking.

"Hey, Manhattan." Arlo offers me a marshmallow and a roasting stick. The mallow puff sits there on his extended palm, his black nail-polished fingers encircling it like a tiny cage.

"I have a name, you know," I snap.

"Do you? You never introduced yourself."

"You called me by my name when we first met. I know you know who I am, but instead I'm just *Manhattan*. Because apparently this is all a big joke. Apparently my life being a giant dumpster fire is a joke to anyone who isn't living it."

He cocks a brow up. Moves the toothpick from one side of his mouth to the other. "Easy there, Nell. I'm just trying to be nice." He holds the marshmallow out a bit farther. "You want this or not?"

I snatch it off his palm and chuck it directly into the fire. It goes up in flames, engorging then melting then charring black.

"Where you going?" he calls as I sulk off.

"To bed. I don't need this."

And I don't.

I head back to Cabin #8 and climb into my bunk. Face the wall. Shiver and pull the blankets high above my chin. Outside, branches scratch at the cabin's siding. The wooden structure groans and creaks. There's a dampness to the evening air that permeates, sneaking through the cracks in the cabin and soaking into my bones.

The girls come back in a bit later, laughing and tripping as they kick off their shoes.

"Nell, you still up?" Viv asks.

I pretend to be asleep.

They go about washing up for the night, the soft light leaking from the bathroom, and then the cabin is swallowed in darkness.

Soon it's quiet, the three of them dreaming like mummies in coffins, me the only soul unable to sleep despite being so damn tired. I stare at the ceiling and pray for it to come.

Finally, *finally*, it pulls me under.

CHAPTER
SIX

I wake almost a half hour before my phone's alarm was set to go off.

My body feels achy, like I've been in bed too long, and it will be good to move. I get changed quietly, dressing in layers so I can peel them off as the day heats up. It's cool when I step outside though. I tug the cords on my hoodie, drawing the neckline tighter.

I beat most of the staff to the kitchen. It's just Dolores, chatting with one of her cooks—a scrawny man in his mid-forties, when I arrive. They're prepping potatoes for hashbrowns, their backs to me as I slip through the rear door.

"Can't believe they still haven't found him," she's saying. "A sighting in southern Jersey and yet he's evaded authorities again?"

I freeze. Dad's been spotted? This is news to me.

"Maybe it wasn't him," the cook says. "Maybe

whoever called in the tip misidentified him. He's probably left the country already."

"Or put a bullet in his brain. He's gonna get life in prison if they catch him."

"The wife could be helping him somehow."

"I feel bad for that poor girl."

I clip my hip on a counter and curse loudly. Dolores and her friend both jerk toward the commotion. Several rolling carts filled with trays stand between us, but I can't hide.

"Nell," Dolores says, trying to act unsurprised. "Morning."

"Morning," I chirp back. Because it's awkward enough already and they know I've heard everything, I ask, "Where are you getting updates? I don't have cell service."

Nor do I want it, I think. Social media apps, I can avoid opening. But emails and texts are harder, and I know the number of unread messages must be climbing.

"Goodwin gets a paper delivered to the office daily," Dolores explains. "It makes the rounds through the head staff after she's read it."

"He was seen yesterday," the potato-chopping man says, as if I didn't overhear it already. "Someone called the tip line. Authorities haven't found him yet though."

I nod, my stomach coiling. I have no clue what Dad would be doing in Jersey and I don't really care. I just want him found. I want him found so this can blow over. It *has* to blow over. Nothing lasts forever. But scandals have a way of fascinating. Of pulling people in. They get invested. If Dad's not found soon, the best thing would be for *another* scandal to break. Something that has nothing to do with him but is just as juicy. If it involves my class-mates, even better. Last year, someone started a rumor that Sadie Dunlop got an abortion and it was all anyone talked about for six months. I remain firmly in the camp that it didn't matter why she went to Planned Parenthood —it was her own business—but it turned out she went for birth control because her parents are extremely religious and she knew they wouldn't take her. The truth didn't matter though. Plenty of people shunned her, or made jokes, or called her a slut, as though having sex was the worst possible thing a girl could do.

I don't wish that sort of vitriol on anyone. But I also wouldn't be sad if the attention suddenly shifted away from me for a bit. Maybe homecoming could get cancelled. Or someone else's father can get caught in an ethical nightmare. I'm not picky at this point.

The metal door bangs behind me. Two more people have arrived. "You got coffee brewing yet, Tom?" one of them asks.

Tom quarters another potato and beams. "You know it."

The metal door rattles again, and there's Arlo, shrug-ging out of his hoodie and slipping his apron over another plain white tee. I wonder if there's anything else in his wardrobe.

"Look at you, Manhattan, showing up early and

proving your dedication to the job." He winks, then pauses. "Oh, shit. I'm supposed to call you Nell now, aren't I?"

A half dozen more staff members step through the entrance, threading between us, heading for the mugs Tom's left out near the drip machine.

"Eh, nicknames are fine," I hear myself telling Arlo. "I don't really care. Sorry I snapped last night. It's just been a lot, all of this." I wave at the air, signifying camp and my life and . . . everything.

"Want a coffee? I'll grab us some."

"Where the fuck are all the spoons?" someone shouts from up front. Dolores pulls open one of the dishwashers and swears. "Looks like unit three never ran last night. Nell, can you hand wash these—fast? We got campers and staff arriving in about ten and we don't have nearly enough clean utensils."

"Gotta pass on that coffee," I tell Arlo. "Thanks though." And then I'm in my typical form, elbow deep in soap suds, scrubbing the grime from utensils as the kitchen fills with the smell of oatmeal and eggs, fresh fruit and coffee.

As the morning stretches on, I can hear some of the staff discussing Dad. They think they're out of my earshot, and for the most part they are. I can't hear everything they're saying, but I can hear enough. His name. His company's name. Mom's name.

When I get a moment, I pull my cell from my back pocket and, bracing, check for messages from Mom.

Nothing's gotten through of course. Not from her, or anyone from school.

I keep hoping Kylie will say something—anything. I'm not going to be the one to initiate contact again. Not after her final response to me Friday afternoon before I left New York.

They lost everything, Nell. EVERYTHING. Your dad fucked us. My college fund is GONE.

Kylie's parents and mine went way back. They were friends before either of us were born and had been investing with my dad for nearly as long. I told her how terrible I felt, how sorry I was on behalf of my selfish, manipulative, back-stabbing father.

Did you know? she shot back.

No, of course not! It's news to me and Mom. We found out almost exactly when the general public did.

I can't believe this. I can't fucking believe this.

Me either, I wrote. *I'm so sorry. Truly.*

I don't give a fuck about your sorrys right now, Nell. This has ruined everything. I need a minute. Don't text me again.

Come on, Kylie.

I'm serious. Don't fucking text me.

And I haven't. But I keep hoping she'll reach out, keep fantasizing that she'll realize my life is a mess from this too. Dad screwed her family, yes, and all his clients', but he screwed me and Mom also.

I don't know what I expected from her, but it wasn't this. How can you be friends with someone since birth and then drop them so effortlessly?

I spend most of the day trying to sync up with Viv, but nearly all her free time is during meals when I'm at my busiest. The entire day passes without us crossing paths. By the time dinner wraps, I'm both exhausted and lonely. Dishwashers, it turns out, are the last to leave the kitchen.

Arlo hangs up his apron.

I rub my cracked and aching hands.

"You coming?" he asks, holding the door open.

"In a minute."

"Suit yourself."

The metal door closes with an ear-shattering crash, and I stand there a moment, reveling in the solitude, the quiet. Just me. Alone. No looks, no stares, no whispers. I breathe deeply, feeling like I could blink into oblivion if I stood here long enough, just disappear into the darkness, vanishing like Dad.

A few minutes later, I flick the lights off and step outside.

"What the hell were you doing in there?" Arlo asks.

I flinch, grab my chest. "What are *you* doing? I thought you left." That's when a musty smell reaches me and I spot the joint in his hand.

He takes a long drag and then holds it out to me. "Want a hit?"

I shake my head. With my luck, Goodwin or Towers will appear and catch me in the act, and I don't need to give anyone another reason to think poorly of me. "You're gonna get busted smoking back here," I tell him. "It's not exactly a low-traffic place."

"Busted. Ha! Like your dad. Good one." He chuckles to himself, and I brush past him.

"Shit," he mutters. "I'm high already. That was in poor taste, sorry. I'll see you around, maybe? Sometime?"

"Yeah, tomorrow," I say with an eye roll. "And the day after that. And every day until camp lets out, unfortunately."

"And here I was, thinking we were starting to get along." He smirks his usual smirk. It's weird to see it without a toothpick wedged between his lips.

"Goodnight, Arlo."

"'Night, Manhattan."

I step beneath the pines, happy to be swallowed by the shadows.

CHAPTER
SEVEN

We fall into a routine that first week, waking with the sun, winding down as it sets. The campers know the schedule. The counselors and staff flit from responsibility to responsibility. And I wash a million and one dishes.

As the week carries on, the stares from the staff lessen. They still whisper though, gossiping about Dad. From what I overhear, there's been no developments since he was spotted in Jersey and it's likely that whoever thought they'd seen him had actually spotted someone else. I check in with Goodwin on Thursday morning, asking if Mom has called or messaged with any updates. But there's nothing to report, which means I'll continue to keep my head down, trying to avoid the rumors and theories swirling around me.

Evenings become my favorite part of the day—the few minutes after organized activities wind down and before lights-out is enforced. It's in this time that Viv and I lounge in our bunks and chat, ignoring Jocelyn and Gretta on the other side of the cabin with almost indifferent ease. Viv will ask me for advice on how to handle this or that with her campers. I complain about life in the kitchen. It's a simple arrangement. Some nights we even talk about our dads. Mostly, she talks and I listen. I envy how she has good memories with hers. Even before mine was exposed, before the proof of his terribleness was blasted all over the news, I knew he was rotten, wrong. He had Mom fooled somehow, but not me.

I wonder if she's still standing at the apartment window, waiting.

I wonder what could possibly be keeping her there.

———

The first week of camp closes with another bonfire on Friday night.

Everyone gathers around the central pit and Mrs. Towers addresses the campers and staff, commenting on a great opening week and outlining all the fun activities ahead, including the Fourth of July celebrations that will take place on Saturday. The fire crackles and snaps behind her. Smoke mingles with the scent of pines and damp earth from a rain shower earlier in the afternoon.

Then it's time for s'mores.

The campers gather roasting sticks and marshmallows, chattering excitedly. The fire casts flickering shadows across their sunburned noses.

Jocelyn waves to me and Viv from across the fire pit, gesturing us over. She's emerged as a sort of queen bee of the counselors during the first week. Gretta stands beside her like a loyal lapdog, the both of them surrounded by the rest of the counseling staff—four other girls who bunk in Staff Cabin #7 and whose names I've learned from Viv: Kayla, Abbie, Celia, and Ryan. I pinch Viv's elbow, nod across the sparking campfire flames. Jocelyn gestures more adamantly.

"Guess we better go see what she wants," Viv says with a sigh. She's confided in me that she finds Jocelyn tiring. "Everything is strategic and calculated with her," she whispered just last night. "She doesn't do anything without a reason. It makes me not want to trust her."

We pick our way across the sea of campers, dodging bony knees, crossed ankles, and discarded marshmallow-roasting sticks.

"We're sneaking over to Windsor Camp tomorrow night," Jocelyn announces when we join her. "You in?"

"Who's we?" Viv asks.

"Whoever's brave enough. Plus Davie and a few other counselors from the boys' camp."

"Davie Prentiss?" Viv makes a gagging noise. "How'd you even get in touch with that ass?"

Jocelyn beams and pulls her cell phone from her back pocket.

"But there's no service up here," I point out at the

same time Viv practically screeches, "How'd you get a signal?!" I've caught her drafting texts to friends back home each night at the cabin, then sighing and stuffing her cell back under her pillow. She'd be better off writing letters. There's a mailbox in the mess hall for dropping off post.

Still, the simple thought that she has friends outside this place—people who talk to her and look forward to hearing from her—makes my stomach twist with envy. Meanwhile, I'm afraid of service, of walking into a pocket of space that causes my phone to suddenly flood with hateful messages. I switch my cell to airplane mode, kicking myself for not thinking of this easy fix sooner.

"Shh," Abbie hisses, her corkscrew curls bouncing as she glances around. "Don't let Towers hear."

"I led the hike to Notch's Point on Thursday," Jocelyn explains to Viv. "If you have Verizon, you get a single bar of LTE at the lookout. Just enough to send—and receive—a text."

"And the boys always have service on their docks," Gretta points out. "Something about not being blocked by the mountains the way we are. Lucky jerks."

"How do you know Davie?" I ask Jocelyn.

"We met on the shuttle bus." She tosses her hair over her shoulder. "Besides, what's it matter? Are you in or not?"

Viv and I share a glance. We're supposed to be in our bunks by ten, exactly an hour after the campers retire to theirs, and then nowhere else until sunup. Counselor cabins and camper cabins are clustered together, but the young girls sleep like the dead, worn out from the day's activities. The rest of the staff and admin bunks are on the other side of camp, between the mess and Goodwin's office. It's not that sneaking out will be hard. It's what will happen if we get caught. There's also the fact that Viv *hates* Davie Prentiss, and I'm pretty sure that if she's going to risk breaking curfew, it wouldn't be to hang with him.

"How are you getting there?" I ask, trying to find a hole in the plan, and easy excuse for Viv and me to back out.

"The canoes. We'll leave them on the boys' beach, then hike to Windsor together. Davie says there's a path."

"I don't know . . ."

"Look, if you guys are too scared—"

"I'm not scared," Viv snaps.

"Good. Eleven o'clock tomorrow night then."

———

Later, when Jocelyn and Gretta are asleep, I kick the upper bunk gently. "I thought you hated Davie. Why do you want to do this?"

Viv's torso appears in the darkness, dangling upside down over the side of the bunk. "Move over," she says. I do, and she hops down and joins me on my mattress. "God, it's freezing," she complains, yanking up the blankets. It's not, but after the hot, humid days, the coolness of evening is always a shock.

"I've been thinking about what Jocelyn said about that place being haunted," she goes on. "And I figure if I can put up with Davie for a few minutes as we hike up to Windsor, it will be worth it." She tells me how she plans to record some noises on her phone—groaning, moaning, maybe even a shriek or two. Then she'll tuck her phone in a corner of the house and make sure it plays while Davie walks by.

"That is genius," I say, dissolving into giggles with her. "And so cruel."

"But so deserved," she says.

And from what I've learned about Davie the past few nights during our chats, it will be. He's bullied Viv since the fourth grade, torments everyone at their school who doesn't fit his image of cool and worthwhile, and treats girls like objects. I used to think people like this didn't exist, that they were extreme caricatures made up for movies and TV shows—an obvious villain that was easy to hate. But maybe it's simply that my world—a private school in New York City, a close-knit neighborhood— showed me a limited bubble.

The other possibility is that I just wasn't looking hard enough. Maybe pure evil *does* exist. Because when I think about what Dad's done—the promises he made to his clients, the trust he elicited only to shamelessly betray— it's hard to not consider him evil. He took what wasn't his. He stole retirements, life savings, and now he's not even decent enough to face the consequences of his actions.

I still can't fully comprehend it. He was never going to win Father of the Year, but I never imagined him capable of the things that have come to light in the last few days.

A distant, feather-light sensation touches the back of my neck. I close my eyes. In the darkness behind my lids I can see Windsor, calm and dark. A peacefulness we will disturb tomorrow evening.

"Hey Viv, do you believe in ghosts?"

She stops laughing. Clears her throat. "Sure," she says after a moment. "Who are we to say what does or doesn't happen after death?"

"It's just . . . that stuff with Avery Jane Windsor is only talk. People turned tragedy into a spectacle. You know that, right?"

Viv frowns. "Yeah. You told everyone that already. But just 'cus people dreamed up a ghost story about the Windsors doesn't mean that ghosts don't—or can't—exist."

I nod, not because I necessarily agree, but more to steel myself for tomorrow night. I'm not afraid of Windsor Camp because of ghost stories, but I don't particularly want to visit it either. I did that once, and once was enough.

Tragedy isn't something to be gawked at. And Windsor . . . it attracts a lot of eyes.

Maybe that's why it felt heavy when I explored it last summer. Something terrible happened there, but only the house remembers the details.

CHAPTER
EIGHT

ourth of July falling on a Saturday means an entire day's worth of celebratory activities. Camp-wide games of Capture the Flag and Marco Polo. A giant scavenger hunt and water balloon fights. I witness very little of it. Instead, I hunker down in the kitchen, where every manner of classic American food and barbecue is served throughout the day. Potato salad and corn on the cob. Hamburgers and hotdogs. Fried chicken and pasta salad. Strawberry shortcakes and flag cake made with cream cheese frosting and rows of raspberries and blueberries for the stripes. We serve it pre-sliced, which defeats the purpose of all that clever work.

Arlo drops off a plate of food for me—a cheeseburger and potato salad and buttered cob of corn—but it sits beside the sink, growing cold because the stream of dishes keeps me preoccupied. Arlo delivers these dishes too, toothpick clenched between his teeth. He winks smugly as he sets them on the counter. He empties and unloads the dishwasher, stacks plates, runs dishes back and forth through the kitchen. The whole time he keeps eying my uneaten meal in annoyance, as if my refusing to eat is a personal slight to him. It couldn't possibly be because I'm so overworked I can't spare even five minutes for myself. Maybe if he bothered to get his hands wet and scrub alongside me it would be different. But that never happens.

When we're finally done for the day, my fingers are so waterlogged I fear I may never dry out.

I make for the central firepit. It's been doused in anticipation of fireworks but still smokes slightly. Young girls sit in tangles, eyes on the darkening sky.

The lone town on Corwin sets off fireworks every Fourth, a spectacle far more impressive than you'd expect of a town with only three hundred residents. But it's tradition. Looking south, Camp Durant's girls will get a perfect viewing of the show from here. The boys across the lake, however, will be on the water, watching from kayaks and canoes.

I find Viv in the crowd. She hooks her arm through mine.

When everyone else lifts their eyes to the explosions, pupils reflecting tendrils of raining sparks, I turn toward Windsor and watch the fireworks glint in the dark windowpanes.

We sneak for the shore. Gretta is a ball of nerves and Jocelyn keeps hissing directions far too loudly.

The moon is impossibly large above us, so bright that if Goodwin or Towers were patrolling, they'd see us easily. We're wearing hoodies, flip flops, and shorts, and —with the exception of Jocelyn and Kayla's darker legs— our limbs gleam like glow sticks.

Viv gets the keys from the pegboard and unlocks the padlock on the canoes. After a bit of grunting and pulling, four canoes are slipping into the water. We break into pairs: Jocelyn and Gretta, Kayla and Abbie, Ryan and Celia. Leaving the fourth boat to me and Viv.

The glasslike surface of Corwin ripples as we glide silently through the water. "No flashlights till we're across," Jocelyn whispers. "Aim for the left of the boys' docks."

It's a non-swimming area, where reeds and plant growth poke up through the water. Where our canoes won't leave visible marks in the damp earth along the shore.

Viv rows, her gaze rooted firmly on the boys' beach. I, however, can't pull my gaze from Windsor Camp.

It seems to get taller as we cross the lake, rising up like a gravestone, stretching for the sky. The windows are dark. The night still. But there is something about the quiet that feels primed to snap—a breath ready to exhale, a trap about to spring. A shiver claws down my spine.

I attempt to rub warmth into my arms, but a coldness has pierced through me, leaving me wide-eyed and rigid. It's like the place knows we're coming. Like it's been waiting for us.

Gretta speaks, her whisper carrying easily across the quiet lake.

"I have a bad feeling about this."

———

Our canoes bump the opposite shore.

We hop out, water splashing lightly, murk and muck squelching beneath my flip flops and between my toes. I wade through the reeds, ignoring how they feel like fingernails scratching my skin. When the canoes are secure, we creep for the tree line.

Lights bob there, soft white and blue. Cell phone screens. Less obvious than flashlights. Safer to use until we are well out of range of camp.

"Took you long enough," a voice hisses. Davie. He's what you'd call attractive on paper—tall, a strong chin, and dark, hooded eyes that look mysterious—but I know the truth. "Thought maybe you chickened out and weren't coming."

"You wish," Jocelyn says.

There are four other boys behind Davie. Their group eyes up ours. Gretta smiles bashfully, unaware that most of guys are ogling Jocelyn.

"Ladies first," Davie says, fanning an arm at the narrow dirt path that weaves through the pines.

Jocelyn straightens, adjusts her bra straps, and starts walking.

Viv and I quickly fall back, bringing up the rear. I hold the flashlight and Viv fiddles with her phone.

"I want them queued up and ready to go," she says, swiping through her recordings. She played them for me earlier—impressively creepy renditions of her saying *help* in a long, drawn-out monotone while fire crackles in the background. She recorded at the campfire, before it was doused for the fireworks.

"Do you think he'll fall for it?" I glance up the line of flashlights slicing through the trees. Davie is telling anyone who will listen how Avery Jane lit herself—and her exorcist—on fire. How the demon that possessed her made her do it, and how her ghost is still terrified of fire to this day.

"I think if he keeps telling ghost stories the whole walk, everyone is going to be so on edge, a snapping twig could send us running," Viv says.

I scratch the back of my neck. Shiver.

I consider telling her that I don't think we should go through with the prank, that Windsor Camp deserves respect. But even if she believes me, the others won't. There's no way to get out of this without looking like a huge wimp.

"Got it," Viv says, tucking her phone away. "Here, I'll

hold that for a bit." She takes the flashlight from me and we carry on, listening to Davie recount the supposed horror of that night. My apprehension grows, creeping over my limbs, spreading and stretching like fire devouring kindling.

CHAPTER
NINE

t emerges between gaps in the trees. Wood siding glistening with dew. Window trim damp with rot. Glass panes clouded with dust and cobwebs.

Approaching from the southeast, it merely looks deserted. We'd have to walk around to the front of the house, where a dirt driveway carves through the wilderness, to see the destruction done by the fire.

Davie leads the group to a set of French doors that face the lake. They're boarded up with planks—an attempt to keep out intruders like the ones who probably broke the glass to begin with.

I try to imagine the French doors as they were a few decades ago, glass panes parting as Avery Jane burst through and skipped down the winding stone steps that lead to the water. Now, those very steps are overgrown with weeds and brambles, the rocks slick with moss.

"Someone's been here recently," Davie whispers, pointing to a gap in the installed planks.

"Local kids, probably," Jocelyn says. "Or some other camp staff came last weekend." She shrugs. "What are we waiting for?" She ducks through the opening, disappearing into shadow. A bold move that silently dares the rest of us to follow. We do, slipping inside one at a time.

When Viv and I finally reach the doorway, I can see that Davie is right to assume the break-in happened recently. Most of the planks installed here are worn, but the edges around the opening shine in the moonlight, not yet weathered by the elements.

I touch the exposed wood.

We shouldn't be here.

This is wrong.

A twig snaps behind me and I twist, staring into the trees like a spooked deer. I wait for the eyes of wildlife to blink back, but there's nothing. Nothing but shadows and an inescapable blanket of dampness that leeches into my bones.

Then.

A gasp. Or maybe a groan.

I freeze, uncertain where the noise came from—the woods, the house, maybe even the audio recordings on Viv's phone, playing prematurely.

I twist to face her. "Did you hear that?"

"Hear what?"

I look back toward the woods, searching, peering.

"You coming or not?" she presses.

I duck beneath the planks and enter Windsor Camp.

———

Inside, the air is stale and musty. I can feel it wrapping around me like a second skin.

Viv sweeps her flashlight across the space. What was once a game room is now littered with evidence of past intruders. Discarded beer cans and bottles of liquor. Cigarette butts. Plastic shopping bags and moth-eaten blankets. Among it all, the wilderness creeps in. Dirt and rubble. Dried leaves. At one window, a tendril of ivy snakes through a crack in the glass, curling over the trim like a claw.

"This way." Davie slinks for the stairs, everyone tiptoeing after him.

We should turn back, but I also want—need—to belong. To not draw attention to myself. Like a fish on a line, I let myself be reeled in. I let myself be tugged after the group, one foot ahead of the other, to the stairs, then up them, and onto the first floor. Wallpaper—now faded and coated in moisture—covers the walls.

"Open that vodka already," one of the boys says.

Davie takes a swig and hands the bottle over. Soon it's being passed through the group, everyone taking swigs, whispering and giggling. Viv turns it down and I shake my head as well. It cycles back to the front of the group.

"Come on," Davie whispers. "Ballroom's this way."

We move through a sitting room, a living room, the

kitchen. The closer we get to the ballroom, the darker the wallpaper becomes, growing stained from smoke. In the dining room, it peels back, brittle, blackened. The abandoned furniture looks like charcoal sculptures.

"Check it out." Davie points his flashlight at a crucifix affixed to the wall. It hangs wrong side up.

Hairs raise on the back of my neck. I twist, looking for Viv, and find her near a built-in opposite the crucifix, where shelves hold a graveyard of picture frames and porcelain dishware—some broken, others whole but coated in ash. Viv hurries to join me, winks. Her phone is now stashed on one of those shelves, hiding behind a serving plate or water pitcher. The recording—with several seconds of silence at the start—has already begun playing.

"Jackpot." Davie nudges a door open with his foot. It cries in protest, and the noise is so impossibly loud in the quiet house that we all freeze as it swings inward. Beyond the open door is a blackened floor with a gaping hole at the center. The far wall is thin plywood. It takes me a moment to realize we are looking at the skeleton of the ballroom, now boarded up.

"Sick," one of the boys whispers.

"She died right there—in the center of the room where that hole is," Davie says, though he can't possibly know this. The bottle of vodka dangles from one hand as he points with the other.

A crackle sounds behind us.

"What was that?" Jocelyn latches onto Davie's arm.

He frowns. "I didn't hear anything."

But then there's the unmistakable sound of wood popping, tongues of fire snapping.

"I heard it. Something's burning." This from Gretta, whose eyes widen in the glow of flashlights.

Davie stills. Cocks his head. "It's coming from over there." He points beyond Viv and me. "Near those shelves."

Everyone shuffles toward us, brushes by. Viv and I feign interest and follow. A groan has joined the crackling fire, low and croaky. Gooseflesh coats my limbs. There's something electric in the air—a surge of energy, a presence. Even when I know it's just Viv's recording, I can't shake it.

"*Shit!* I saw something!" Davie yells, and I turn back toward the others.

"Where?" Jocelyn cries.

"What was it?" Gretta screeches.

"A sh-shadow," Davie stammers. "Moving. In that mirror."

Viv's recordings are everywhere now, echoing in the room, surrounding us as we cluster closer, shoulders jammed together, all peering into the mirror mounted beside the built-in. It's old, the glass partially fogged. A dozen faces stare back at us, our reflections, wide-eyed and spooked. All of them slightly blurred on account of the aged glass.

And then . . .

Behind us . . .

At the very back of the group . . .

A figure.

Dark hair that hangs in her face. Brow dripping with blood.

I scream. Davie swears.

Like fish scattering when a rock drops through the surface, we bolt, bodies bumping and staggering. We flee. Through the rooms, back to the foyer, down the stairs, out the French doors. My heart is in my throat, pulse pounding, blood white-hot. I run after the others, tripping on the root-covered path, choking on the fresh pine-scented air. It's only when we approach the boys' camp that we finally slow, then stop. Hunched over, palms braced on our knees, we pant and wheeze for air.

"I saw her," Davie gasps out. "I saw Avery Jane Windsor. She was in that room with us."

"You don't know what you saw," Viv says, rolling her eyes.

"It was a girl. I one-hundred percent saw a girl in that mirror," Davie insists. "She was bleeding everywhere."

"Cut it out, Davie," Jocelyn says.

"I'm not kidding! She, like, flickered into view. Did you honestly not see that?"

Everyone exchanges glances. It becomes obvious that they all ran immediately, spooked by my scream and Davie's outburst. No one saw what we did.

"I heard noises," one of his friends supplies.

"Yeah, what was that?" another chimes in. "It sounded like a fire."

"Yeah, can we at least agree we *heard* that possessed bitch?" Davie says.

"Don't call her that," I say. There's still an electric tension to the night, thrumming through my veins, and it feels like the house is listening. Like it can hear Davie insulting her. This girl that was just a kid.

Davie bats a hand at me and bears down on Viv. "You didn't hear those sounds?" His eyes narrow, his face has gone red. "You calling me a liar?"

"Why would she be bleeding?" Viv asks, ignoring the question. "Avery Jane burned to death."

"So what—You think I'm crazy? Think I imagined it all?" Davie is really close to Viv now, practically foaming at the mouth as he towers over her.

"I . . . I thought I saw something too," I cut in. Not because I want to side with Davie but because I want him to stop attacking Viv, and I *did*, indeed, see something.

She looks at me wide-eyed, wounded.

"But . . . I don't really know what I saw," I add. "It all happened so fast. You freaked out"—a glance at Davie—"and then I freaked, and then we were all running. Maybe we imagined it."

"Fuck this," Davie grumbles. "I'm going to bed."

He stalks off, his friends following him like loyal lap dogs, one of them elbowing him and laughing at how he got spooked. We girls skirt down the hill to the beach to fetch our canoes.

The water is freezing, like a razors slicing into my calves.

—————

"I left my phone," Viv whispers when we're safely back at our cabin. "At Windsor. It's on that bookshelf still, behind a serving plate." I hear her roll over in the bunk above. "We all just . . . ran."

"We can go back for it. You and me. Tomorrow night."

I offer it even though the thought of returning to that place makes the hair on my arms stand on end. On the other side of the cabin, Jocelyn rolls over in her sleep and Gretta snores. The vodka was catching up with them by the time we got back. They passed out almost immediately.

"Did you really see something?" Viv asks. "In that mirror?"

"Yes."

"So he wasn't making it up?"

"I don't think so. Her hair was matted, covering most of her face. There was blood dripping everywhere."

"I didn't see," she admits. "I was too busy watching Davie for his reaction."

I shiver beneath the sheets.

"Let's be quick when we go back for your phone," I say. "I don't think we should spend any more time there than necessary."

"Sure."

Long after her exhales lull and shallow with sleep, I'm still thinking about that mirror in the dining room, the sensation that we were not alone, the human-like groan I heard long before Viv started playing the recording on her cell.

I don't believe in ghosts, I tell myself. But it feels like a lie.

It takes a long time for sleep to find me.

CHAPTER
TEN

I wake to complete and absolute darkness.

The cabin is silent. No creaking frame, no tree branches scraping the siding. Even when I hold my breath, I can't hear a single exhale. The sleeping girls might as well be corpses.

But in the quiet is . . . something. I sit up, listening, straining.

I think I can make out the lap of the lake, slapping the shore. But no, that's just the beat of my heart. It's not a sound I'm reaching for, I realize. It's . . . something intangible. The ghost of a sunburn. Featherlight, but there. Beckoning. Summoning.

I'm overcome with a need to move, so I climb from bed and slip outside. I follow the pine-needle-carpeted path away from the cabin. The needles give way to dirt and roots, and then I'm stepping from the woods and crossing the dew-covered grass field that leads to the beach.

The sand is damp, cool. I'm barefoot. I've forgotten my shoes.

I step into the water. Wetness creeps up my sweat-pants. Sand particles swirl around my ankles and settle over my toes. The lake is freezing, but I don't retreat. I've become an anchor in the shallows, mesmerized by the ripples I've created when entering the water.

The evening, which I first thought to be so quiet, is anything but.

The water laps.

The leaves and pines rustle.

The wood docks groan, like floorboards creaking. Like a canoe tugging against the weight of a rope tethering it in place.

Pull, tug, creak . . . Over and over. Louder and louder, until my skull is pounding.

And just as suddenly as the thrumming noises built, they stop.

The water is still as slate, as if I never stepped into it. My ripples are gone.

Far across the lake, a patch of orange glows on the smooth surface. A patch of orange in the dead of the night.

My head snaps up, to Windsor Camp. There's a light on in one of the upstairs windows.

A breeze caresses the back of my neck.

And then, in my ear, at the softest volume . . .

Eleanor . . .

I stagger from the water, spin around wildly.

"Viv?" I whisper back toward the trees. I wait for her to step from the shadows, buckling with laughter, maybe even with the other girls, all of them gasping, "You should have seen your face!" But there's no one here. I'm alone. Completely and utterly alone.

I turn back toward Windsor.

The light has been extinguished, the house now indiscernible from the dark hillside on the opposite shore. But I can feel its presence still.

I know it's there.

And I can feel it watching.

————

Come morning, I think I've imagined it.

It must have been a strange dream. A waking nightmare.

After all, I can't remember returning to the cabin or climbing back in bed. My sweatpants are dry. My feet inexplicably clean for someone who walked through sand and pine needles barefoot.

But as I make my way to the mess hall at dawn, leaving the other girls still sleeping in their bunks, the sensation returns: a subtle pull, as gentle as a strand of spider's silk, coaxing me toward the beach.

I indulge it, then pause when it releases its hold on me.

I'm standing just inches from the waterline. There's a low fog hovering over the lake and the sun hasn't quite broken the mountains to the west, so the entire world is drenched in a faded shade of purple, like a bruise. Directly across the water, Windsor Camp stands out like a dark scar among the pines. The window that was aglow last night regards me like an unblinking eye.

There was someone there last night.

Probably just local kids, messing around in the abandoned house on a dare. Or a cop, called in to chase out a squatter. Maybe Davie even returned later that night, angry that everyone had laughed at him and determined to find something that supported his girl-in-the-mirror story.

That still doesn't explain the voice. The person who called your name.

My mind drifts to the story Jocelyn told—the fire and the exorcism and the ghost of Avery Jane. I know it's not real. I know how whispers and speculation become rumors, how they morph into stories greater than themselves. How the very setting of this summer camp, with its towering pines and curling mist makes for perfect tinder, ready to ignite as ghost stories are shared around a campfire.

But even still, I wonder.

The house, the mirror, the light in the window.

Beside me, a dock groans. I stare at the estate across the way and feel an unbearable coldness emanating back.

I grab a rock from by my feet and hurl it into the

water. Ripples billow out in a circle. I watch them trem-ble, slowly overtaking the reflection of Windsor Camp on the surface, wiping it clean until all that remains are streaks of color atop the water, rusty and dark, glistening like blood.

———

Reveille plays later on Sundays, but I'm anxious for the day to start. I need a distraction. I walk, drifting through camp like a speck of dandelion fluff.

By the time I have to report to the kitchen, I feel like I've lived a thousand lifetimes.

There are no updates on Dad—Dolores is sure to tell me this the instant I walk through the door—and I spend the morning rush with my hands in soapy water, thinking about Avery Jane. Her story took on a life of its own, becoming a joke to people like Davie, a spectacle to girls like Jocelyn. I feel guilty for participating in it.

The whole thing makes me wonder if my family will be the same in a few decades—a scandalous story to whisper and recount, the people in it reduced to mere characters. Roles, more than human beings.

I go through the day in a daze. Arlo tries to engage me in conversation a few times, but I'm lost in my own thoughts, a mental loop that cycles through what might have truly happened in that house, to what people whisper happened, to whatever strange experience played out for our group last night.

When the sun finally sets in the evening, I'm feeling less than thrilled about having to return to Windsor with Viv.

"Davie likes me," Jocelyn says as we're washing up in the cabin. "That's why he was trying to freak us all out. It was a joke, a prank."

"I saw something too," I remind her.

"Suuure you did, Nell." Jocelyn winks at me, smiling.

I'm not sure if this is some type of coping mechanism for her—pretending our bone-chilling experience at that house didn't happen—or if she truly believes that Davie pretended to see something in the mirror.

"If Davie likes you, why is he trying to terrify you?" Viv asks.

"That's what boys do. When they like you, they're mean."

"I think that's just called being an asshole."

Jocelyn blows out an aggressive puff of air. "You wouldn't understand."

"Davie's been cruel to Viv since fourth grade," I point out. "But shockingly, he still hasn't asked her out. So maybe it has nothing to do with liking you and everything to do with the fact that he's a douche."

"I thought he was fine," Gretta interjects. "They all were."

I have a feeling Gretta would say any boy that paid her a fraction of attention was fine. She doesn't seem to have the highest standards, but I also can't blame her for it. When everything around you seems to imply that the most important thing is to be beautiful and to be loved, it's easy to forget to love yourself first.

I'm not exactly innocent here either. I've gone along with Kylie's plans plenty of times all with the hope of fitting in, being admired, and holding someone's attention. Dad never made me feel worthy, so I went looking for proof of my worth everywhere.

"Are we gonna get together with them again?" Gretta asks, clearly hopeful.

"If I can get in touch with them, sure." Jocelyn checks the signal on her phone. "Maybe I can lead a hike again soon, send a text."

"Can't wait," Viv grumbles under her breath.

Jocelyn and Gretta go on chatting, but Viv and I climb into our bunks. At a whisper, so the other girls don't hear, I tell her about feeling drawn to the shore, the light I saw in Windsor's upper window.

"Maybe I was wrong," I say softly when I finish.

"About?"

"That place. The ghost stories." I swallow. "Maybe she does haunt Windsor."

"It was probably someone messing around in the house. Just like we were," Viv says, but her voice isn't terribly convincing.

Out on the lake, a loon cries, mournful and stoic, a sad lament.

"I thought you said you believe in ghosts."

"I do," Viv says. "But that doesn't mean there's a ghost in the house across the lake. You could have dreamed the light in the window. You said your pants were dry when you woke up in the morning, your feet were clean. Plus I didn't see anything in that mirror the other night and neither did anyone else."

"Except for Davie."

"Except for Davie," she concedes. "Supposedly." She says the last bit with an air of disgust. I wonder if she doubts my word also.

"Did you at least feel something there?" I ask after a moment. "Something unnatural?"

"The place is definitely creepy," she concedes. "Now shh, let's pretend we're sleeping so they finally go to sleep also."

It takes the girls awhile to call it a night. Part of me hopes they won't, that they just stay up rambling until dawn and Viv and I never have the opportunity to sneak out. I'm not prepared for what awaits across the lake.

But eventually the cabin falls silent, and Viv nudges my arm, urges me up. Reluctantly, I slip from bed, edge out the door, and follow her to the shoreline.

CHAPTER
ELEVEN

We are utterly alone. Me and Viv. Two girls in a canoe that feels no bigger than a grain of rice against the gaping width of the lake, the stillness of the night so permeant we stay silent as we retrace our steps.

Back to the boys' beach.

Back up the twisting path.

Back through the half-boarded French doors and up the steps and into the dining room.

Viv goes straight for the built-in. "It's not here," she says, fingers searching.

"You sure?"

"Positive. It's gone."

I move closer with the flashlight, casting the beam over the shelves. She pushes aside pitchers and cups, dishes and bowls. Dust dances in the illumination.

"It was right here," she says, pointing toward a

serving dish that stands in a display easel. On the shelf surface, there's a subtle rectangle in the dust, the phone's footprint from last night.

"Where would it have gone?"

"I don't know."

A shiver hits between my shoulders and snakes down my spine. "Can ghosts touch things? Pick them up?"

"No clue. I believe in them, but in the same way I kinda believe in aliens or dark matter. Doesn't mean I get how they operate. I think I read somewhere that they don't like salt. Or iron? Maybe it was both." She keeps searching the shelves, moving faster, frantic. In her panic, she knocks a saucer from a tiny easel-frame. It spins on its side in slow motion, twirling like a dancer, teetering toward the edge of the shelf and then plummeting for the floor.

We watch it fall in what seems like half-time. And then it's shattered, tiny shards twitching to a standstill, the tinkling of broken china ringing in the silence.

Overhead, the floorboards creak.

Viv freezes. "What was that?"

I shake my head and click the flashlight off. Darkness swallows the house.

For what feels like an eternity, it's pitch black. We are drowning in ink, a bottomless abyss. Then my eyes adjust. Viv becomes visible first. Then the framework of the built-in. The glass mirror—a muted, silver disc on the wall. It's too dark to see either of us properly, but I stand there, pulse pounding, expecting a third figure to appear behind the dark silhouettes of me and Viv. The bleeding girl.

It's just us.

I nod toward the stairs.

"What?" Viv whispers.

I put a finger to my lips, lead.

"No," Viv says. "Come on, Nell. Let's go."

But I'm on autopilot, already ascending the first few steps. They are carpeted, thick with dust and dirt, and who knows what else pushed deep into the fabric. It softens our footsteps. On the landing, I pause, gathering my bearings. The noise came from the right.

Viv tugs at my wrist, but I pad down the hallway. Find the door to the room. Push it open.

It's a bedroom.

Maybe *her* bedroom.

The bedframe is still there, but the mattress is gone, exposing rusted coil springs. There's a dresser, a rocking chair, a nightstand. A blanket lies crumbled on the floor beneath the window.

She called this place home once. Does she still?

A creak on the stairs now.

Then below, in the dining room.

Like she's gone down to find us, just as we've come up to find her.

"Let's go, Nell," Viv whispers. "I'm scared."

I am too.

But I stand bone still a moment longer, breath held, waiting.

When all I can hear is the beating of my own heart, I link hands with Viv and we descend the stairs together.

———

"I just don't know where it could have gone," Viv laments as we paddle back across Corwin.

"Maybe one of the boys grabbed it," I offer, because I know we're both disturbed by the other possibility.

"They didn't even know it was there."

"Someone else exploring the house might have found it."

"But it was hidden *really* well."

I swallow, gooseflesh coating my limbs.

"I think she's real, Viv," I whisper. I'd wondered just earlier today, but now I feel sure. We weren't alone in that house tonight.

Viv glances over her shoulder, staring at Windsor as it shrinks behind us. "Maybe."

"I still don't know why she'd take your phone."

"Could she want something in exchange for it? Help moving on? Isn't that why ghosts get stuck in our dimension—because something keeps them from passing on?"

"If she wanted help, she could have shown herself. We heard her moving around tonight."

Viv shudders. "God, this gives me the creeps."

"I'm not afraid of her." It's only when I say it aloud, that I realize it's true. The house is unsettling. Her story is scary. Her appearance in the mirror even more so. But I don't think she means us any harm. If she did, she's now had two chances to inflict it. "I feel sorry for her—what happened, how she's stuck."

Our canoe bumps against the beach and sags to a stop. I help Viv drag it out of the water and back to the rack. We slide the chains back in place, lock the boat up, and return the key to the pegboard.

"So what do we do now?" she asks me.

"We need to learn more about her before we reach out again. Research what happened." For the first time since arriving at Camp Durant, I look west down our shoreline, toward Bradley House. "I know a place that has internet."

"I meant about my phone."

"Oh. I'll text it when we're researching. I'll have service via the Wi-Fi. Maybe we'll be able to reach whoever picked it up."

Viv's eyes narrow. "Where do you know that has Wi-Fi?"

I tell her about my family's summer house, watching her brows rise a fraction in the moonlight.

"All right, fine," she agrees finally. "But only because we're trying to get a hold of my phone in the process."

"It will take two hours, round-trip. We should go when we have daylight."

"I won't be able to get away during the week," Viv says. "The schedule is tight with my campers."

"Same for me with kitchen duties."

"Saturday then," she proposes as we slink through the trees, heading for the cabin. "My girls have an outing with the girls from Moss Lodge. Fly fishing excursion on the river that feeds the north end of the lake. They'll be gone all day. Jocelyn and Gretta are overseeing it with two other fishing guides. It's my afternoon off."

I try not to think of how many dishes will pile up at the kitchen while I'm gone. Enough that Dolores will definitely notice that I'm not "pulling my weight."

"I'll ask Arlo to cover for me."

"Think he'll agree?"

I shrug. I'm not sure where Arlo and I stand. We're friendly, but I'm not sure we're actually friends. "Guess I'll find out."

CHAPTER
TWELVE

The week passes slowly, days bleeding together like a sunset. Reveille in the morning. Taps at night. Owls in the evening and the itch to move finding me in the darkest hours.

When the rest of the camp is sleeping, Windsor calls to me. I'm certain, deep in my bones, that if I slipped from bed and slunk toward the shore, I'd find Avery Jane in that bedroom window, backlit by a square of light, her gaze turned toward our beach. I'd hear her whispering my name again.

But I don't dare get out of bed. If I go to the water in the dead of the night again, I won't be able to turn around. I'll either canoe straight across the lake to confront her, or I'll head to Bradley House, needing to do something productive with my time to distract from the ghost trying to communicate with me. And I don't want to go to Bradley House without Viv.

All the pictures of Dad on the walls.

All the memories of life before.

I already faced it alone once. I don't know if I can bear to do it again.

The sticky weight of summer settles in, and the campers are coated in sweat by lunchtime each day. The kitchen is a sauna, nearly unbearable. I keep my hair piled atop my head in a messy bun. Arlo continues to smoke at the end of each day and somehow, miraculously, hasn't been caught. On Friday after dinner, once I hear his lighter flick to life on the other side of the door, I finish the last batch of dishes quickly and slip outside to join him. I've been meaning to talk to him all week, and now I'm nearly out of time.

"Hey."

He startles like a kid caught stealing. "Fuck, don't do that!"

"Do what?"

"Sneak up on me like that. You're too quiet. You're like a mouse. Or a . . ." He pauses, then grins, all teeth. "A moth."

"You're high," I say plainly.

"Not untrue."

"So . . . Can you do me a huge favor and handle dishes tomorrow?"

"All day?"

"Just lunch and dinner. I'll make it up to you."

"How's that?"

"Not sure yet. Your call."

He considers this while he takes a long drag, then puffs out perfect little rings of smoke. They float upward, stretching and wobbling until they dissipate into nothing.

"That could be dangerous," he says finally. "Giving me so much power."

"Well, I trust you won't be an ass about it, otherwise the deal is null and void."

"Void," he says, smirking. "I like that word. Voooooid."

"Arlo, will you do it or not?"

"Yeah, sure. You got it, Manhattan."

"Thanks."

I glance back when I hit the dirt path that leads to the cabins. Arlo's leaning against the wall, sending smoke rings toward the slivered moon.

———

Back at the cabin, I find Viv in the bathroom, brushing her teeth. Her hair is wet from a shower and poking up in all directions, and she's wearing sweats and a tee-shirt for some band I don't recognize. The lone mirror is thoroughly fogged, which makes me wonder how long she'd been soaking in the hot water and how pissed Towers would be if she knew. Part of her monotone speech during orientation had mentioned conserving water and the need to take quick, efficient showers.

"Arlo's going to cover for me on Saturday," I announce.

She flashes me a thumbs-up and keeps brushing vigorously.

"Afternoon and evening, so we can go anytime after I finish the breakfast rush."

"Great," she says through a mouthful of toothpaste.

"I'll owe him."

"Mhmm." She spits, rinses, then starts flossing, never once looking in my direction.

"Why are you being weird?"

"Weird? I'm not being weird."

"Yes you are. You're flossing, for starters. That's something you're supposed to lie to the dentist about doing but not actually do. And also? You won't even look at me."

"People who want to avoid cavities floss."

"Viv."

She leans closer to the mirror. Tries to examine her teeth through the obscured glass.

"Vivian."

"I just . . . overheard them today," she says, twisting to face me. "Talking about you. It made me feel shitty."

"Who?"

"Goodwin and Towers."

"What did they say?"

Viv throws her floss out and grabs her toiletry bag. I follow her back to our bunks.

"Come on, Viv. I can handle it."

She sighs heavily. "They were discussing the news, some update in the paper. From what I caught, it sounded like Towers thinks the feds have given up finding your father. That he's been sneaky and smart and they're only going to find him if he slips up at this point. Oh, and that the spotting in Jersey might have been false." Viv shrugs. "She said something about how they're keeping the hotline open for tips and they're hopeful this will all end well."

I scoff. "End well. How can it end well? He screwed so many people out of their retirement funds. And no one will even talk to me back home, not unless it's to curse me out."

"Goodwin said, 'I feel so terrible for Rachel. My heart breaks for her.' I'm assuming that's your mom?"

I nod.

Viv's mouth contorts, something between a frown and a grimace. "That's bullshit. The way all the adults are acting like this is so awful for your mom, but not for you. It's awful for everyone involved."

"Thanks, Viv."

I slump onto my bunk, staring at the overhead mattress. I wonder what Mom's doing right now. Maybe she'll drive up here and Mrs. Goodwin can hold her hand and tell her everything will be fine, and I can just keep dealing with this absolute fuckfest on my own, unaided, with zero support from any adults in my life. I still don't know how I'm going to face everyone in the fall, when school starts up again. Mom's never been the easiest to talk to about . . . well, anything, but I expected her to check in with me by now. If not by heading north, at least by coordinating a phone call through Goodwin's office.

Though perhaps that goes both ways.

Perhaps she's sitting in the apartment, sulking, waiting for me to call her. Or write to her. I'd told her I'd write.

Viv sits beside me, pats my shin. "You okay?"

"Not really." It's not the answer I want to be giving, but it's honest.

"I'd say we could watch something on my phone, but . . . a ghost stole it."

That makes me smile.

"I'd have lost my mind by now if not for you," I tell her.

"I really am a saint. It's so hard being decent and treating you like a human being. You're gonna owe me."

"You *and* Arlo? This is unjust."

"I'm only going to ask for your firstborn child. Nothing too big."

"Maybe you'd like my inheritance too. Assuming there's any left."

"That sounds fair."

Jocelyn and Gretta burst into the cabin, talking about activity points and how the boys' camp has pulled ahead of the girls' in the Cross-Camp Competition. "They're going to be gloating and insufferable by the mid-summer talent show," Gretta complains.

"Who cares about gloating," Jocelyn responds. "I'm just excited to see the guys again."

"What about your boyfriend?"

"Looking and talking isn't cheating, Gretta."

I roll my eyes. Viv shouts goodnight to them.

It's not late, but we have a big day ahead of us. The sooner we sleep, the better.

———

The morning brings building humidity that is downright brutal by the time Viv and I lug a canoe to the shore shortly before noon. The sky is cloudless, an endless swath of deep cerulean. Once on the water, Viv slathers on sunscreen. I squint in the glare off the lake.

There's no breeze today and the water is mirror-clear. Our canoe sends ripples billowing outward as we slice through the shallows. Soon we're leaving the beach behind us and following the curve of the shore south.

When the camp is swallowed from view, the remoteness of Corwin Lake overwhelms. Pines, rolling and climbing around us. Water and sky and trees stretching out forever. A bit farther south, we'll find the occasional house. But for now, in this small moment, Viv and I might as well be the only beings in the world.

"My mom wrote me," Viv announces, breaking the quiet. "Said she's started seeing someone."

"That's good, right?"

She does that frown-nod thingy that means she agrees but is kind of *meh* about the whole thing. "Our neighbor.

He's a vet and pretty boring, but entirely decent. She could do a lot worse."

I picture Mom standing in the apartment foyer, looking down on the sidewalk, stuck in the past, waiting for someone entirely un-decent to return home.

"Think your mom might start dating again?" Viv asks.

I shrug. "She needs to accept that Dad's gone before she can do that. Maybe file some divorce papers, too."

"Maybe she needs a five-year plan."

"Five years is being generous. She is the most unadventurous woman you will ever meet and she doesn't do well with change." I swat a mosquito away from Viv's shoulder. "I should probably write her. I said I would, and she might be worried."

Viv nods. "How much farther you think?"

I take in the shoreline and everything that was hidden by fog on my last trip along this stretch. A few small cabins—home to fishermen that have been in the same family for generations—are visible through the trees. Their shingled roofs are covered in moss. Forest-green shutters hang off-kilter.

"Forty minutes, maybe. We should have taken the kayaks. They'd be quicker."

"But then we couldn't take turns resting. Or snacking." Viv pulls an apple from her backpack and shines it on her shorts. The skin gleams, red and tempting. "Want one?"

My stomach twists. "Thanks, but too anxious."

"Anxious?"

"My mom could be there."

"Wouldn't she have told you if she was coming up?"

"No one tells me anything."

Viv shrugs. "More for me, I guess." She bites down on the apple, the skin breaking with an audible snap as her teeth sink into the juicy flesh.

CHAPTER
THIRTEEN

When the house finally comes into view, Viv draws a quick breath.

It's impressive on a normal day, but after weeks of camp cabins and bunkbeds, it's extravagant, bordering on gauche. At least to my eyes.

Mom's never been fond of the logs—whole, split, peeled or otherwise—that are used in classic Adirondack architecture. She says they're too irregular, too rustic. That the result *looks like a drunken deer tried to decorate a chalet.* She has, however, always approved of the granite stonework that makes up many of the boathouses, chimneys, and foundations of the Great Camps, and that's what makes up the foundation of Bradley House, too. Above the stone foundation, the siding is an ashen gray, as though color alone can trick someone into thinking it's made of logs felled from the native forest, peeled, and left to weather beneath the sun and rain. The windows are massive, taking up most of the facade that looks over the water. There's the central A-frame that screams *look at how impressive I am*, two chimneys, and wrap-around deck.

Bradley House tries to look like a Great Camp, but at best, it merely imitates. Even still, it screams wealth and money.

"So, you're like . . . rich-rich," Viv says. "I mean I figured, after you told me about your dad, but now I can *see*."

We glide toward the boathouse, which is set into the hill beneath the house. The three doors are closed, the windows of the suite above, pulled tight. The windows on the main house are secured too. Mom, always quick to crack windows so a breeze can chase out the stale air, is clearly not here.

I'm both relieved and disappointed.

We hop out at the dock beside the boathouse, then pull the canoe onto the shore.

"Follow me." I jerk my head toward the house and Viv follows me up the winding steps. The same steps I took down to the dock when I headed to orientation.

The shade provided by the upper deck is a relief after an hour of canoeing in the blistering sun. I locate the spare key from beneath a flowerpot near the slider door.

"Shouldn't there be a cop here?" Viv asks.

"What do you mean?"

"Don't people on the run often return to places familiar to them? Shouldn't someone be staking this place out?"

"Huh." She's right. But there wasn't a soul here when I arrived before orientation and the place still looks deserted. "Maybe they're just watching the security cameras. Dad set a few up a couple years ago. I bet Mom gave them access to the feeds."

I unlock the door and give it a good shove with my shoulder—it's swollen from the humidity—and then we're spilling into Bradley House, the security alarm chirping at us angrily. I punch in the code, and the house falls silent.

"Wow," Viv says.

The family room we've stepped into could hold the entire staff cabin we've called home the last weeks, plus two more. Wide-planked wood floors gleam, and carpets split the room into separate functional spaces. Lounging (sectional sofa, flat-screen TV), drinking (bar, stools, wine cooler), socializing (pool table, dartboard). The art on the walls is everything Dad bought that Mom decided wasn't up to her standards, her least favorites. But a gallery light still hangs above every frame.

"Wait till you see upstairs," I groan.

We head up. I try to witness the home as if I'm seeing it for the first time, through Viv's eyes. It all starts to feel ridiculous. The high ceilings, the exposed beams, the massive fireplace. Everything three times larger than necessary.

Dad once said that Mom was compensating for apartment living when Bradley House was built. She spent the majority of her days in what most New Yorkers would consider an ample footprint for an apartment, but when it came time to build a second home, she built for the space she wished she could have in the city, then multiplied it by five.

It's one of the few things he's ever said that I agreed with.

"It's over-the-top. I know. Please don't hate me?"

"Why would I hate you?" Viv's turns in a circle beneath the A-frame window, looking up into the beams. The sun catches off the face of her watch and flickers on the floor.

"Computer is in the library."

"There's a library, too? Weren't you only up here during the summer?"

"Yeah. Mostly."

She whistles.

The curtains are drawn when we step into the room that served mostly as Dad's office. I boot up the computer, then open Chrome and stare at the blinking cursor in the browser bar.

"Where do we even start?"

"Death of Avery Jane Windsor?" Viv suggests. "I'm afraid to touch anything," she adds, nodding at the impressive collection of books that fill the built-ins.

I peck at the keyboard, entering Viv's suggested search term, then scroll through the results.

It's all stuff I've heard before but can now confirm with reliable sources: reports on the fire, obituaries for the family, quotes from townsfolk lamenting over the tragedy, follow-up articles months later when the investigation ended and the fire was confirmed to be the result of a horrible accident. Everything is dated late 1985, early 1986. After that, there's nothing. I click to the second page of search results. And there, at the top: "Avery Jane's real and I can prove it."

I click the link and cringe. The site is all black, with bright white text and ads flashing in the sidebars recommending ghost tours and cemetery guides. A logo at the top reads *The Ghost Hunter's Haven,* with a font that looks ripped directly from the Ghost Busters movies, a white apparition poking through the O and everything. The site's subtitle proclaims it to be the "#1 online destination for hunters of paranormal activity."

The link I've followed has dropped me into a forum, or more specifically, into *Real Encounters > New York > Adirondacks > Avery Jane,* and the OP's *Avery Jane's real and I can prove it* entry.

I scroll quickly. The thread is hundreds of comments long. No, thousands. This will take ages to read.

"This is going to give me a headache," I moan. My eyes are already aching from the white on black text. I print the discussion so I can read it later, then select "Browse by Map" from the main menu. There, I drill down through New York, then the Adirondacks, and find an entry called "Avery Jane (The Girl in White)."

Another page of white text on black loads. The post lays out the twisted version of the Windsors' story. The same one Jocelyn presented as fact that day at the bonfire, in which little Avery Jane was possessed by some sort of spirit. An exorcism was performed and the ballroom was inexplicably engulfed in flames, the entire family killed by a vengeful demon.

This story is completely at odds with the news articles, and yet, I'm starting to believe that this dramatic version of the tale may actually hold a kernel of truth.

"Check this out," I say, and begin reading aloud. "'Avery Jane supposedly haunts the remnants of Windsor Camp in the white dressed she died in. Some believe she lingers because she is not yet free of her demon. One theory is that her burned and mutilated body was buried wearing a possessed item that still binds the spirit to her, such as a ring or necklace, while others believe a far less likely possibility, and one not supported by many facts: that Avery is possessed not by a spiritual demon but by a need to reveal that she was murdered by her own parents. Believers of this theory claim the fire was started by Mr. and Mrs. Windsor in an effort to destroy evidence of their crime, but it burned too hot too quickly and delivered them all to an untimely death.'"

The figure in the mirror flashes before my eyes—the straggly hair, the way it dripped with blood. A fire wouldn't result in blood, but a murder might.

"That's twisted," Viv says, looking somewhat pale. "I think that might be even worse than being possessed and dying during an attempted exorcism."

I nod in agreement. "'The truth,'" I keep reading, "'may be lost forever. Many who enter Windsor Camp say the Girl in White is nowhere to be found and the story is nothing but an urban legend. Those who swear to have crossed paths with Avery Jane claim she is fitful and untrustworthy. If she needs help moving on, she'll have to accept the help of ghost hunters, not chase them from the remnants of her charred home.'"

The article ends with a bold call to action. *Have you made contact with this ghost? Share your experience in the forums.*

Viv clicks her tongue. "Say her ghost really is trapped and wants help—what would we even do?"

"Figure out which theory is true, I guess. If she was murdered, we try to prove it and get the truth out. If she was possessed, we find her grave and separate her from the cursed object." I should feel ridiculous proposing these plans, but it fills me with purpose. There's a way forward now. This proves that I've been feeling drawn to Windsor Camp for a reason, that I'm not seeing things.

Avery Jane is trying to reach out to us. She's *called* to me.

And we need to help her.

I navigate back to the forums and check for other threads that may be of use, but there's no recent activity. In fact, the pages I've printed are the most recent discussion about Avery Jane, and they're from nearly a decade ago.

On the shelf above the desk, the printer finally sputters to a halt. "Maybe the forums will give us some ideas of where to begin," I say, gathering the thick stack of pages from the tray. "We can read through them back at camp and—"

"Hey, I've seen this bag," Viv interrupts.

She's pointing to a framed picture hanging on the wall beside the desk. It's a shot from a Cornell alumni reunion a few years ago. Dad's standing with his arm hooked around the neck of an old baseball teammate. They'd reunited for a friendly game and are dressed not in formal uniforms, but casual Cornell athletic gear. Branded tees and hats. *Go Big Red!*

Dad's friend is still wearing his baseball mitt, and Dad has his duffle bag slung over his shoulder, the handle of a bat poking out one end. It's his Cornell-branded duffel bag that Viv's pointing at. The Big Red logo sits front and center—a brown bear entangled with a large letter C—but it's far from the only logo on the bag. Patches from various National Parks also cover the material. Dad had a short-lived life outside finance and investing, and it happened during college and the two years after, when he traveled to every national park he could possibly arrange to see, hiked and backpacked with school buddies, and then ironed a patch from each park onto the duffel at the end of each trip. At least that's how Mom explained it.

"You've seen *that* bag?" I repeat, thrusting a finger at it for emphasis. "Where?"

"In Glens Falls. I was heading home from the library, waiting for the bus. A guy walked by with that exact duffel. I remember thinking it was weird—a sports bag, but covered in parks patches."

I freeze. "You don't happen to know when this was, do you?"

"Actually, yeah. It was on my birthday."

"And that's . . . ?"

"June twenty-sixth."

I shoot out of the chair, stuff the printed pages into the back of my jean shorts. "We have to go. Right now."

"Why?"

"We have to get back to camp. You need to talk to Goodwin, ask to use the office phone so you can call the hotline."

"What are you talking about?"

"The sighting in Jersey was false, just like everyone has been theorizing. But June twenty-sixth? That's the day the scandal broke, Viv, the day he went missing. You saw my dad, running."

CHAPTER
FOURTEEN

Viv talks to Goodwin without me. She thinks it
will be best.

I watch her cut up the hill after we secure the
canoe, the ends of her pink hair bobbing above her shoulders. Then I head to the beach and sit on one of the docks,
dangling my feet in the water.

It's fairly quiet. Most campers are back from their
activities but too exhausted from the day's outings to do
anything other than lounge in their bunks now that
dinner is over. A few are getting a final swim in before the
sun sets. One dock over, Jocelyn and Gretta are chatting.
Gretta sits with her legs crossed beneath her. Jocelyn is
half-reclined on the dock but propped up on her elbows,
staff shirt discarded in favor of the bikini underneath,
working on her tan. The way Mrs. Towers glares at her
from where she stands on the shore, chatting with one of
the on-duty lifeguards, makes me wonder if she thinks

wearing a bikini isn't role-model behavior. Which is infuriating. We're at a lake, and it's hot. What's she supposed to wear to swim—a track suit?

Jocelyn gives me a little wave. I wave back.

She's not my favorite person in the world, but she's also not as bad as I originally thought. The scandal has been awful. People judged me unfairly, but I understand I'm just the punching bag for the anger they feel at Dad's actions. And at least Jocelyn hasn't said much about him since that first day.

I stare at the house across the water.

I have felt eyes on me since I arrived Corwin Lake. From my very first paddle from Bradley House to camp, I felt something among the trees. Then again outside the cabin, a presence watching me step inside for the first time. And then the house itself—the way I've been drawn to it, to some entity I can't place. The things I felt while standing inside its walls, the light I saw in the window that night.

Is it her? Has it been here this entire time?

I say her name in my mind, narrow my eyes, will her to call for me.

Birds sing in response.

The water laps.

My vision tunnels and the sounds of early evening are suddenly sucked into oblivion, as though I've stepped into a vacuum. My eyes are locked on Windsor Camp. They burn, ache. I couldn't blink even if I wanted.

Something touches my shoulder and I flinch, startled.

Everything is as it was. Only it's twilight now, Corwin Lake painted in musty, faded hues. The birds have stopped singing. Jocelyn and the other staff members are gone.

How long have I been sitting here?

I look up to find it's Viv who's touched my shoulder. "Hey, how'd it go?" I ask as she plops down beside me.

She hangs her feet over the edge of the dock, lets her toes dip into the water. "I told her I think I saw your dad in Glens Falls on June twenty-sixth."

"And she called it in?"

"Not right away. First she got all serious and put her hands on my hips and said, 'Are you positive, Vivian? I can't call in this tip unless you're absolutely positive.'" She bites her lip, looks at me sideways. "She asked me how I knew, and I . . . I had to lie a little."

"What? *Why?*"

"Well, I realized if I told her we'd been to your house she could fire us. We're not supposed to sneak off camp property. So I said that were talking about your dad this morning and you mentioned his sports bag. Your description was so unique I said, 'Wait, show me a picture!' And you had one on your phone—please tell me you have one on your phone—and once I saw it, I knew I'd seen that same bag being carried by a someone in Glens Falls on my birthday."

"It's one of his old profile pics on Facebook," I say. "So it's not directly on my phone, but I could have showed you *on* my phone."

"Phew," she says. "That works perfectly then."

"Except I don't have service at camp."

Viv's expression deflates. "I guess I'll figure out that wrinkle if it comes up again."

I nod, agreeing. "So what now?"

"Now I wait for the cops. Goodwin thanked me for coming forward and said she'd call it in immediately. I bet it's only a matter of time before they arrive. Hey, you didn't remember to text my phone did you? While we were at your house?"

"No, sorry. We bolted so fast after you recognized Dad's bag that I forgot. I'll do it soon. I promise."

She looks unconvinced, and I wonder if I'm that transparent. I have no plans to return to Bradley House any time soon.

———

I read the forums that night by flashlight, Viv passed out in the bunk above me. Two cops showed up maybe an hour after Goodwin called the tip line, and Viv spent most of the night answering questions in the main office.

What time did you spot him?

Where exactly in Glens Falls?

Was he hitchhiking? Walking? On the north- or southbound side of the road?

What was he wearing?

Explain the bag again?

Was it the duffel in this picture?

They had a printout from Facebook. Viv told me how they'd set the photo on the wooden desk in Goodwin's office and slid it toward her. In the end, she said they thanked her for speaking up and would take her information to the right authorities. Within five minutes of recounting the evening to me, Viv is passed out and snoring in her bunk.

I flip to a new page of forum printouts, the paper crinkling in my lap. There's nothing concrete in the fifty-plus pages I printed from the Avery Jane forum on *The Ghost Hunter's Haven*. Speculations. Gossip. Rehashing of the legend itself—how Avery Jane stopped eating that summer, then heard voices, then lost control of her mind and body to the spirit that would be her undoing. Of course, there are posts from folks debating this, claiming she was never possessed at all and her death was a murder. And then there's comments about actual encounters with her ghost, the bulk of which are little more than stories from people who snuck into Windsor Camp and got creeped out by a creaking floorboard or the whining wind outside. But the original poster mentions something that stands out to me, something that is mentioned by a half-dozen other ghost hunters later on in the discussion.

They all claim you can only see Avery Jane in mirrors. She'll appear as a flicker, or a face, or a blur of pale clothing. The Girl in White. Lurking in the reflective surfaces of Windsor.

None of the descriptions exactly match what I saw that night we first broke into the estate, and the most recent sighting is from nineteen years ago, but the hair on my forearms still rises.

The only thing everyone seems to completely agree on is that all ghosts fear iron and salt, and that Avery Jane is no exception. One commenter claims he spooked Avery Jane by blowing a handful of salt from his palm. Another swears he struck something invisible while swinging a metal chain around in the ballroom—something that screamed, then fled, causing the doors to blow open.

With a shudder, I fold the papers in half and tuck them beneath my pillow.

I'm cold. Restless. I need to move. I slip from the cabin and walk to the shore.

Fog curls over the water, hiding the reflection of stars. Across the lake, Windsor Camp is hidden among the trees, the entire shoreline painted a giant swath of shadow.

Avery? I call to her in my mind.

The only answer is an owl, hooting deep in the woods behind me.

Did someone murder her? Was she possessed by a demon? Was it all just a tragic accident? The majority of the forum's posters leaned toward possession. It was clearly the most popular theory, but it's also the most sensational. The sort of set up that makes for a good movie, and if I've learned anything these past weeks, it's that people love a dramatic mystery.

A breeze passes over the lake, rippling the water.

Every hair on my arms stands on end.

Eleanor . . .

It's a girl's voice, soft and gravelly.

I freeze, staring at the house.

It remains dark, invisible.

Eleanor Bradley . . .

"Were you murdered?" I whisper into the darkness. "Possess—"

She doesn't even let me finish the word. A square of light comes to life across the water—her window aglow. It's like a beacon, a magnet, a response to my question.

A fist tightens around my heart. I want to look away, but I can't. My eyes water, burn. I think I can hear fire cracking, flames snapping. Screaming, even. I stagger away, run for the woods. When I reach the first of the pines, I grab a trunk for support and gasp, breathless.

When I glance over my shoulder, the window is dark, the shore cloaked in shadow.

Somewhere in the woods, the owl calls again.

CHAPTER
FIFTEEN

The morning brings rain thundering down on the cabin's roof and turning the paths outside muddy. Pine needles ride the water like little kayaks in a raging river.

I pull on my raincoat and sprint to the kitchen. Running does me no favors; my jean shorts are still drenched by the time I arrive. The kids will come in rushes this morning, driven in like cattle by the first bad weather of the camp season, but for now the mess is filled only with staff.

"Manhattan! How'd your little excursion go?" Arlo asks.

I shake water from my limbs and shed my jacket. "Fine. How were things here?"

"The usual." He shoots me a grin and it makes dimples appear. This seems like a feature I should have noticed before, but I realize that he doesn't have a toothpick in his mouth today—or a joint between his lips—which changes the entire shape of his smile. It brings his whole face to life. He's . . . not bad-looking, I realize. Kinda disheveled in that I-don't-care-how-I-look way, but he pulls it off.

If I wasn't in the midst of trying to make contact with a ghost while my reputation goes up in flames on account of my father's scandal, I might be concerned what these realizations mean.

"So what do you I owe you?" I ask him.

He shrugs.

"I do owe you, right?"

He shrugs again.

"Riveting conversation, as always." I roll up my sleeves and get to work at the sink. Already, dishes are starting to pile up.

Arlo disappears to help Dolores with something.

I scrub and clean.

Later, when the breakfast rush is over and the dishes are slowing, Arlo reappears. "So I decided how you can pay me back," he announces, leaning against the wall beside the sinks.

"M-hmm?"

"Let's hang out sometime. Maybe tonight."

I cock a brow at him.

"Oh, come on. This place is boring as hell. The guys I bunk with are all pushing forty. Instructors for rock-climbing and fishing. And then one of the facilities crew. They all crash at, like, nine p.m."

"Maybe because they are a responsible adults and want to be well-rested come morning."

Arlo reaches a long arm out and turns off my faucet. I look up, annoyed.

"Come on, Manhattan." He blinks his brown eyes at me. "What's the harm?"

I twist the faucet back on. "For one, I barely know you. Maybe you're a creepy stalker. Why do you work in the kitchens at a girls' camp, when you could be doing the same job at the boys' camp across the lake? Or better yet, be a counselor? It pays better. And secondly, I said I'd owe you a *favor*. Not a date."

He scoffs. "Who said it was a date? I just want to hang with someone who isn't a few years off from a mid-life crisis."

Well, now I feel dumb.

"And it's because of my mom," he adds.

"What?"

"That's why I'm at the girls' camp and not the boys'. Mrs. Towers, the director? She's my mom. She got me this job."

Arlo Towers.

"Oh." It's all I can manage. He looks nothing like his mother.

"Just consider it, Manhattan. It could be fun. And you're not against fun, are you?" He's doing that smirking thing again.

"You're insufferable."

He winks. "Great. Meet at the campfire tonight."

Before I can argue that I never actually agreed to hang out, he's slipped outside.

————

Sunday passes lazily, as it tends to do at Camp Durant. Outdoor activities like pick-up games of basketball and ultimate frisbee are called off due to the weather, but campers congregate inside, doing crafts, reading books, and chatting with friends.

After lunch, the pouring rain has relented to more of a spitting drizzle, and I can't stay inside any longer. I pull the hood of my raincoat up and head out.

I walk without a destination. Viv's busy with her campers, and I don't know where I want to be except that I want to be there alone. I drift by the waterfront, cut behind the instructors' and admins' cabins, and hit the Notch's Point trail.

The air is thick and humid, but I have a chill I can't shake. Probably on account of my absolute drenched sneakers and soaked socks. I'm a smudge moving through the woods, the pines towering around me. I'm the wreckage left behind from Dad's chaos.

Awhile later, the trail turns sharply, breaking from the pines and ending at the summit that overlooks Corwin. From here, the camp is hidden behind the trees and the curve of the shore, giving the sensation that I'm truly lost in the wilderness. The water ripples and dances beneath the spitting rain. In the distance, the horizon is a blurry cloud of moisture, the opposite shoreline obscured in shadow.

The last time I came to this lookout, I was a camper and Kylie was with me. We were wearing matching friendship bracelets that we'd made earlier that day in our arts session, and tee-shirts that we'd stitched our initials into along the hemline.

My initials are embroidered into the right rear pocket of the jean cutoffs I'm wearing today. I touch them absent-mindedly, feeling the shape of the letters beneath my thumb— E and B. Somewhere in Manhattan, Kylie has a pair bearing her initials, too. She insisted on us embroidering a pair of shorts every summer, a tradition from our camp days. It was the only manner in which she stayed young. For years, we were obsessed with being older, sexier, more independent, but some part of us must be afraid to let go of childhood, of the absolute carefree nature of it all, because we never questioned this ritual. It was just a thing we did. Initials. Every year.

I kick a rock off the ledge, watching it plummet into the water below, once again furious at how quickly Kylie deserted me when Dad's crimes came to light. Even still, I find myself missing her, and I hate myself for it. Why am I worrying about a friend who treated me as disposable when I have a true friend in Viv here at camp?

I think I might understand, finally, how Mom can wait for someone who shows no interest of reengaging. People leave imprints on us. They can sink in their hooks and even once they're ripped free, the wound remains.

It's hard to ignore that.

It's hard to not wish to become tethered again.

———

The rain clears out during dinner and Towers announces that the evening festivities are on. It's the girls from Pine Knot's turn to start the campfire, but the tinder is damp and it takes a lot of help and patience from Viv before they get it burning. When tongues of fire start cracking and smoke drifts lazily upward, the clouds are finally breaking. I can see a slash of inky black overhead, a few stars glinting in the gap.

Viv hooks her arm in mine and drags me nearer the fire. "What'd you do this afternoon?"

I swallow, guilt pinching my side. I should have checked for service at the summit of Notch's Point, tried to text Viv's phone and learn who picked it up. But without any answers, I'm hesitant to tell her I spent my afternoon hiking.

Jocelyn saves me, launching into speculation about the talent show that's happening next weekend—a joint event with the boys' camp to mark the middle of the season. Ryan strums a guitar and Viv seems to forget about her question, joining Gretta in bobbing her head to the rhythm.

The marshmallows are pulled out and a group of campers across the way start singing. I can feel the warmth of the fire pulsing out from the pit, but I still can't shake my chill. I changed when I got back from the trail, but it's like I'm wearing a damp second skin still, like my very bones are cold.

On the other side of the fire, Goodwin is chatting with Towers. Some of the staff are huddled near too—facilities coordinators and activity guides. But no Arlo.

I don't even know why I'm disappointed. Until recently, I could barely stand the guy.

———

People start retiring around 8:30. The youngest campers go first, ushered off to their cabins. Then the older girls at nine, followed by the counselors and staff.

"You coming?" Viv asks.

I glance up, startled. Everyone has cleared out. The fire has been reduced to a pile of glowing, pulsing embers.

I rub warmth into my arms, then pause. A shadow approaches from the opposite side of the fire. His hands are deep in his jean pockets, the hood of his sweatshirt pulled up over his hair. He pauses when he spots me. Raises one hand in hello from the opposite side of the fire pit and smile around the toothpick wedged in his mouth.

"Ahhh," Viv says, and winks at me. "Have fun."

She runs off before I can say anything. Arlo crosses over to join me and sits beside me on the log. Tosses his toothpick into the embers.

"I thought maybe you bailed," I say.

He touches his chest in mock surprise. "Leave you hanging? I would never."

We sit on one of the logs and I steal a peek at Arlo. He's watching the glowing embers.

A few months ago, I wouldn't have given Arlo the time of day. Kylie had rules about the type of people we could invite into our inner circle; the amount of money in their parents' bank account and the brands they chose to wear were highly prioritized. Stoners in unmarked, gray hoodies who work at summer camps would not have fit the bill. Viv wouldn't have, either. But in an unexpected turn of events, now the people who have been kindest to me since the scandal broke are the very people Kylie and I used to ignore.

I can hear Kylie in my mind, trying to talk me into bailing on Arlo. *He's a stoner,* Nell, she'd say. *He's not going anywhere.* But every rich, trust-fund kid she approved of over the years had their vices—namely alcohol. Most were arrogant and cocky. Add that with drinking and the results always got ugly. The number of parties I attended with Kylie that ended in guys throwing fists was pathetic. Those guys weren't going anywhere either. They coasted. They were cruel. They were selfish. They were getting everything handed to them and had never worked a day in their lives.

You're missing the point, she would argue. But I don't think I am. I think maybe I missed the point right alongside Kylie for a very long time and it took Dad's scandal to wake me up.

"All right, I gotta know," Arlo says, pulling me from my thoughts.

"Huh?"

He's staring at me, one corner of his mouth quirked up. "What you're thinking. You went someplace just then."

I glance at the fire, change the subject as fast as possible. "Do you know anything about Avery Jane?"

"Avery Jane Windsor? From across the way?" He jerks his head toward the lake. "Sure. I grew up just a few towns south of here. I've been hearing ghost stories about her since I was a kid."

"I think there might be some truth to them."

He bites his lip. "They are definitely, one hundred percent, just stories. I promise you. But I understand why people like to believe. Especially here, at camp."

"You've heard all the different versions? Like how some people say she was murdered by her parents and the fire was meant to cover it up?"

"Yeah, I've heard that one and it's completely bogus. Definitely the most far-fetched of the tales."

I nod. "Yeah, I think it's the other one. The exorcism gone wrong. I think she was possessed and she haunts that place because she's still not free of the demon."

He laughs. "What'd she do—tell you all this?"

I think about how the light illuminated her window before I even finished speaking the word *possessed* last night.

"Something like that."

Arlo nods slowly, licks his lips. He hasn't said I'm crazy yet, so that's something.

"Is there a local cemetery around here?" I press. "Someplace she might be buried?"

"Yeah, sure. There's a cemetery. But the fire was so bad there were no bodies to bury. There's a family plot *at* Windsor though, on the grounds. At least that's what I've heard."

I turn this piece of information over in my head. How am I supposed to find whatever item still possesses Avery if there was no body to bury? Maybe she has a headstone in this family plot at Windsor. Maybe her ashes were even scattered there. Or some sort of item was buried in place of her body and that *item* is what's holding her ghost in place.

I glance toward Windsor Camp. The sky is still cloudy from the earlier storm, blocking the moon.

I'm going to have to go back. To search for the family plot.

Maybe Viv will come with me.

Maybe—

"Nell?"

I jerk toward Arlo. He hasn't used my name like that before—my actual nickname as opposed to the city I call home. His wide, brown eyes sweep over me. He reaches out ever so slowly, brushes a tendril of hair away from my face. I have been rendered a statue. He's very close suddenly and I worry I've given him the wrong idea.

I scoot back on the log. "Look, I have a lot going on

right now. I'm not looking for anything like . . ." I motion between us awkwardly.

He smirks, drops his chin to his chest.

"I'm sorry. I didn't—"

"Don't apologize," he says. "You didn't do anything wrong." It's quiet for a beat, then: "You know people can just be friends, right? It doesn't have to be anything more?"

I frown. "But weren't you just . . . I thought you were going to . . ."

"Make a move?" He shrugs. "Can't blame a guy for trying."

I shiver.

"Come on. I'll walk you back." And just like that, he shifts gears, back into the carefree, nothing-can-fluster-me guy I've come to know from the kitchens. He spreads the coals and tosses water on them—a camp rule when a fire is left unattended—then grabs my hand and pulls me to my feet. "You're freezing," he says. "You want my hoodie?"

"No, that's fine. Thank you, though."

We walk in silence, his hands deep in his hoodie pocket and mine swinging at my sides. I can't tell if the silence is awkward or comfortable, which I'm pretty sure means it's awkward. I don't want it to be awkward. I like the casual, ribbing, sarcastic relationship we've had up until this evening and hope we can go back to that.

"I didn't ruin anything tonight, I hope?" I say when

we reach the cabin. "It's not going to be weird tomorrow, is it?"

"Only if you keep asking questions like this."

I cock up a brow.

"I swear, Manhattan. I'm a big boy. I can handle it. See you bright and early, okay?"

"Okay."

He winks and saunters off.

I stand there like a deer in headlights, shivering as he disappears between the trees.

CHAPTER
SIXTEEN

"What a weirdo," Viv says when I finish telling her about my evening with Arlo. It's early Monday morning. Pale gold light filters through the pines and into the cabin, creating subtle shadow play on the walls. Jocelyn and Greta are still asleep. "No guy I know is *that* much of a gentleman about being turned down. Half the time they get pushy or call you a bitch. And then there's a shocking number that just straight-up ignore what you say and try something anyway."

I nod, understanding all too well. There's a club back home (popular among my classmates because it's 18+ and doesn't card so long as you look at least twelve), and it's frequented by the type of guy Kylie adored and I pretended to adore too so that things were easier between us. The guys there never asked for anything. They took. If they wanted to kiss you, they'd grab your arm and smash their lips to your face, and then try to tell you it was romantic. Like you existed solely to please and entertain them.

"So why *did* you turn him down?" Viv continues. "He's cute!"

"I don't know," I say, momentarily doubting myself. "There's just a lot going on right now, with my dad, and I'm not in the right headspace for . . . well, basically anything but surviving."

"That's fair," she says plainly.

"If you're interested in him, definitely don't let me stop you."

"Oh my gosh, Nell, that's not why I asked."

"I'm serious though. I would fully support you."

"And I appreciate that, but I will give him a generous twenty-four-hour period to mourn you turning him down . . . and for you to change your mind."

I kick the bunk overhead, laughing.

"Besides, I'm kinda seeing someone back home," she adds.

"Oh, I didn't know."

"How could you? I never mentioned it." Viv scrambles down the ladder and starts getting ready for the day. "We're not very serious. She's headed to college in the fall, and we agreed to an open relationship for the summer. It will likely fall apart completely after that."

"I'm sorry."

She shrugs. "Don't be. I'm serious when I say it's *not* serious. Why do so many people think relationships have to be serious? They can just be fun. Plus, now I have Arlo as a prospect too." She waggles her brows playfully and I find myself laughing again.

A few minutes later, we're dressed and headed for the kitchen. Viv's planning to go for a run before breakfast, so she'll do that once we split ways.

"I was thinking we should go back to Windsor and look for it," I announce before she can jog off.

"My phone?" Viv's face scrunches up.

"No, the family plot Arlo told me about."

"Right. Sorry. I forgot about that the instant you told me he tried to kiss you." I roll my eyes and Viv adds, "Didn't Arlo say there were no bodies to bury?"

"Yeah, but I still think we should check the plot. Maybe an item was buried for each person—something meaningful. And in Avery's case, maybe something cursed."

"Do you think you're maybe getting a little obsessed with all this?"

"What? No. I thought you wanted to try to help her too."

Viv sighs. "I do. But at the same time, I know it's just a ghost story that keeps freaking us out, and I'm wondering if it's a giant distraction for you from . . . well, you know. Your dad and the news. And distractions are fine, so long as they're healthy."

"You don't have to come. I can do it alone." I sound defensive. And I am. Just the other day she'd wondered alongside me if Avery Jane was real and now she's implying my plan is unhealthy.

"I don't want you to have to do it alone. But I also don't want you to waste your whole summer chasing a ghost." Viv pauses. "Look, I'll come and keep you company. It's just . . . paddling back across the lake, hiking to a creepy-as-fuck house, digging around in the family graveyard?" She raises a brow. "It's like you're trying to scare off your best friend."

My chest tightens. That term used to belong to someone else. I didn't expect to make friends this summer, and now I'm terrified of driving her away.

"You don't have to come," I insist again. "Really. I can go alone."

"No, no. I'm in. Morbid curiosity is my specialty."

I'm not sure if I believe her. It seems just as likely she's coming with to keep an eye on me, as though I'm a child that needs babysitting.

We reach the mess hall and Viv pauses. "Good luck in there this morning. Don't make it awkward." She waggles her eyebrows.

"Good luck on your run," I respond, not taking the bait.

She gives me a small salute and breaks into a jog, heading uphill toward Goodwin's office. She'll do a loop around the place, then run along the shore, back around the cabins, and return to the mess just in time to meet her campers for breakfast.

"Think about when we should go back," I call after her.

She raises an arm above her head and gives me a thumbs up.

———

Bustle and chatter fill the kitchens, but Arlo is nowhere to be seen and dishes from food prep are already piling up beside the sinks. I sigh, shrug out of my flannel overshirt and pull on my apron. The water is warm, but I feel chilled again, like my bones have iced over, like I'm just a few degrees away from freezing solid.

When Arlo finally shows his face, the breakfast rush is upon us. He sets a stack of dishes down and reclines against the counter. "Morning," he says brightly.

He was right last night. It isn't awkward. It will only be awkward if I make it awkward, which I don't want to do, but there's also a part of me that's ticked off knowing that if things sour, the blame will be placed squarely on me.

"Where were you this morning?" I ask a bit more forcefully than intended. "I had to do a shit ton of dishes on my own."

"I was busy," he says evenly.

"Getting high?"

He moves his toothpick from one side of his mouth to the other. "Frankly, it's none of your business."

"When I'm picking up your slack, it is absolutely my business."

"Oh, sort of like when I covered for you on Saturday?"

"I asked you about that. In advance. That's totally different. And if you just bailed to—"

"Look at me," he says, pointing to his eyes. They are wide and clear and definitely not bloodshot. "I'm capable of functioning without pot."

"I didn't mean to imply that you weren't."

His eyes narrow. "Oh, I think you did. I think accusing me of something was easier than accepting that when I said I was busy, I was just that—busy. Maybe even with something personal that you are not owed an explanation about."

I open my mouth, close it. Somehow everything has gotten turned around and now I'm the bad guy. I sigh, frustrated. "I'm sorry about the interrogation. It was just a lot of dishes and I felt abandoned."

"Not my intention. Let me make it up to you." He grabs my flannel off the hook and tosses it at me. It hits me in the face and I barely gather my wits quickly enough to catch it before it falls to the floor. "Take the rest of the day off. I've got this."

"You sure?"

"Limited time offer again, Manhattan. If you snooze, you—"

"I'm going, I'm going!" I dart for the door. "And thank you," I call over my shoulder.

Outside, the sun assaults me. I stand there a minute,

the door banging shut behind me, uncertain what to do with my newly acquired free time.

A tickling sensation spreads over my limbs. That invisible line tightens in my navel, calling me toward the shore. Toward Windsor. Toward her.

Not today, I think to myself.

I'll deal with Avery Jane later. I can't waste a gorgeous day like this sitting on the dock and staring at her window. I turn east and start walking.

———

The cove where campers do paddle boarding is a bit of a walk from the mess, but I know it will be deserted at this time of the morning, which sounds ideal. It's on the other side of Goodwin's office, where the shoreline tucks and turns northeast, making a view of Windsor Camp impossible. Another plus.

By the time I reach the cove, the sun is strong, the temperature is steadily climbing, and I feel like a swim. I strip off my shirt and jean shorts, kick off my shoes. I'll be swimming in my sports bra and underwear, which seems like a recipe for landing in Towers' office for a lecture, but there's no one around to see.

When my toes enter the water, it's ridiculously warm, the shallows heated like bathwater by the sun. A few more steps and the cold sets in, slicing into my calves. By the time the water is cresting my thighs, it's torture. I dive forward just to make it end.

The water is a shock at first, stealing my breath. I sputter, move quickly to warm my limbs. After a few strokes, it's not so bad anymore. I swim out about thirty strokes, then turn and head back for the shore. Turn and do it again. Out. Return. Out. Return. I lose myself in the rhythm, swimming until I'm breathless. Eventually I roll into a back float and stare up at the sky.

It's a cheerful blue today, flawless and sprawling. Wherever Dad is, he can see this sky, too. Unless he managed to hop a flight to the other side of the globe and is currently staring up at the moon. I wonder if he's thinks of us ever—me and Mom—or if he's too focused on staying hidden, running from his demons, outsmarting the authorities.

A crow flies overhead. I sit up and tread water, watching as the bird lands on the branch of a dead tree along the shoreline. It cocks its head at me, ruffles its wings, and screeches. The caw rattles the stillness of the morning, piercing into me like a nail. Suddenly, it's too quiet. No breeze, no swaying grass. Even the water seems to have stopped lapping. The crow keeps staring at me, its beady eyes glinting and flashing like fire-play.

I find myself mesmerized, hypnotized.

When the crow lifts off the branch without warning, it doesn't make a sound. I watch as it flies south toward Windsor, wondering if it's truly a crow or if ghosts can take other forms. If even here beyond Windsor's reach, I'm somehow being watched.

Something grazes my leg beneath the water.

I jerk back, peer into the depths. A ripple of white. Like fabric.

I swim like a panicked animal, lurching for the shore. The fabric grazes my foot again, and I scream, swallowing water. I kick, and something swats back at me, slick and cold, like long-dead fingers, pawing at my ankle.

I reach the shore gasping. Scramble out on all fours. Twist back, my hair dripping water into my eyes.

The thing moves beneath the water, bubbling up, wanting air. It's the hem of a child's white dress, mushrooming as it approaches the surface.

I stare, horrified, unable to move.

It breaks the surface . . .

And it's only a plastic grocery bag.

Litter.

I back away, heart still pounding, blinking water from my eyes. What did I expect? Avery Jane didn't drown in the lake. Why would some bloated, dead, floating version of her corpse be rising from the deep to torment me? Unless she's everywhere—at the house, in the trees, under the lake.

I squeeze out my hair, gather my clothes and wrestle them on. The sun beats down, but I shiver, the chill settling back into my bones.

Maybe I'll never shake it. Maybe it's this place, her ghost, something unseen fated to follow me. Like a shadow, unable to be shed.

CHAPTER
SEVENTEEN

The week is uneventful, a predictable schedule of breakfasts, lunches, and dinners at the mess hall, my fingers pruning in dishwater as Arlo passes by, smirking around a toothpick, sometimes bumping his shoulder into me playfully as he goes. We haven't hung out again, just the two of us, and I don't think we will. But that seems fine.

I thought he'd been playing off my rejection the other night. I thought it couldn't possibly *not* bother him. But he hasn't given me the cold shoulder or pulled away. Things continue as they had before—his gentle ribbing, sarcastic comments. "Eat up, Manhattan," he says at least once a day as he delivers me a plate of whatever is being served out front.

The whole of camp is busy preparing for Saturday's talent show. Viv's girls are perfecting their acts, which range from comedy sketches and musical performances, to a card tricks and a disturbing number in which one of her girls, gifted with numerous double-joints, plans to contort herself into an oddity of positions. I see Viv mainly in the early mornings and the evenings, when she's not busy with counselor responsibilities. But on Friday afternoon, in between my lunch and dinner shifts, she gets a break as the campers run through a dress rehearsal.

"Tell me something about your dad," I say. We're walking the shoreline south of the beach. My sneakers dangle from my fingers, the warm water surging over my toes with each step.

"What kind of something?" Viv asks.

I don't quite know how to answer. I only know that I've been thinking about Dad lately, about fathers in general.

"Did he enjoy spending time with you?" I ask. "Or did you have to schedule time with him?"

"Unless your dad is like, the president or a congressman or something, I don't think he should have to pencil you into his calendar."

"Tell that to mine. Actually, he didn't even do the penciling. Mom scheduled me into his calendar weekly and then forced him to attend the appointment."

"Pardon the bluntness here," Viv says, "but some people really shouldn't have kids."

"You know, that might be the crux of it all. I don't think he ever wanted a kid. My mom did. Maybe it's not completely his fault that he's a terrible father."

"Nell, he isn't just a bad father, he's a bad person. I'm sure there are lots of people out there who weren't sure if they wanted kids but put on their adult pants when the baby arrived. Your dad sounds selfish and entitled." She cringes, glances at me sidewise. "Sorry."

"You're not saying anything I don't already know. He was shitty to me. He was even worse to his clients." Pain explodes through my foot and I grab onto Viv's shoulder for support.

"What?" she gasps.

Still holding on to Viv for balance, I pull my foot from the water and survey the damage. There's a fishing hook embedded in my heel.

"Ouch," Viv hisses. "We really shouldn't be walking her. This is where they do fishing, isn't it?"

"Yeah, I think you might be right."

"Do you need the nurse?"

I grab the hook, twist, and pull.

"Okay. Guess not," Viv says, looking at me out of the corner of her eye.

Before any blood can well up, I stick my foot back in the water and swish it around.

"Not sure that can count as a proper cleaning." Viv pauses. "You wanna go back?"

I shake my head. I get so little shared downtime with Viv that it seems foolish to waste some of it in with the nurse, especially when I can clean the puncture wound properly on my own and put a Band-Aid on it back at the cabin. So I point at a shaded picnic table a few yards back from the shore. "Let's just rest for a few." We make our way to it—Viv striding confidently, me half-hobbling—and sit on the bench with our backs resting against the table so we can look out over the water.

Viv launches into a story from shortly after her father's injury, when they were stuck inside due to a stretch of bad winter weather. He was on pain meds, but not yet hooked. They passed the time by doing puzzles.

"We did every single one we owned," Viv explains. "Somewhere around the fifth puzzle, I started hiding a piece somewhere in the house. He'd be so furious when we got to the end. 'All that work and there's a piece missing?!'" She chuckles to herself. "He'd refuse to box up the puzzle until the piece was found, so we ended up with mostly completed puzzles on every surface of the house. The dining room table, coffee tables, every spare counter. Eventually we started doing them on plywood he pulled from the garage so that we could stack them on top of one another."

I smile at the image. "And the missing pieces stayed missing?"

"No. Sometimes he'd find them on his own. And if he didn't, I'd eventually move a piece into his jacket pocket or wallet. And then he'd find it and be like, 'I did not take this piece, I swear!' But the puzzle would then get completed, and we could box it up, and move on to a new one. We ran out of puzzles by the summer, and he started buying more online." She pauses, looks at her hands. "We were halfway through this massive six-thousand-piece one when he died. I tried to finish it, but it's missing a piece. I think he hid it somewhere, but I haven't found it. I don't know if I ever will."

"You will," I insist, because the alternative is too painful to imagine.

"You can't know that. And honestly, I'm not sure if I want to find it. If I find it, then the puzzle's done and I have to box it up and put it away and it'll be like he's really, truly gone."

She falls silent, staring out over the lake, and in that moment, I finally understand Mom. If she stops waiting at the window, if she stops looking for Dad, it's like she's accepted his disappearance, his guilt, his crimes. It will be like letting go of him for good.

Then again, he's still out there somewhere, hiding.

But Viv's father . . . He's gone forever. She'll never see him again, whereas I might be lucky enough to reunite with mine. *Lucky.* I consider that word, wondering if I even want such a reunion to happen. Would I be able to forgive him if it came to it? Could I move past what he's done, love him despite everything?

I honestly don't know, and I think that's okay. It's complicated, and like Viv said the night we met, *love's weird.*

Viv makes a small sound and I realize she's crying. "Hey," I say, throwing an arm around her shoulder. She leans into me and lets it all out. Her body heaves and shudders.

"I'm sorry, Viv," I say when she's through.

"Me too." She sniffles. "For myself. Also for you."

"Why? I don't have memories like that with my dad. I don't even miss him."

"But you still lost something," she says, and I can't argue with that.

———

As the Friday-night bonfire unfolds, I find myself on the beach. I don't remember intentionally walking away from the fire pit, and yet here I am, sand infiltrating my sneakers, my toes just inches from the edge of the lake.

It's warm tonight, muggy. Moisture lifts off the water in delicate curls. Windsor Camp stands across the way, waiting.

We have to go back. *I* have to go back.

Viv said tomorrow night would be good, that she can probably sneak away during the talent show without anyone noticing, but I wish we could go sooner. I want to go now. I pull the hood of my sweatshirt over my hair, stick my hands deep into the pocket. Muffled laughter and cheers drift down to the beach from the bonfire. Somewhere out on the lake, a loon calls.

And then . . .

Eleanor.

I squint through the mist.

Eleanor Bradley . . .

Trees sway in a subtle breeze, branches pawing at Windsor like hooked claws.

"Too busy up there for you?"

"Jesus!" I clutch the front of my sweatshirt and side-eye Arlo, who's appeared out of the dark like a ghost. "Where the hell did you come from?"

"What are you doing down here?" he asks, ignoring my question.

"To be honest, I don't know. Just needed some time alone, I guess."

He nods at this, face solemn. "Nell, I have to ask you something." There it is again, my real name, not his nickname for me. I look at him sharply, thinking maybe I was wrong, that he's going to push for us to be more than friends. But he's pale as the moon. He looks like someone died. He was confident bordering on cocky that night at the fire pit. This is something else.

Arlo bites his bottom lip, exhales. "I don't want you to get mad at me. This is coming from a place of concern. 'Cus I care about you."

I blink at him, waiting.

"Are you . . . okay? Like, healthy, I mean?"

"What?"

He drags a hand through his floppy hair. "Are you eating? I haven't seen you eat a single thing since you got here."

"Because I'm always washing dishes during meals."

"So you eat after then? Or before?" He moves the toothpick from one corner of his mouth to the other. It's such a strange question that I just stand there, staring. "I just want to make sure you're not anorexic and starving yourself or something."

I feel my mouth fall open. "You think I have an eating disorder?"

"I don't know. That's why I'm asking. But you're always cold, and I know that can be a sign—poor circulation—and I've never seen you eat a single thing."

"What the fuck, Arlo?"

He grabs my arm as I try to turn away. "Nell. Nell! I'm sorry. I'm just . . . I'm concerned, okay?"

I yank my hand from his. "You're being nosy. I'm cold because I'm cold. I'm skinny because I'm skinny. That's all there is too it."

"Really? When was the last time you ate something?"

I rake my memory and honestly can't remember, but I'm too ticked off to admit it. "Will you just drop this?"

"Yeah, of course. I'm sorry." He takes a step away. "I hope this doesn't change anything. I— I don't want you to be mad at me or . . ."

Across the lake, Windsor's window illuminates. The patch of light flickers and warbles, distorted by the evening's fog.

"Look!" I grab Arlo's arm and point across the lake. But by the time he turns, the house has fallen dark once more.

Arlo's forehead wrinkles. "What?"

"There was a light. In that window. It's Avery Jane. She's been trying to communicate with me, I swear."

A breeze rushes across the pond, like an exhale.

Eleanor, it says.

Eleanor Bradley . . .

"Maybe it was some kids messing around," Arlo says, showing no sign that he's heard a strange voice whispering in the night.

"It wasn't kids, Arlo. Something's wrong with that place."

"Have you been seeing anything else weird? Are you feeling faint?" He tries to put a palm to my forehead and I dance out of the way. "Please just eat something, Nell." He holds a granola bar out to me, brandishing it like a sword.

"Will you drop it?" I bat it out of his hand.

"Nell, come on."

"Leave me alone." I break away, run up the beach. There's a figure where the sand meets the grass. Viv, come to find me.

"What's wrong?" she asks.

"Arlo," I pant, "won't leave me alone."

I can hear him following, his feet clumsy in the sand. Viv holds her arms up to stop him, pushes him in the chest. "Uh-uh. That's close enough."

"Nell, come on. I'm sorry. Let's just talk, okay?" His eyes are pleading in the darkness, wide and glossy.

"Maybe tomorrow, Arlo. I'm going to bed."

"Yeah, okay," he says, stepping away from Viv, holding his palms up in surrender. "Whatever you want. I'm sorry, truly. I only brought it up because I care."

Viv grabs my hand and leads me away from the beach like a lost puppy. "Brought what up?"

"Nothing." I touch my temple. "My head hurts." Maybe I should have taken the granola bar after all. But I'm not hungry. If anything, I feel sick, like I'm going to puke.

"She's doing something to me, Viv. Avery Jane. I don't feel right. And I keep hearing her, calling my name."

"Calling your name?" she repeats doubtfully.

"We have to go back, find the grave," I murmur. "I need to make this stop."

Her expression is fearful as she holds my gaze. But I can't tell if she's afraid *for* me or *of* me.

"Tomorrow," she says finally. "During the talent show." She rubs my hands vigorously, then blows on them. "God, you're cold."

CHAPTER
EIGHTEEN

I t threatens rain all Saturday and finally delivers come dinner time.

I avoid Arlo in the kitchen and he makes it easy. He seems truly remorseful for his accusations and pushiness, and he gives me plenty of space. The only words he's spoken to me came at breakfast, when he first slipped on his apron. "I'm sorry. Again. Whenever you want to start over, I'll be around."

When the talent show begins, it's pouring. Despite the warmth and humidity of the evening, the droplets still sting with cold. I pace for Viv outside the hall, the hood of my raincoat pulled up over my head.

She's five minutes late, then twenty, then sixty.

Soon the whole thing is over, the campers filing out in a rush of chatter and linked arms. I catch Viv toward the end of the crowd.

"What happened?" I whisper.

"I couldn't get away. Almost all of my campers needed something. Support or help with a costume or whatever. We'll go later, after lights out. I'm sorry."

By the time we're finally creeping for the shore, the rain has let up to a mist, which is preferable to the earlier downpour, but it somehow makes me colder.

"Why do we have to do this tonight?" Viv grumbles, pulling her hood up to shield her eyes.

I unlatch one of the canoes and tug it off the rack. Thrust an oar at Viv. "Because."

"That's a crummy reason."

"Help me get this in the water."

She pauses a moment, frowns. "Are you okay?"

Yes. No. I'm not really sure anymore. I blink mist from my eyes and zip my rain coat a bit higher. A shiver rakes my limbs.

I grab a shovel from the lifeguard office and place it in the belly of the canoe. Then I give the boat a shove, forcing it into the water. "Let's go."

———

Windsor waits as we paddle across Corwin. The mist pricks our faces. Once we're out of the boat and slipping beneath the cover of the pines, we finally get a reprieve from the elements.

I follow Viv, my eyes on the shape of her backpack. Her multitool keychain glints in the glow of my flashlight. I'd told her to bring the bag in case we find something we need to carry. Now in the woods, it seems foolish. If Avery Jane's grave holds a possessed item, it's unlikely it will be too big for our pockets.

As we approach the back of the estate, I cut in front of Viv. "You go left around the house, I'll go right," I propose. "Yell if you find anything that looks like a family cemetery."

"No way we're splitting up. That's how vengeful spirits kill stragglers in horror movies. I'll follow you."

"Fine."

I nod and lead the way. Like Bradley House, Windsor Camp is built into a steeply sloping hillside. Working our way around it is treacherous in the wet weather. When we reach the front, I get my first view at the fire damage from outside the house. A wide scar of weathered plywood mars the facade, boarding up what was once a cavernous hole in the estate's siding. The front door remains undamaged, the brass knocker still hanging there, glistening in the rain.

On the other side of the house, the hillside has been landscaped. Retaining walls create a tiered yard, and when we make it to the third and lowest level, we find a wrought-iron fence. The gate hangs from one hinge, partially open. I sweep my flashlight into the space beyond and the beam falls on a small grave marker, low to the ground.

"Bingo," Viv whispers.

We squeeze through the entrance, the gate creaking in protest. Rain patters around us, striking wet earth. The smell of damp soil and decomposing leaves hangs heavy in the air.

I stoop beside the first marker. *Alfred Theodore Windsor II, 1902-1973. Beloved husband and father.*

I imagine Dad's headstone will bear similar words one day, even if they are entirely untrue. It makes me wonder about Alfred's true character. We tend to remember people more fondly in death.

I move to the next marker, searching for Avery Jane's name, or at least her parents', but the only headstones I can find are for Alfred's wife, Beatrice, and another set of Windsors even older than the first.

"Nell?" I hear Viv say from deeper in the plot.

I step over the next two rows of markers and meet Viv near the rear section of fence. She's pointing toward her feet. There is no headstone, but the soil looks different here—darker, free of weeds and growth.

"It's fresh," I realize aloud.

She nods. "Nell, I don't like this. I think we should go."

I raise the shovel up and bring it down with force, sinking into the damp soil. I lift up dirt, toss it aside.

"Nell, come on. We can't be doing this. We're trespassing."

"No one even lives here."

"It's still trespassing. *Someone* owns the land."

I force the shovel in again, step down on the blade. This could be her grave, unmarked. Whatever has tethered Avery Jane to the demon, to this house, could be right beneath my feet. I dig faster.

"I don't understand why it looks fresh," Viv mutters.

Because someone disturbed her grave recently. A ghost hunter maybe, from the forums. Avery Jane could have rested quietly for years and then some meddling hunter dug up her plot and now she's active again, sending out signals from bedroom windows, begging for help, desperate to sleep.

Dig, heave, toss.

Dig, heave, toss.

Again.

Again.

Deeper into the earth, the rain spitting on the back of my neck, Viv begging for us to leave, until suddenly the shovel hits something.

"What was that?" Viv breathes out.

It doesn't feel solid enough to be a coffin. "Bring the light nearer." I start clearing away the dirt best I can, revealing the hidden shape. An assaulting smell hits me and I nearly vomit.

"Oh, God," Viv mutters. "What is that?" Her flashlight sweeps into the hole. There's a blanket wrapped around something. The pattern is Southwestern—geometric arrows and Xs. A coldness spreads over my limbs as I reach for it.

"Nell, don't."

But corner of the blanket is already in my hand, the

rough fabric scratching at my fingertips like a familiar itch. I grip it firmly, yank it back.

Viv screams. I scramble out of the hole, hands flying over dirt, scrambling backwards like a crab.

"Oh my God, oh my God, oh my God," Viv says through her fingers.

I grab the flashlight from her, send the beam into the hole. The body is belly down, head turned to the side. And it's moving. Squirming. No, those are only maggots, white and pallid. Feasting. The clothes hang on what remains of the decaying corpse.

White All Star sneakers stained with dirt and blood.

Cut-off blue jean shorts with an *EB* embroidered into the rear pocket.

A lightweight, soft blue raincoat, bunched up around the torso, mangled from an unceremonious shove into this shallow grave. It's an exact match to the coat I currently wear. So are the shoes, the shirt. All of it. I'm wearing the same outfit, only clean and blood-free.

"Nell," Viv whispers, and her eyes are unnaturally wide as she stares. "Nell, that's you. In the grave. Your body is in the grave."

But I'm standing right here.

Maybe it's Avery Jane in the dirt, her body somehow distorted and contorted to look like me. Maybe whatever possessed her is making us see this awful image, some warped trick, a way to scare us off, to keep us from freeing her.

But the smell. It's real, and everywhere. This body

isn't old; it hasn't been here nearly long enough to belong to Avery Jane.

"We have to go," Viv says, grabbing my hand. "We have to go *now*."

We flee down the trail, roots threatening to trip us, branches clawing at our arms. Back to the canoe. Across the lake rippling with rainwater.

As we paddle, I think about the chill I can't shake, the coldness of my limbs.

I think about how I can't remember the last time I ate something.

I think about the fishing hook I stepped on just yesterday and the way I never saw it draw blood.

As Viv locks the canoe to the rack, I grab the multitool from her backpack and flip open the blade. I have to check. I have to be certain.

I touch the blade to the top of my thigh and press down. Gently at first. Then a bit harder.

The tip of the blade goes in, and I immediately regret everything. It hurts—burns. But then the blood doesn't come. I curl my fingers around the handle more firmly and drag the blade down the length of my thigh. I stifle a cry, clamping my mouth around the pain. My skin is on fire, flaming, throbbing. But there is still no blood. It should be streaming down my leg, but there's nothing.

I pull the blade free and stare at my skin. There's no sign of the cut. No wound.

My leg is unmarred.

I stab into my thigh, pull it free.

Nothing.

I'm about to try a third time when Viv returns and spots me with the blade raised. "Nell. Stop!" She lunges, grabbing the knife from me, trying to wrestle it free. It nicks her forearm and the blood wells up instantly, dark and glistening beneath the moon. She slaps a hand over it, applying pressure.

"I'm sorry, I didn't mean it," I blubber.

"I know."

She stares at me, the blade, then me again. "What the fuck were trying to do?"

"This is im-impossible," I stutter, sinking to my knees. "This can't be real. This isn't happening."

My fingers ache with cold.

My lips tremble.

Finally, I say it. "Am I . . . Am I dead?"

CHAPTER
NINETEEN

I run for Goodwin's office, Viv on my heels. She's shouting that of course I'm not dead. That I'm right here. That we saw something that wasn't real in that graveyard plot.

But Viv didn't see the knife in my thigh. The lack of blood. She's not forever cold or uninterested in eating.

I pound on Goodwin's door before Viv can stop me.

"What are you gonna tell her?" she asks, breathless.

"Exactly what we found—a body."

A light flicks on in the second floor of the office. It's a tiny space, that second level; a single room shaped like a triangle on account of the sharply sloped roofline.

"But it was *you*. I mean, it sure looked like you, which is impossible. Do you have a twin or something?"

"No. I'm an only child."

Footsteps clomp down the stairs. First-floor lights flick

on. I can hear Goodwin fumbling with the lock on the other side of the door.

"She's gonna fire us," Viv grumbles as the deadbolt turns. "We're screwed."

The door lurches open, and there's Goodwin, her hair a disheveled mess atop her head, her eyelids heavy. When she realizes it's us, she's instantly alert. "What happened? Are the campers okay?"

"Uh, yeah," Viv says. "It's not that. It's. Well, Nell and I were . . . We went to . . ."

"We found a body," I interrupt.

Goodwin clutches the font of her bathrobe. "I'm sorry. You what?"

"A body. A corpse. In the family plot at Windsor. It was me."

Goodwin frowns. Her gaze falls to my hands, my feet. I realized I'm covered in wet soil, dirt wedged beneath my fingernails, my clothes damp with rain. "What on earth were you doing over there?" she asks, as if her staff leaving camp is somehow more horrific than uncovering a decaying body.

"Who fucking cares why we were there!" I erupt, and Goodwin's brows raise in disapproval at my language. "Did you not hear me? It was a body. A girl, a teen. It looked just like me. It *was* me."

Now Goodwin looks annoyed. "Is this some type of prank?"

"Call the fucking cops or I'm going to wake the whole camp and tell them about this!"

Goodwin grabs my arm and tugs me forward, across the threshold and into the office. "That's obviously not necessary." She glances at Viv. "Come in. Sit down. I'll call them right away and we'll get to the bottom of this."

———

About two hours later, I jostle Viv awake. She'd fallen asleep in front of the cabin's small hearth, curled up on the floor like a cat. I didn't sleep a wink because I was too anxious. Instead, I sat beside Viv, wide awake, listening as Goodwin called the cops, watching as red and blue flashing lights appeared beyond her windows, waiting as she stepped out to speak with the officer. When she returned, it was to announce that someone would be in to talk with me and Viv in a few minutes, but those minutes stretched into hours and it's not until the clock on the mantel reads 2:34 a.m. that the front door finally cracks open and two cops step inside.

The first is an older man whose salt-and-pepper beard makes me think he's rapidly approaching retirement. He's followed by a middle-aged woman with auburn hair pulled into a tight bun at the nape of her neck.

Viv sputters when I elbow her, and wipes drool off her lip. "Ow, my neck." She grabs the back of it and cranes it left and right, stretching. Then she spots the officers entering the room and clamps her mouth shut, sits straighter.

"Vivian Carter? Eleanor Bradley?" the female cop says. She's a large woman, easily six feet tall, with a solid torso but pencil straight legs. A badge on her uniform reads "Sheriff."

"Viv," Vivian says, raising a finger.

"Nell," I add, identifying myself.

"I'm Sheriff Ashmore. This is Officer Murkowski." She nods at the man behind her. His pale fingers are hooked on his belt as he eyes us with disdain. Something about his expression says that we've committed a crime, not discovered one.

I wait for them to ask us where we found it, what we noticed first, how we might have disturbed the scene. I wait for them to stare at me in horror, unable to comprehend how a body that looks like me could be decomposing across the lake while I also stand right before them in Goodwin's office.

Instead, Ashmore crosses her arms and says bluntly, "Do you want to tell us what's really going on? I might be able to smooth things over with the feds if you come clean."

"The feds?" Viv asks, her voice high and panicked. "Why are there feds involved?"

"There's been a federal agent staking out the Bradleys' summer house ever since Nell's father went missing," Ashmore explains. I catch Viv's eye and can tell by her confused expression that she's as startled by this as I am. We didn't see a soul when we stopped by Bradley House the other weekend. "When a couple kids say they found a recent grave and the body inside looks like Eleanor Bradley, well, we called that agent immediately. 'Course, we didn't know you were working at this camp, Eleanor. Mrs. Goodwin failed to mention who reported discovering the body. She just said it was a staff member." Ashmore gives me a piercing look. "Anyway, the federal agent's not that happy with you right now. And frankly, neither are we. Just 'cus there's not much to do in Hamilton County doesn't mean we need to waste resources searching the grounds of Windsor Camp at one in the morning."

"How could this be a waste of time?!" I erupt.

Just then, the door cracks open and yet another person enters. A tall, broad-shouldered, clean-shaven man. His blue jacket has three white letters on the front. FBI. The jacket is wet from the elements, his hair thoroughly soaked, his boots a bit muddy. Even still, he reminds me of every Hollywood detective to grace the screen. Clearly in shape despite the bulky jacket, a bit annoyed to be here, with a confidence that drips off him like rainwater.

His steely, shadowed eyes sweep over us, softening briefly with . . . shock? Concern? He wipes the expression away before I can make sense of it and closes the door behind him. "Sorry for the interruption," he says. "Carry on."

Sitting at her desk, Goodwin observes this new player in horror. She looks about two seconds away from fainting.

"I was just explaining to these girls how we don't appreciate our time being wasted," Ashmore says.

"There was a decomposing body!" I practically scream. "My body!"

Ashmore's eyes narrow, her mouth thins. "We went to Windsor," she says bluntly. "There's nothing there."

CHAPTER
TWENTY

I feel my jaw drop open. "Did you check the cemetery? The family plot?"

"Did you check the cemetery," Murkowski mimics with an eye roll. "Of course we did."

"There was a decomposing body," I insist. "Someone was killed and dumped there."

"Then they've managed to vanish, maggots and all. Isn't that right, Donovan?" Ashmore looks to the FBI agent.

"There was nothing suspect except a recently dug hole and a bunch of footprints," he confirms. "And I'm pretty sure those footprints will match Eleanor's and Vivian's if we check their shoes. But that doesn't seem necessary. Kids pull pranks all the time, don't they?" He smiles at us, lips pressed together. He's trying to give us an out, and I know we should take it, but I just can't.

"How can there be nothing? How could all that evidence just vanish?"

Agent Donovan holds my gaze. "I did find a few hairs. They look roughly your shade, Ms. Bradley."

"Maybe we should involve forensics, see if we can get a DNA match," Murkowski grumbles.

"Of course you'll get a match," I erupt. "It was my body in that grave. I was dead!"

"How could you be dead?" Donovan says. "You're standing right here. Clearly something spooked you girls and you saw something that wasn't really—"

"You guys are missing something! There was a body there. My body! Look, I can prove it." I grab the multitool off Viv's backpack and flip open the blade.

Murkowski pulls his gun. Goodwin screams.

"Easy, Nell," Ashmore says, reaching for the grip of her weapon.

"I'm dead. Look." I bring the blade toward my arm. "Just watch."

This time, the tip of the blade has barely broken the skin on my forearm when the blood bubbles into view, red and gleaming. I stare at it, horrified, my arm burning in pain.

There's a flash of movement in the corner of my vision, and then Donovan's diving at me. The air goes out of my lungs as I'm tackled to the floor. The knife clatters from my grasp and Donovan pushes it toward Ashmore.

"Have you lost your damn mind?" the sheriff yells,

grabbing the multitool. "What are you—high?" She searches my eyes.

I thrash in Donovan's grip, but he's too strong. My arms stay pinned down by my sides, immobile as he bear hugs me. "I'm dead!" I scream. "My body is in that grave. Someone murdered me!" Spit flies from my mouth. Hair sticks to my face.

Murkowski screams to cuff me. Viv repeats my name, pleading for me to calm down. Ashmore jumps to action, helping Donovan restrain me. Soon I'm pinned face down, the floorboards scratching at my cheek.

I go limp, panting.

"I'm gonna take her in," Ashmore announces.

"I don't think that's necessary. She's calming down," Donovan says, his voice close. It's him holding me down, I realize. "You're calm, aren't you, Nell? No need to spend the night locked up or to get an arrest on your record."

I raise my head slightly so I can look at him. He's smiling reassuringly at me, but there's something fearful in his eyes, like he knows just how much an arrest could fuck up my future.

My future that may or may not exist.

Because I'm dead.

Or was.

I don't know what to make of the blood that appeared on my forearm just now, the echo of the pain from where the knife cut me.

Viv stands just before the hearth, her eyes brimming

with tears. "Nell, please," she begs. "Maybe we saw something that wasn't there. Maybe we imagined it. It's the only thing that makes any sense."

"I think that's exactly what happened," Donovan says. The pressure lets up on my back and he helps me sit. Then he pulls a handkerchief from his pocket and wraps it around the cut on my arm.

I feel like I'm losing my mind.

"Why would the girls pull a prank like this," Donovan says to the cops, "when all it would do is get them in trouble?"

"Yes, exactly," Viv agrees.

"Nell, if you can get a hold of yourself and stay cool, I think we can just put this behind us. Something spooked you out there." Donovan glances toward the sheriff. "Ashmore, if what you've told me is true, this wouldn't be the first time kids broke into Windsor Camp and got themselves worked up."

"I can't have someone unstable working at this camp," Goodwin interjects, white-faced behind her desk.

"You're not unstable, are you, Nell?" Donovan's deep blue eyes bore into mine. "You're just a bit scared. Worked up. A good night sleep and you'll be right as rain."

He's giving me another out, and this time, I take it.

"Yeah. I just need to sleep it off. I'll be okay in the morning. We got scared. That place . . . it's disturbing."

"You are on thin ice, Eleanor," Goodwin warns,

fiddling with her necklace. "You so much as blink wrong, and I'm sending you home. Do you understand me?"

I nod, feeling numb.

"Look, I've left my post long enough as it is," Donovan says to the cops. "You guys think you can handle the rest of this?"

"Nothing left to handle, I don't think," Ashmore says. "Just a couple kids wasting our time, like usual." Murkowski grumbles in agreement.

Donovan gives me a half smile as he leaves. The pity lurking in his eyes reminds me of the feds that showed up at the apartment to arrest Dad, the looks they cast toward me and Mom.

After Goodwin lectures me and Viv for what feels like an hour, promising to watch us like a hawk, we're finally free to leave her office. As we head for our cabin, I glance toward Windsor, but it's hidden in the darkness.

"We didn't imagine anything," I say, breaking the silence. "You don't really think we imagined it, do you Viv?"

She's quiet longer than I expect. Too long.

"There was a body," I go on. "And that smell."

"Yeah, but if there's no body now . . ."

"Someone—or something—moved it."

Her eyes move to the bandage on my arm. "Why did you try to cut yourself?"

I can read the confusion on her face, hear it in her voice. She's starting to doubt me, to question my sanity. If

I tell her about what I did to my thigh, how it didn't bleed, she'll lose faith in my completely.

"You know what we saw there, Viv. You said it was me in the grave. You recognized me instantly."

"It's that house, that place." Viv trembles slightly in the pale moonlight, shaking her head back and forth. "It's making us see things. Things that aren't real. Maybe whatever possessed Avery Jane all those years ago is still in that house and it's messing with us."

I'm at a loss for words. Just the other day she worried I was getting too obsessed with the Windsor legends, and now she's suggesting they're responsible for what we saw.

Our cabin appears between the trees. I pause, glance over my shoulder. I can't see the shore from here, let alone Windsor, but I feel it watching me. Viv might be on to something. Maybe it was never Avery Jane I was feeling in that house, but something else. Something bigger, more dangerous. Something lurking in the dead of the night that should be feared. Something Avery Jane once feared as well.

We wash up in silence, climb into bed. I hear Viv's breathing lull within minutes, but I'm unable to sleep. When I close my eyes, I see maggots, squirming. Did we really imagine that? Did something make us see it?

I grab my thigh in the dark, picturing how the blade went in so easily, how the pain was immediate but the blood never came. Until it did, suddenly, in Goodwin's office.

I wonder if I actually stabbed myself on the shore or if I only *thought* I did.

I squeeze my eyes shut in the darkness, terrified by the possibility that I can't trust them.

I feel like I'm losing my mind.

CHAPTER
TWENTY-ONE

'm up before anyone, including the sun.

In the dark gray pre-morning glow, I stagger for the shore. My eyes burn. My lids are heavy. I haven't slept despite my absolute exhaustion. An entire night spent turning and thrashing while the girls dreamt beside me even when I desperately wanted to join them. My brain simply wouldn't let me.

Now at the beach, the sand is cold against my bare feet. I walk straight into the shallows, watch the water ripple outward as an icy coldness creeps over my skin.

I stare at Windsor. It's visible just above the mist that rises off the lake, lurking in silence. That horrible sensation pinches in my core again, an invisible line tugging me forward. Like I can't escape it. Like the house—or something inside its damp walls—owns me.

The more I try to ignore the sensation, the stronger it gets. I take another step into the water. A third.

No, I think. And the tug intensifies, almost in response.

I grit my teeth, refuse to move.

It pulls at me again. *Eleanor . . .*

"What?" I scream. I thrust my hands into the water, search around until my fingers close over a smooth rock. I fling it toward the house. "What do you want from me?"

My voice bounces back, a ghostly echo. *From me-me-me . . .*

Heat pierces through my skull. The headache is violent and precise, drilling into the space between my eyes. I stagger out of the water, drop to my knees in the sand, and clutch my temples.

My scalp is wet, sticky. I yank my hands away, only to find them covered in blood.

A scream rips from my mouth as I wipe my palms frantically on my shirt. I swipe at my forehead with my arm, expecting to see more blood on my skin. But there's nothing. My forearm is clean, dry. I turn my palms toward the sky, then the ground, then the sky again. The blood is gone, my skin covered with nothing but damp, clinging sand.

I push myself to my feet, pulse racketing in my ears and edge toward the shoreline. I bend forward, cautiously, fearfully.

On the rippling surface, my face is reflected back to me. There's no blood, just my wide, bloodshot eyes, and a mouth that hangs open in horror.

———

"You're here early," Arlo says as he slips into the kitchen.

I've already been here a solid hour. Desperate to get away from Windsor and not wanting to wake Viv or the girls, I'd fled to the kitchen, where I sat with my back against one of the dishwashers, my head hanging between my knees, breathing through the pain in my skull. The headache still lingers, but it's not as intense now, almost as if the distance between me and Windsor is directly proportional its intensity.

Arlo hangs his backpack on a hook by the door. "Did you hear? Someone spotted your Dad in South Carolina. They called in a tip."

My first thought is that it will be just like the other spotting—a false alarm, a misidentification. But Dad does have a brother down there—my uncle. Maybe he went to him for help. Maybe this sighting is legit. Even still, I can barely muster the energy to care.

"The staff's been talking about it all morning. I guess it was in the paper and—" Arlo freezes. "Hey. Are you okay? You look like you've seen a ghost."

And suddenly I feel not okay at all. This is more than a bad headache.

"I need to talk to you," I say, as I scramble to my feet. I grab Arlo by the wrist and tow him outside. We walk a few yards into the woods, so that anyone else arriving by the walking path won't see or overhear us.

"Something's wrong," I blurt out. "With me."

"Is this about the eating disorder stuff? Because I don't want to say the wrong thing again."

I blink at him.

"I mean, it doesn't mean something's wrong *with* you, just that you need help. It's sadly really common. It's—"

"No. I saw something. Last night. At Windsor. Viv and I snuck over there and." I press a hand into my mouth, shaking. "Fuck, Arlo. I feel like I'm going crazy."

He frowns. "What did you see?"

"We found the family cemetery. And there was a freshly dug grave. So I dug it up and . . . there was a corpse. Like, a new one. Decomposing. Maggots everywhere." I gag at the memory.

"Holy shit."

"Yeah. And the worse part was it was me. My body. It looked just like me. It was wearing what I was wearing."

"I . . . I don't understand."

"I know. That's why I feel like I'm losing my mind."

He rubs his chin. "What did you guys do? After finding that?"

"I went to Goodwin. We found a *body*. A clearly murdered body. But then the cops said there was nothing there. No corpse or evidence or anything. But I know what I saw." I leave out Viv's multitool and how the knife didn't cut me until the cops were there to witness it. I worry it will make me sound even more unhinged than I already do. "Arlo, what is happening to me? I can't stop thinking about that house. It's calling to me, I swear it.

Something's not right." I grab at the hair beside my temples, squeezing.

"All right, all right. Calm down." He takes me gently at the wrists and brings my hands to his chest. They fist into the front of his hoodie almost against my will, as though my body knows that I need purchase, something to keep be from unraveling completely. "What did Viv make of it all?"

"She thinks we must have imagined it. But the smell, Arlo. It was real. And just this morning . . ." I tell him about the blood on my hands that wasn't there. The voice that calls to me from across the lake.

"Hey, hey." He cradles my face, holds my gaze. "You're all right. Look at me."

I do. His eyes are a deep warm brown. He has a small scar on the bridge of his nose. I hadn't noticed that before.

"Maybe all you need is a distraction." He pulls a joint from his pocket and wiggles it before me like a dog treat.

The tiniest bark of a laugh escapes me. "You are a terrible influence."

"We don't have to smoke it if you don't want. I just thought—"

"No, I absolutely want to. I need to chill out." I grab the joint from him, my fingers brushing his wrist in the process, and he flinches slightly.

"How are you always so cold?" he asks.

"I don't know. It's like I can't shake it." A thought hits me suddenly. "What if you were wrong about the eating thing, but also close?"

"What do you mean?"

"The legend says that Avery Jane stopped eating that summer."

"Please don't tell me you still believe that ghost story," he interrupts. "I promise you the place isn't haunted."

"I know. I think you're right on that. No one has 'spotted' her in almost twenty years according to the ghosthunters' forums I've been reading. But all ghost stories start somewhere, and everyone on those forums mentioned that Avery Jane was possessed by *something* that summer, and that the very first sign of that possession was that she'd stopped eating. Then she started hearing voices. And some people say *she* started the fire in the ballroom because she was so cold that summer. Cold. In the middle of August."

He looks at me, clearly, horrified. "You think you're possessed?"

"No. Maybe? The similarities are concerning. It could be the start of . . . something. How else can we explain everything that's happening to me?"

"I don't know. But I assumed you came to me so I could tell you everything was fine. Not push you farther into wild-theory land."

"Sure, but sometimes what we want to hear isn't what we need to hear."

"Oh, you *need* to hear that you've somehow become possessed by whatever supernatural power once took control of Avery Jane Windsor?"

His refusal to even humor this possibility makes me

grit my teeth. "I'm just saying it's a possibility . . . that something could be trying to get its hooks in me. That place isn't right, Arlo. Local kids avoid it like the plague."

"They break in all the time," he argues.

"Do they? Or do they break in once and then don't come back because it's so creepy, and then a new batch of kids break in the next summer?"

There's an awkward pause.

"Look, I'm not trying to gaslight you, Nell. I believe you—that you've seen something, that you don't feel quite right. But you're not possessed. You've been through a big trauma with your dad's baggage and stuff, and it's probably—"

"Made me susceptible to evil spirits?" I finish.

"I was going to say 'put you under a lot of stress and it's manifesting in nightmares and strange visions.'"

I groan. My headache has mellowed from violent jackhammer to distant thrum, and the experience at the beach this morning feels like a strange fever dream. Maybe it even was. Maybe I'd finally managed to fall asleep and my exhausted mind delivered and extremely vivid nightmare. Arlo could be on to something.

"What I really want is to be able to trust my own eyes," I say. "I want to be able to relax."

"I can help there." He sits on a large rock, motions for me to join him, and finally lights the joint.

I've only smoked a handful of times in my life, always with Kylie, during a period when she had a fling with a freshman at Columbia who smoked more often than he went to class, burning through his parents' money and eventually dropping out just after the New Year. It always made me mellow and sleepy, something I desperately need now, but I must be doing something wrong and not taking big enough hits, because I feel more or less the same, just a touch less jittery.

"Any better?" Arlo asks when he snuffs out the joint on the bottom of his shoe.

"A little," I admit.

Laughter filters through the trees—campers making their way in for breakfast.

"We are definitely late," he says. "Come on." He offers me a hand and then pulls a bit too hard as he helps me to my feet. "You're gonna be okay. You know that, right? Whatever this is, it will pass."

"I hope so."

We hurry to the kitchen, only to find Dolores waiting to pounce on us the instant we sneak through the back door.

"Where the hell have you two been?" she snaps.

"Sorry. Nell was helping me with something," Arlo says quickly. "It was my fault."

"You can make up for it by dealing with the dishes." Dolores points a rigid finger toward the sinks, where a stack of dirty cookware is already piled precariously. "No, not you, Bradley. You're wanted up at Goodwin's office. There's a Mr. Donovan looking to speak with you."

CHAPTER
TWENTY-TWO

When I arrive at Goodwin's office, she informs me that she has some important phone calls to handle and that she sent Agent Donovan to the Performing Arts Building, which is vacant on Sunday mornings, and I can speak with him there.

I make the trek over and find him leaning against the stage, the blue sleeves of his plainclothes Henley pushed up to his elbows, scrolling through something on his phone. He's wearing sunglasses despite being indoors, and pushes them onto his forehead when he hears me enter. His gaze is piercing, his mouth in a suspicious frown.

"Ms. Bradley. How are you this morning?"

"Fine." In truth, I'm nervous my eyes may be bloodshot from the pot, and even though I feel fine, the last thing I want is for an FBI agent to ask me if I'm high. Or smell the weed on me.

"Why don't you come have a seat?" He nods to the benches that line the space in front of the stage. If I refuse, I'll only look more suspicious, so I start moving.

"What's this about?"

"Just some follow-up questions. Thought it would be better to do it without the sheriff and her lapdog around. They were riding you kind of hard."

"They were. Thanks." I sit on the second bench from the front, leaving a bit of space between us. He doesn't seem to mind. In fact, he's leaning away from me slightly, as though he worries I might lash out with a pocket knife again.

He swallows—hard—then unwraps a stick of gum, folds it in half, and pops it in his mouth. "I'm trying to put a timeline together," he says, chewing slowly, his eyes still glued to me. He extends the pack of gum in offering. I shake my head. "When did you come up to camp?"

"Oh." I pause. I'd thought he was going to ask about the other night, and the question catches me off guard. "Friday night before orientation. Technically Saturday morning by the time I got in. I think I arrived at Bradley House around two a.m."

"And that would have been"—he checks his phone—"the twenty-sixth and twenty-seventh, then. Of June?"

"Yeah."

"And how did you arrive?"

"I took public transit out of the city. Then hitchhiked the last bit."

"Your mom told us your friend Kylie drove you. But when I spoke with Kylie, she said she hadn't heard from you since Friday afternoon." He uncrosses his legs, pushes off the stage. Any unease he'd projected earlier is gone, replaced with stoic confidence as he adds, "Why the lie?"

This has definitely taken a turn into interrogation land.

"I'm sorry. Am I in trouble for something?"

"No, not at all, just trying to piece things together and figure out why you weren't honest with your mother."

"Because she worries, and I knew she'd freak if I told her the truth."

He pops his gum, regarding me down the thin line of his nose. "Why not just come up Saturday and take the shuttle bus Camp Durant provides?"

"I had to get out of there—the city. I told Mom all this. The attention, the noise—it was too much."

He takes a step toward me. Another. His thumbs hook on his belt. "Funny thing is, there's no video footage of you leaving the city. I couldn't find you on anything. Not feeds from the subway or Penn Station or even any bus terminals. So I'm wondering how a girl without a license managed to drive herself from Manhattan to middle-of-nowhere Hamilton County."

"I'm . . . I'm not lying. I took public transit." My heart is beating so hard, I can feel it between my ears. I feel like

I'm about to be arrested simply for breathing. "Why would I lie about this? I just wanted out."

"Did you see him at all that day? Maybe travel with him?"

"Dad? No! I hadn't seen him since Thursday, the day before the news broke."

"You're sure?"

"Positive! I have no clue where he is. Maybe South Carolina? I heard someone just spotted him there."

"Yes, we got that tip around six p.m. yesterday. We have local agents there looking into it. Seems credible, too, unlike the previous tip. His Cornell duffel has been found in a park but he's still missing." He peers at me through slitted eyes, as if he's expecting me to know something about this. "This is the same bag that your friend Vivian apparently spotted him carrying in Glens Falls. On Friday the twenty-sixth."

I grab the edge of the bench, the coarse wood scraping at my palms. "That's right," I say, even though he hasn't asked anything.

"I find it odd that she saw him but didn't say anything until almost a week after he was reported missing. Almost as if she was covering for someone." He says *she* but he's staring at me when he says it. As though *she* should be *you*. As if he thinks I told Viv to tell this story.

"You think I helped him?"

"I think maybe you got caught up in something and you felt torn between family and duty. Maybe you wanted to give him a head start. Let him head south before you called in a tip that placed him much farther north."

"And now I'm protecting him?" I practically screech.

"You tell me."

Donovan's steely eyes bore into me. He was so kind last night in Goodwin's office. Concerned. He held Ashmore and Murkowski at bay, perhaps only to win my trust so he could get to this moment right here.

"I think I should have a lawyer present," I say thinly.

He frowns, clearly frustrated. "You're a minor, Nell. You likely wouldn't be charged as an adult and I doubt you'd be judged harshly for helping him. There's a power imbalance and the fact that he's your father. The courts would go easy on you. We just want to find out what happened in those final hours . . . between when his crimes broke and he vanished. We want to know what you know."

"I know nothing or I would have said something weeks ago."

"Why don't you give me your phone and I can confirm your story by checking your calls and locations."

"Pretty sure you guys have ways to check that without getting your hands on the physical phone." I stand up. "Also? This is over. You want to talk to me again, call my mom and get the family lawyer to come up here. I'm not saying another thing until they're both present."

"Suit yourself," he says with a shrug. His fingers dip into his jacket pocket and he pulls out a pack of cigarettes. Grumbles, stuffs them back in, goes to his pant pocket.

Out comes a shiny metallic Zippo lighter, then finally, the thing he was looking for all along. He passes it to me. It's a business card, with his name and contact info. His first name is Cormac. The *o* is a solid black circle. I run my finger over the oddity.

"Printing mishap," he grumbles. "But of course I can't get it corrected until I go through the five-thousand-card order first." He smiles at me for a beat, like he's waiting for me to say something. I'm reminded of a wolf flashing its teeth before the kill. "Anyway, you think of something you want to share, you can call my cell. Or just swing by your summer house. You know where to find me."

I pocket the card and leave, pausing only when I reach the door. I glance over my shoulder. "You know, maybe this whole timeline mess is your fault."

"I beg your pardon?"

"I swung by the house about a week ago with my friend Viv. Just wanted to get away from camp for the afternoon. We didn't see a soul."

"I've been watching from the road."

"It's a good thing no one can come by boat then, like we did."

Frustration flickers over his face.

"But you're doing a good job on the main road, detective. You saw me come in at two a.m. that Saturday morning in the rain. Hard to miss a hitchhiker and their car."

"I wasn't set up until midday Sunday," he snaps, "once they knew your father was for sure on the run. And they sent me alone. I should have a partner for something like this. Do you know how ridiculous it is that I don't have a partner?"

"Lucky for Dad. He always had a lot of luck, got everything he wanted. Right up until he didn't, I guess."

Donovan scoffs. "Yeah. Right up until he didn't." He looks at me sadly, runs a hand through his hair and sighs. "Sorry to put so much pressure on you. It's just the longer we go without finding someone in a case like this, the less chance there is we'll get the outcome we want. I just wanted to make sure you weren't hiding anything."

"Believe me, if I knew where he was, I'd tell you. I want this to end as much as anyone."

He gives me a farewell smile-nod and begins punching something into his phone.

I slip outside. Just as the flimsy wooden door bounces shut behind me, I can hear him say, "She doesn't know anything. I'll be in touch."

CHAPTER
TWENTY-THREE

That evening, while everyone is at the bonfire, I slip away and head back to the Performing Arts Building. I've spent the whole day wondering how Donovan managed to make a phone call when all of Camp Durant is notoriously awful with service. Do FBI agents have fancy service boosters or something? Cells that pack an extra punch?

The building is closed, but not locked. I pull the door open, step through the frame. Without daylight filtering in the windows, the place is pitch black. I use the light of my phone to walk up the aisle.

Something glints at the front of the stage. It's Donovan's chrome Zippo lighter, standing on the edge of the stage like a miniature headstone. My phone light reflects off the metallic case, making it appear to blink.

I turn the lighter over in my palm. It's cool to the touch and impossibly smooth. I flip it open, flick it on.

The flame jumps up, casting a tiny golden glow around me.

I'm transported back to our New York City apartment, to a November evening when I was five, sitting on the balcony in the rocking chair Dad likes to smoke in. The ashtray on the table beside me held three cigarette butts and a tiny mountain of ash. I picked up his Zippo and flipped it open. My fingers were too small for the wheel, but I thumbed it again and again, trying to make the flame spark to life.

The slider door lurched open and I flinched. Dad appeared, an unlit cigarette perched between his lips. "There it is," he said, eyes finding the lighter in my hand. "You shouldn't be playing with that, you know. It's like matches. Fire can be dangerous."

I handed it over silently. He sat in the chair beside me. I watched the end of his cigarette pulse and glow as he burned through it.

We didn't speak, but there was a comfort to the silence, an impression that the not speaking made the shared time more special. We didn't have to talk or play a game or do anything. He was always so adamant about me going to bed at exactly seven so he could get back to his work, uninterrupted, and here he was, letting me stay up in the chair beside him, his phone shockingly not in his hand, watching the few stars bold enough to compete with the glow and glare of the city wink to life in the sky.

A bit later, the slider creaked open again. "Duncan,

you can't be smoking with her right next to you! She's inhaling all the secondhand smoke."

"We're outside, Rachel." He was annoyed, bothered. I could hear it in his tone—a tone usually reserved for me. I was glad tonight it was aimed elsewhere.

Mom grabbed me beneath the arms and lifted me from Dad's chair. "Bedtime, Eleanor."

Dad flipped his Zippo open and lit another smoke. He shot a small smile at me and winked, as though our time together had been a secret. Then the glass door slid shut, swallowing him from view.

I snap the lighter closed now, throwing the Performing Arts Building into darkness. I hadn't remembered that evening with Dad until picking up the Zippo and it makes me wonder how many other tolerable moments with him I may have forgotten. Maybe he's not as awful as I've made him out to be. True, he's done something unforgivable, and he was never going to win Father of the Year, but there were moments when we enjoyed each other's company, weren't there? There must have been moments when he liked being my father.

I pocket the Zippo, making a mental a note to return it to Donovan the next time I see him. Despite the ultimatum I gave him, I have a feeling he'll try to talk to me again, even without the family lawyer present.

I unlock my phone and check for service. Nothing. I wait a moment, two, and for an instant, a single bar appears on my screen. I lock every joint, standing there like a statue, waiting to see if anything comes through—a message from Kylie, a text from mom updating me on the latest sighting of Dad. Still nothing.

I pull up my contacts and select Viv's name. We'd swapped numbers the day after orientation, thinking we wouldn't need them until camp was over, but now I'm glad for our proactiveness.

The owner of this phone wants it back, I type. *Text me so we can meet up.*

I hit send and watch the progress bar crawl across the top of the screen. It makes it about three quarters of the way before stalling.

I wait for fifteen, thirty, sixty seconds. The bar of service disappears, then blips back on, then disappears again.

"Not delivered" appears beneath my text.

I sigh and head for the cabin.

———

The other girls are asleep. I pull off my shoes and tiptoe soundlessly for the bathroom. The tiniest sliver of moonlight cuts through the lone window, painting a slash of white on the shower curtain. Otherwise, the room is dark.

I turn for one of the two sinks, moving by memory. They each have an age-fogged mirror above them, and between the mirrors, a yellow, dust-covered lightbulb with a pull chain. Before I can grab for the chain, a muted *plip* sounds behind me, near the shower.

I freeze.

Plip. There it is again.

Plip-plip, like liquid dripping on stone.

The temperature in the room plummets. It's suddenly freezing. The hairs on my arms raise.

The lightbulb's pull chain feels miles away, my limbs heavy like stone. I reach into the pocket of my hoodie and retrieve Donovan's Zippo instead. I flip it open, flick the wheel.

A faint light fills the room, and something scuttles in the shower stall in response.

It's in your head, I tell myself. *There's nothing there.*

The muted dripping continues.

I extend my arm, moving the lighter toward the noise, and shadows stretch and contort with my motion. The shower curtain is pushed to one side but nothing in the stall appears wet—not the curtain or the floor tiles or the space around the drain. The dripping sound has stopped. I grab hold of the curtain and rip it back farther, revealing the whole of the stall.

It's empty.

And dry.

I lower my arm, turn around to face the mirror. My wide-eyed reflection stares back, rippling in the flickering glow of the Zippo.

I blow out the flame. Darkness engulfs me. And almost immediately, there it is again, a muted, wet dripping. Something moves behind me, scuttling. I'm certain of it this time. The shower curtain swishes, and then it's nearer, right behind me, it's breath hitting my neck.

I flick the lighter on.

And there she is. The girl from Windsor's mirror. Her eyes hidden behind a mop of dark hair that drips with blood. A gash on the side of her head pink and glistening, her skull split open like a ripe melon.

I scream rips from my throat. I drop the Zippo in my panic, and it claps shut.

"What is it?" Viv yells, bursting into the bathroom. "What happened?" Brightness floods the space as she yanks the pull chain between the two mirrors and the lone lightbulb flickers on.

I shield my eyes with my hands.

Jocelyn and Gretta stand in the doorway, rubbing the sleep from their eyes.

Viv crouches beside me, helps me stand. I grab at the porcelain sink for support, shakily lift myself to full height, and force myself to look in the mirror. It's just me again—my own wide-eyed reflection staring back—and an empty shower stall behind me. "She was right here," I mutter, pointing. "In the mirror. I saw her."

"Saw who?" Jocelyn says, annoyed.

"When I— When I looked . . ."

Jocelyn rolls her eyes. "I'm going to bed." Gretta follows, yawning.

"Nell?" Viv asks, still helping me stand. My legs are weak and quavering.

"It was the girl from Windsor. The one I saw in the mirror the night we went with Davie."

"With the blood?"

179

I nod. "It felt like someone was behind me, but in the mirror, she'd taken my spot. Like she'd replaced me." Viv helps me to my bunk and I collapse on the mattress, shaking in a cold sweat.

"You should go see an exorcist," Jocelyn teases from her bed.

"Yeah, sounds like you're possessed, Nell. Like the house got a hold of you." Gretta waggles her fingers and makes a cartoony ghost noise. They both cackle and howl.

"Not helping," Viv snaps.

"Oh, chill," Jocelyn says. "We're just joking around."

But joke or not, their comments bring my own fears into sharper light.

What happened at Windsor Camp all those years ago . . . Maybe it's happening again—this time to me.

CHAPTER
TWENTY-FOUR

About an hour after the sun rises on Tuesday morning, basking Corwin Lake in shades of golden honey, I find myself heading into town in Arlo's car, a 2011 Honda Accord with red paint that's chipped along the bumpers and door seams.

Town is perhaps a generous word because there's not much of anything surrounding Corwin Lake. On the southern end there is a marina though, and surrounding it, a small general store, a bar, and a few homes. This is where Arlo is taking me.

I spent the better part of Monday lamenting to him about my predicament. I told him what I'd seen in the mirror, the "joke" my bunkmates had made. At first he looked at me like I was pulling a prank. When my story about the mirror didn't change, his expression grew deeply concerned. "Don't you see what's happening here?" I snapped when he refused to agree that something might be possessing me, driving me mad. Finally, late during the dinner rush, he pulled me aside and told me to call in sick in the morning. Not with a fever or cold —that would land us in the nurse's office, trapped on campus. But if we both claimed to have eaten something that disagreed with us—some food that had sat out a bit too long as we cleaned up—that just might do the trick.

"Why do we need to be sick?" I asked.

"Because you need a day off, Nell," he answered. "You desperately need a day away from all this."

I sent word of my food poisoning to Dolores via Viv. Arlo sent it through one of the maintenance workers that bunked with him. Dolores bought it—or at least she didn't send a message back demanding we show up to work regardless—so we waited until our cabins cleared out and then met up in the parking lot.

And now we're driving.

"You want the radio on?" he asks as the car passes beneath the giant wood archway that marks the entrance/exit to camp. The words "Camp Durant" are fashioned from meticulously cut pieces of birchwood, looking down at us from the highest point on the arch. A small, whitewashed sign with the words "for girls" etched into it hangs beneath by a few rusted chain links.

"Sure, if you do."

"Not really. Nothing comes in up here anyway." He jerks his head at his cell, mounted on one of the vents. "You can pick something from my phone."

"I kind of like the quiet," I admit.

"Oh, okay."

I suddenly feel like I've said the wrong thing. I've snapped at Arlo quite a bit recently and he hasn't deserved it. The silence in the car is now piercing and I find myself wishing I'd said yes to music. I crack the passenger window, letting a tiny roar of fresh air permeate the cab.

The Accord bumps over ruts in the one-lane dirt road. We wind through the towering pine trees for about a half mile, until we hook up with the main road. It's paved, but just as deserted.

Arlo turns right. The tires hum on the asphalt.

"So you're from around here?" I ask.

"Inlet."

"That's what? An hour away?"

"Depends on which end of Corwin you're measuring from. The very southern end—where the marina is and we're headed? That's only like twenty minutes from home. But the north end? By camp? That's an easy hour."

"And what's the plan once we get to the marina?"

"Walk a bit," he says. "Enjoy time away from camp. Maybe see a friend of mine."

"You have friends?"

"Har har," he deadpans.

I steal a glance at him. His gaze is rooted on the narrow, winding road. He has one palm on the top of the steering wheel, the other arm hangs out the window, which he opened when I turned off the A.C. His shaggy hair blows in the wind.

He catches me watching and smirks. No, that's not quite right. It's more of a smile that quickly morphs into a conflicted frown.

"You're gonna be okay," he says. "You know that, right? Everything that's happening is just—"

"I'd rather not talk about it."

"Right. Good plan. A day away, all that on the back burner."

"Exactly."

But even as I say it, I can't keep my leg from bouncing with nerves, my fingers from twisting together. Arlo reaches for me, his left hand taking over the steering wheel while his right hand grabs mine. He threads his fingers between my fidgeting ones, and I freeze. He keeps his eyes on the road, and I stare at our entwined fingers, the way my hand looks small in his, the way the back of his hand rests against my bare thigh.

The chill that has plagued me for weeks seems to fade away, my core thawing. Soon it's downright hot in the car, and stuffy, but I don't want it to end.

We drive the whole way with the windows down, the muggy July air blowing on our faces.

———

Arlo parks behind the general store, in a tiny lot where weeds grow in the cracks of the faded pavement. I can see the shore from the lot; the pines have been felled to make room for what can barely be considered a town. There's a single street running parallel to the shore, and the street we drove in on bisecting it.

That's it. That's the extent of the roads.

Down by the marina, a man fuels up his boat. His outfit—Patagonia pullover, crisp swim trunks, and glinting designer sunglasses—give him away as a summer resident. The marina owner, however, is clearly local. A faded flannel, an even more faded Yankees hat, and work shorts that have been patched and mended and still have a hole near the hem. He accepts the cash payment with a quick nod, then watches the boat pull away from the marina.

"This way," Arlo says. We take the road along the shore, moving away from the marina and toward a string of buildings. Chipping paint adorns nearly every house. Most lawns are in need of a mow. And then there's a small white chapel, its steeple piercing the sky. The front double doors are robin's egg blue and one of them hangs slightly off-kilter, giving the impression of a crack in an egg. A squat sign out front reads "Corwin Lake Chapel" in rose-pink letters.

Arlo takes the steps two at a time, then glances back over his shoulder. "You coming?"

"Inside?"

"It'll make sense in a minute, I promise." He motions for me adamantly.

I sigh and climb the steps, but the closer I get to the door, the less I want to go through it. I've never been even remotely religious and places of worship make me uneasy. I feel like a fraud here, naked and exposed.

Arlo grabs the door handle and heaves. It doesn't give. "Locked," he says with a frown.

Good, I think. I'm about to tell him to I'd rather not go inside anyway, when a voice calls out to us. "Can I help you two with something?"

We twist in unison, turning toward the voice. A wrought-iron fence surrounds the chapel, and standing on the opposite side, in the neighboring property, is an elderly man in black slacks and a black dress shirt. A Roman collar is visible at his throat.

"Father Williams?" Arlo asks.

"Yes." His bushy, gray eyebrows rise, causing a dozen wrinkles to spread across his forehead.

"I'm Arlo. This is Eleanor. We work at Camp Durant and have a few questions for you."

"About?"

"Evil spirits. Possession."

"We do?" I say, angling toward Arlo.

He drops his voice to a whisper. "I thought it would be good to talk an expert on this kind of stuff. Hear what a possession might look like and see if there's a perfectly reasonable explanation for whatever it is you're experiencing."

"I just said in the car I didn't want to think about this today."

"I didn't know that at the time I planned the trip," he

says apologetically. "And to be honest, you probably wouldn't have come if I'd proposed this."

"Because you don't believe me. You keep trying to convince me that what I'm experiencing isn't real."

Father Williams lifts a latch on a section of the fence and pushes a gate open. It swings toward us, creaking. "You can keep arguing"—he jerks his head toward the small home behind him—"or you can come inside and talk. I'll let you work it out." He leaves, disappearing inside his house.

"Let's just see what he says, Nell." Arlo touches my arm.

I shake him off. Twist away. "I can't believe this. I can't fucking believe this."

"I'm just trying to help. I do believe you're going through something. And hey, maybe I'm entirely wrong and you're one hundred percent right. Maybe Father Williams will look you in the eye and say you're possessed and know exactly how to fix your problem. But I really believe he'll be able to tell us something that explains all this, and then you'll be able to finally relax. Either way, you'll get answers."

I *do* need answers, I can't argue with that.

"Fine," I grumble, brushing by Arlo. "Let's see what Father Williams has to say."

CHAPTER
TWENTY-FIVE

"The chapel was built over a hundred years ago," Father Williams says as he shows us into his house. "Chapels don't typically have dedicated clergy—did you know that?—but I've always lived next door." There's a nonchalance to his tone. I get the impression it's intentional, as though he's trying to distract from the awkward argument outside. "Can I get you anything to drink? Water? Tea?"

"No, we're fine, thanks," Arlo says.

We pass through a crowded entryway where the priest's jackets and coats hang from hooks, and into a living room that hasn't been updated since the seventies. The couch is mustard yellow. The carpeted floor borders on shag rug. There's a brick fireplace and olive-green walls, and windows flanked by floral-patterned curtains. A picture above the mantel shows Jesus with his eyes closed, a thorn crown drawing blood. It makes me shudder.

Religion wasn't a thing Mom or Dad grew up with, so neither did I. We never attended Mass or said prayers, something Dad's strongest critics latched on to quickly after the scandal broke, saying it demonstrated an utter lack of ethics and morals. They weren't wrong about his morals, but religion had nothing to do with it.

Arlo and I sit on the mustard-yellow couch, our knees nearly touching a walnut coffee table with an oval top and four spindly legs that splay out at slight angles. It's decidedly vintage and in style again, though I doubt Father Williams is aware of decor trends. He sits opposite us, in a wooden rocking chair, and laces his fingers together. "What, exactly, did you care to ask about?" The conversational tone from earlier is gone, replaced with something more weighted.

Arlo looks at me, nods encouragingly. When I don't say anything, he sighs and asks, "What causes a possession?"

Father Williams considers this carefully. "God is a powerful force," he says finally. "So is Lucifer. Oftentimes, someone will unknowingly invite in spirits with malicious intent."

"And if someone was possessed," Arlo presses. "Would they know it?"

At this, the priest frowns. "Theoretically, they would become a host for the spirit, entirely unaware of what has happened."

"So someone possessed wouldn't be able to question if they were possessed?" Arlo suggests. "Simply asking that question would be proof that they're fine."

"I don't know about *fine*, but yes, I would imagine that wondering such a thing is proof, in a sense, that they haven't lost control of their own body or mind." Father Williams pauses briefly. "Now what is this really about?" His gaze slides to me, as if he knows.

Arlo gives me another encouraging nod.

This time, I bite. I take a deep breath and start talking, laying it all out between us. I tell Father Williams about the pull I feel toward Windsor Camp. The light in the window, the voice in the night. The things I've been seeing—*impossible* things. Like a corpse that has vanished, a reflection that isn't there, blood that doesn't exist.

Arlo interjects at the end, explains the stress I'm under, mentioning my family drama without going into the actual details.

Father Williams rubs his palms together, his brown eyes working over me. "It could be a dark force at play. Or it could simply be your own insecurities running rampant. Your brain showing you things to distract from a trauma—or even make sense of it. And it sounds like your family is dealing with quite a bit of trauma currently."

"But when I see these things, it doesn't feel like a dream or a vision. It's visceral. Raw."

Father Williams reaches across the table. "Here, give me your hand."

When our fingers touch, I expect a reaction—something jarring, sudden. But there's nothing. He holds my hand a moment, turns it over, looks at my palm. He curls my fingers around his and closes his eyes. He begins to mutter something softly—a prayer, I realize after a moment. *Our Father.* The way his lips move so quickly, the words tumbling out in punctuated staccatos. It makes me feel hot, flighty. I want to leave. I try to retract my hand, but he only holds on tighter.

My vision begins to tunnel. I feel faint, sickly. In my mouth, I can taste blood.

"Father, I—"

But he's already dropping my hand, his eyes flying open. "Something is deeply wrong."

"What?" I manage. "What do you mean?" I blink several times, trying to hold the room in focus. Everything still spins.

"Father?" Arlo says.

"Please leave. Immediately."

Arlo looks to me, baffled.

"Now!" Father Williams yells. He thrusts a hand toward the door violently. I lurch from my seat so quickly that static dances across my line of sight. I need to get outside. I need fresh air. "Nell, wait!" Arlo calls, but I'm already fleeing, staggering. I lose my footing in entryway and bump the wall. My eyes are burning. My vision tunneling. A crucifix I hadn't noticed earlier slips from its nail, scraping the back of my hand as it falls. I wince, hissing through my teeth.

Then I'm finally pushing out the door, stumbling down the steps. The fresh air is a lifeline. I can breathe again. I inhale deeply, brace my hands against my thighs. I think I narrowly avoided a panic attack in there.

A hand lands gently between my shoulder blades. Arlo. "You okay?"

I nod, silent, then straighten.

The door bangs open behind us. Father Williams is standing on the front stoop, one hand clutched to the front of his shirt, the other hanging idly at his side.

"We give power to the things we fear," he says. "Half of staying in the light is believing in it. Do not let your fears lead you astray, Eleanor. Do not walk toward the darkness. Choose the light."

Sermon complete, he disappears inside without another word, the door slapping shut and the lock audibly clicking.

Arlo looks at me, the door, and back again. "What was *that* about?"

"I have no idea."

But I do. And I think Arlo does too, given the way he's staring at me—like he's not quite sure if he should be helping me or running for the hills.

He brought me here to put me at ease, to show me there was nothing to worry about, and now we both know that couldn't be farther from the truth.

Something is wrong. Something inside me. Something Father Williams most definitely sensed.

I might be possessed after all.

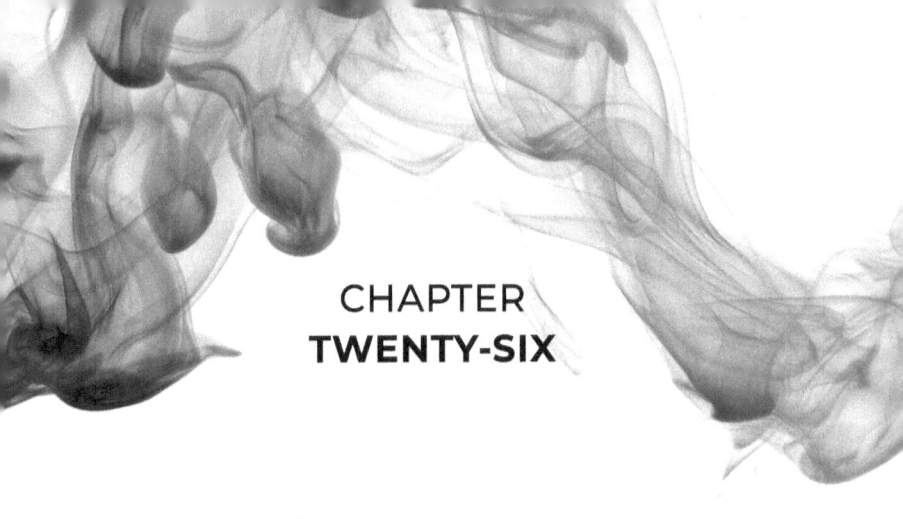

CHAPTER
TWENTY-SIX

"Take the other way around the lake on the way back," I say as we pull out of the parking lot. "I want to stop by Windsor."

Arlo jerks toward me now, eyes wide. "You really think that's smart?"

I blink at him. "Why not?"

"'Do not walk toward the darkness,'" he quotes. "Nell, he straight-up told you not to go back there."

"He also said that we give power to the things we fear. I'm not afraid of that place." Even as I say it, I know it's a lie. But I don't know how else I'm supposed to beat this if I don't face it head on. Maybe staring the darkness in the eye is exactly what I need to do. I need to see it and not be afraid. I need to feel it and then walk the other direction.

"But do you really think—"

"Just drive by the house!"

It comes out louder than I wanted. My hands are fisted in my lap.

"Okay, okay," Arlo says. "Take a deep breath."

"Don't talk to me like that," I snap.

"Like what?"

"Like I can't control my own emotions."

He raises a brow silently. He hasn't said it, but the challenge is there. *Can you?*

We drive in silence. Any warmth I'd felt when Arlo held my hand earlier is long gone. The car is an icebox now and the farther we travel, the worse it becomes. When we finally reach the north end of the lake, closing in on Windsor, I'm chilled to the bone. Almost as if it's this place that's caused the ailment.

"I don't think we should go in," Arlo says. "I think you should just stay at camp and make it through the summer, and then go home. Don't let it get its hooks in deeper."

"So you *do* think I'm possessed?" I ask, narrowing my eyes at him. "You believe me now."

"I never didn't believe you; I just thought there could be another explanation." He regards me sadly. "But after talking with Father Williams . . . I don't know, but it's obvious something isn't right."

The road takes a sharp turn, and there in the shadows ahead, is the driveway. A wooden sign hangs from a nearby tree, the words "Windsor Camp" etched into the grain and painted white. I've seen it only a handful of times, when Mom orchestrated scenic drives around the lake. If we follow the driveway through the trees, it will lead to the front of the house, the one that faces away from the lake and has been boarded up since the fire. But we can't turn down the driveway even if I beg Arlo, because a black SUV is parked there, blocking the way. The rear hatch is open and the someone is digging around in the back of vehicle.

"What the . . . ?" Arlo says.

"Let's stop," I tell him. "See who it is."

"Nell . . ."

"Please."

He humors me, rolling to a halt. The person hears us approaching and turns toward us. It's a woman in her mid-thirties, wearing a striped sundress and sunglasses that make her eyes look as wide as an owl's. I catch sight of what she'd been wrestling with—a real-estate sign with her picture and the Coldwell Banker's logo on it. A second white panel hangs from beneath, reading "SALE PENDING" in bloodred.

"Hi," I say in what I hope is a carefree tone. "When did Windsor Camp sell?"

"Just last week," the woman replies, giving the sign another yank.

"I didn't even realize it was *for* sale," Arlo says.

"You and most of Hamilton County. It was a private sale, handled between two parties with no public show-ings or listings. Of course, now that we're in the process of closing, my boss wants a sign here because it's good publicity." She blows a flyaway out of her eyes. "Not that many cars drive this stretch of road." She eyes us through the open window. "Say, since you're here, you wouldn't mind helping me get this thing in the ground, would you? It weighs a ton."

"No problem." Arlo puts the hazards on and slips from the car. I follow. He lugs the sign out of the rear of the SUV. Bracing it against his shoulder, he carries it over to a hole the woman has already dug and lowers the post into place.

"Who bought it?" I ask the agent. Her name is Stacey DeStefano according to the sign.

"I'm not sure. I'm just here to put up the sign."

"But you're the selling agent. How can you not know?"

She scowls. "It was a private sale and purchased through an LLC. That's all I can say."

"There you go," Arlo announces, wiping his hands together. The white sign stands out like a beacon against all the bark and greenery of the woods. I frown at the red "SALE PENDING."

The house has sat vacant for years—as long as I can remember, even. Why did it sell suddenly? Why was it even up for sale?

"When are the new owners moving in?" I ask.

"You are extremely nosy," Stacey says through a forced smile. She turns to Arlo. "Thanks for your help."

He climbs back in the car, and I stand there a moment,

waiting, but it's no use. The woman won't leave until we do. I won't be able to visit Windsor today. Or any day, really, if it's about to become private property.

I join Arlo in the car. As we drive off, I can't help thinking that he's happy about this turn of events.

CHAPTER
TWENTY-SEVEN

The week passes uneventfully. Or at least as uneventfully as my maybe-possessed body will allow.

The daylight hours are the easiest, the time I feel most comfortable. I still feel the tug of Windsor, but I don't hear strange voices or see things that aren't there. Remembering how Avery Jane's failure to eat was one of the first signs of her possession, I force myself to snack often. Nothing tastes right—coffee, fruit, meat. It doesn't matter. Anything I put in my mouth tastes spoiled or dry to the point of being ash-like. I spit it all out. Rinse my mouth with water. Spit that out too, because even water seems foul.

The nights are the hardest. When everyone is sleeping, the pull to Windsor becomes strongest, my fears and insecurities louder than ever. I begin tying myself to bed, a rope around my ankle, the other end around the post of the bunk beds, just to make it harder to go anywhere. I'm afraid of the bathroom, the smooth surface of the mirror in the darkness. I'm terrified of the path that snakes away from the cabin and down to the shore. A destination my feet want to reach even when my brain screams that everything I find there will only confuse me further.

I sleep very little. Each morning when the sun rises, there's a sense of relief that I've survived the night, but it comes paired with dread that the sun will inevitably set again, and I may not be so lucky twice.

I feel in control, but only barely.

By the time the weekend approaches, I'm exhausted from merely existing, and desperate to do something proactive. Despite Arlo's suggestions to just ride things out, I cannot go on like this for the rest of the summer— barely surviving, pretending everything is normal.

When Saturday morning breaks, I have a plan, and much to Arlo's delight, it does not involve returning to Windsor Camp. Not yet at least. When I tell him I need to head to Bradley House after the breakfast rush, he happily agrees to cover my afternoon shift.

Viv is on an off-campus excursion with the girls from Pine Knot and Topridge, Kayla's campers. They'll spend the afternoon hiking to a set of picturesque waterfalls about an hour from camp, meaning I won't see her again until dinnertime. But that's fine. My goal today—to find out who's purchasing Windsor—doesn't require a second set of hands.

I dart down to the shore, grab my kayak, and head south alone.

As I paddle, questions about Windsor's sale cycle through my mind. Why was the property sold after so much time sitting vacant? When will the closing happen? Does the new owner know anything about what happened there all those years ago? If so, maybe they can help me with my predicament. If not, the very least I can do is give them a warning about the place they are about to buy. Not that I'm certain they'll believe me.

By the time I reach Bradley House, the humidity has peaked. The whirligig loon flaps its wooden wings in greeting as I anchor the kayak to the end of the dock. Then I skirt up the rise, picking my way around the house, and jog down the dirt driveway.

As expected, a dark sedan with tinted windows is parked on the edge of the road, right beside the mailbox. Donovan.

I expect him to see me coming, but when I reach the idling car and tap on the window, he jumps about a foot, flipping shut a manila folder in his lap. Then he rolls down the window. A cool blast of A.C. hits my cheeks.

"Wow, I really scared you there. Sorry."

He leans away from me slightly, as if he expects me to shout *Boo* for good measure. "Ms. Bradley," he says thinly. "Why are you not at camp?"

"I've got the afternoon off. Just wanted to get away for a bit and thought I should let you know that I'm heading inside. Don't want to startle you or anything."

"Oh, thank you. I appreciate that." He sets the manilla folder on the seat beside him.

"Also, you left this in the Performing Arts Building the other day." I pull the Zippo from my back pocket and pass it through the window.

"Again, thank you." He takes it gingerly, turning it over a few times. There's a long pause where I think he might ask me something about Dad's case but ultimately decides against it. "Well, I'll just be out here," he says finally, "trying not to suffocate in the heat."

"Should I let you know when I leave?"

"No, no, that's fine. I've got surveillance set up."

I nod in parting, and jog back down the driveway, wondering how he didn't see me coming if he has surveillance set up, how I was able to startle him.

I enter Bradley House through the front door and turn off the alarm. Maybe *this* is what Donovan meant. Perhaps he can see a report of every arming and disarming of the security system.

In Dad's office, I wake the computer from sleep and Google "Coldwell Banker" and "Stacey DeStefano." She works at an office in Inlet. I pull out my phone and connect to the Wi-Fi.

My phone explodes with messages and alerts after weeks of being without service. I refuse to check any of my social media accounts, but curiosity gets the best of me, and I look at my texts. There's nothing from Mom, but there is something from Kylie.

My heart kicks faster in my chest.

Hey, is all I can see on the preview.

I tap her name with my thumb. Her follow-up texts load.

> An agent called asking when I drove you to camp.

> I can't believe you, pulling me into your family's lies.

> You can fuck all the way off.

> Don't bother responding, I'm blocking your number.

I read it several times, expecting it to change, but of course, it doesn't. The messages are timestamped a week ago, which would be when Donovan started asking questions about my arrival at Corwin Lake in order to "create a timeline." I feel like screaming, like crying, like throwing my phone across the room.

Instead, I take a deep breath and call the real estate office.

"Coldwell Bankers, how can I direct your call?" a chipper voice says.

"Hi, I have a question. Gosh this is embarrassing. See, I'm a summer intern and feel like I keep screwing everything up." I laugh nervously. "Anyway, my boss is in the process of closing on a property on Corwin Lake—the old Windsor residence? I was supposed to make sure we got a copy of the inspection report, but I can't find it anywhere and I was wondering if maybe you guys have the wrong address on file?"

"Hmm, let me see." On the other end of the line, I can hear her keyboard clacking.

"This is for NexusCapital—all one word—LLC?"

"Yes, correct." I scribble the name on a Post-It.

"The address I have on file is 1350 6th Ave, Suite C, New York, New York. Wait, hang on. Our records show that the inspection was waived, so that explains why you can't find a copy of the report."

"Ha! It absolutely does. Thank you for your help, I'm sorry to have been a bother."

"No trouble at all. Anything else I can help you with?"

"No, I'm all set, thanks."

"Have a nice day." The woman hangs up.

I underline the address I've added to the Post-It Note, then I type *NexusCapital LLC* into the search bar and hit return. I scroll, frowning, and dig some more, but for all I can tell, the company doesn't exist. No website, no Facebook page. Nothing. When I type in the address the secretary gave me, Google Maps returns what appears to be an office building holding numerous businesses.

I realize, with a sinking feeling, that I should have asked the secretary to confirm Nexus' phone number, that way I could at least try to contact these people. But I can't call back and ask for it now without looking suspicious.

I tap the pen to my bottom lip, thinking, then Google *How to find the owner of an LLC.*

After a little research, I'm on the New York's Secretary of State website, where a Corporation and Business Entity Database allows me to search by name. A query for *NexusCapital* returns three results, only one of which is based in Manhattan. I click through, scroll down, skimming, scanning, and there. A name. Under registered agent: Sophia Mackel.

Disappointment flutters in my chest.

I'd hoped to recognize the name, but perhaps that was naive of me. Someone is buying Windsor Camp. Just because something in that house has sunk its claws into me, doesn't mean that the person buying it is involved in whatever it is I'm experiencing. Then again, they did go through an awful lot of trouble to keep their name off paperwork, to hide behind an LLC. Maybe they know *exactly* what they are getting into with this purchase.

On a whim, I pull up Facebook and type in the registered agent's name. Dozens of results come back, but the top result causes me to suck in a breath. *One mutual friend.* I click on her name. The info on Sophia Mackel's profile page is limited because we're not friends, and her picture tells me very little. In it, she stands facing away from the camera, hands on her hips, looking out over fall foliage from what must be the summit of a mountain hike. Each clothing choice feels purposeful—the kind of outdoor gear that is selected for fashion as much as for function. Black leggings that tuck into navy socks and hiking boots. A blue puffer vest over a mustard thermal. She's wearing a baseball hat, and even though her hair is in a low pony-tail, it falls in perfect, loose beach curls.

I scroll down the page to her friends list.

And there, the first image in the grid, is our mutual friend.

Dad.

hat the fuck?

  I click on Dad's picture. His profile loads.

Much like my social media accounts, any public post that Dad made before he ran has become a dumping ground for people to air their opinions about him. But unlike me, who went private as soon as possible, Dad didn't lock down. Everything is still online. Accessible. Hanging there in the open, waiting to be attacked and dogpiled.

His most recent post from June 21st is a link to an article he'd shared about rising inflation rates and how they're squeezing middle-income families. It's riddled with angry comments, some only a few hours old.

Like you'd know anything about pinching pennies, you fucking hypocrite.

I hope you rot in hell.

Your family is what's wrong with America. If you all dropped dead no one would miss you.

They get worse. Violent. Full of death threats.

I have to stop reading. Even if he deserves the outrage, there comes a point when vitriol slips into something inhuman, and the entire thing makes me uncomfortable. Worse still, it makes some of the worst comments I received rise to the surface of my memory. The things strangers dropped in my DMs—what should happen to me, what they'd do to me—simply for being related to Duncan Bradley.

The internet is a Godawful place.

Dad's profile photo is his work headshot, taken several years ago. It must have commenting permissions set only for his friends, because the comments posted on it are few—and civil. The most recent one, shared the day he disappeared, is from my Uncle Spencer, Dad's brother in South Carolina. *Duncan, if you read this, please turn yourself in. The only way out of this is to make things right. Much love.*

If Dad's running to him for help, he might not find it.

I spend the next hour going through the rest of Dad's photos, ignoring the comments as best I can as I try to find the connection between him and Sophia Mackel. There isn't one. At least not that I can see. What I do find are memories, many of which I hadn't recalled until looking at the pictures, almost as though I'd tried to bury them.

A trip to Disney World when I was six, me riding on

his shoulders, Mickey Mouse ears on my head, both of us captured mid-laugh.

A getaway to Ithaca for his alumni weekend, our whole family wearing Cornell tees, my gangly limbs and too-big teeth and general middle school awkwardness on full display for the camera.

A Subway Series game from a last summer, when Dad scored us seats right behind home plate at Yankee Stadium. The selfie he took shows Mom in Mets gear and me and Dad wearing Yankees caps. We're squinting from the sun, our faces shiny with sweat.

There's even a photo from as recently as this past Christmas. Me and Mom decked out in holiday finery, posed in the foyer of our apartment and ready to attend the *Nutcracker*—an annual tradition. The lighting is terrible, and Dad clearly took the photo, because the framing is a bit wonky. He never was good with cameras. The caption simply reads, *My whole world.*

I don't know what to make of these photos. They paint a picture so opposite the narrative I've told myself since the scandal broke. But perhaps that's intentional. This is the reality he always wanted to project.

I remember these outings now that I'm faced with the proof of them. I can even admit that they were fun. He was present when he wanted to be, decent—even great— if he decided to put in the effort. But social media is a highlights reel, isn't it? We chose what pieces of ourselves to share with the world, and Dad was never going to post about the time he chose to work on my thirteenth birthday rather than make it home in time for cake. He's not going to show the world that he spent every weekend stroll through Central Park with his phone glued to his ear. He's not going to post about how Mom drowns her loneliness with wine because it's there for her more often than him.

Recently, I've clung tightly to a narrative that will help me survive this scandal: that my dad is terrible, awful, the worst. But the truth is that he is two things at once. He is both absent *and* attentive. He is both a stranger *and* Dad, the only one I've ever known.

Something wet touches my arm and I look down to find a tiny drop of water on my skin. My cheeks are wet. I'm crying, I realize. Over him. For him. I swipe the tears away, gritting my teeth.

The nostalgia I feel when looking at the pictures, the way I miss him so fiercely . . . It's not real. It's conjured up by grief. It's me missing the type of father he *could* have been all the time, not the one he was only on rare occasions.

I click away from his profile, navigating back to Sophia Mackel. This mystery woman who somehow knows Dad and who recently purchased Windsor Camp.

I click on her profile photo, opening her profile photos album. I hit the right arrow key. Her second profile photo is a selfie in a salon. Her eyes are a deep brown that match her hair. She's wearing bright red lipstick. She looks about Mom's age, maybe a bit younger.

The next photo jumps me back farther in time. She's

wearing a wedding gown, her hair swept up into a beautiful, cascading bundle of curls. Her dress fans out around her feet as she shares a dance with her husband. They're both captured in profile, foreheads touching, twin smiles gracing their faces.

I freeze.

My heart seems to skip a beat.

I know this man.

He's younger here, his cheeks fuller, his hair not as thinned. But his eyes are just as steely, even when smiling. I move the cursor over his face, hoping he's tagged, but he's not.

It doesn't matter.

The caption confirms it.

Love you now and forever, Cormac.

Sophia Mackel is Agent Donovan's wife.

———

I don't know what it means. This is not what I expected to discover when researching Windsor's buyer. A historian, perhaps? A local who always loved the estate's location? Maybe even a renowned ghost hunter. But not this.

I'm practically trembling as I walk down the driveway. His car is still there, the tinted windows rolled up.

I'd searched him before signing out of Facebook, but he didn't have an account, not one that I could find at least, and he wasn't in any of Sophia's other profile pictures. If he exists in her other albums, I can't see them. She has them hidden from non-friends.

I flex my fingers, squeeze a fist, flex again. It does nothing to calm my nerves.

Donovan sees me coming this time and lowers the window.

I bend down and put an elbow on the open edge, hoping it makes me look relaxed. "I'm heading back now. I locked everything up and set the alarm."

"Great. Thanks."

He doesn't mention how he told me I didn't need to check in with him when leaving. His computer sits on his lap, but the screen is angled so that I can't see what he's working on. The manila folder from earlier rests on the passenger seat, just inches away.

"Hey, did you know Windsor is for sale?" I say nonchalantly.

"I did, actually. I saw the sign when I stopped by the night you and Vivian got yourself spooked over there."

"I wonder why someone would want to buy that place. It's seriously creepy."

"Maybe because it has beautiful bones and is in a great location." He checks his watch, as though he has something to do other than sit in this driveway from now until forever.

"I guess. Are you gonna tell the buyers about that place's history—Avery Jane and the haunting rumors?"

"Plenty of houses are rumored to be haunted and people buy them every day," he says with a shrug. "It's not my place to speak up about it, and I wouldn't know who to talk to even if it was. My focus is your father's case."

"Right. Okay, well have a good one, Agent Donovan."

"You too, Eleanor."

My fingers tremble all the way down the hill and for most of the kayak ride back.

He lied. Even if he has no clue that his wife's company bought Windsor, which I doubt, he still lied. The sale sign wasn't there the night Viv and I dug up the cemetery. The agent only put it out a few days ago, when Arlo and I drove by the place after visiting Father Williams.

Cormac Donovan is hiding something. And his wife is in the process of buying Windsor. The real question is *why*.

CHAPTER
TWENTY-NINE

tell Arlo about Donovan and Sophia Mackel as we clean up after the dinner rush. There's a connection I can't see, a reason he must have lied. I wonder aloud if perhaps I shouldn't trust him, and when I mention that I'd like to go back to Windsor and poke around, Arlo cringes.

"Just sit tight. The truth always rises to the surface eventually."

"It won't if Donovan's purposely trying to hide something," I argue.

"It's possible he doesn't even know Sophia bought the place. They could be divorced. I mean, she doesn't have his last name. Maybe it means nothing." The toothpick clenched between his teeth moves from one side of his mouth to the other, punctuating this thought.

"It's just too big of a coincidence," I say firmly. "It means something. It has to."

"Just promise me you'll stay away from that place. Remember what Father Williams said about how we give power to the things we fear, how you shouldn't go back there, how you need to not walk toward the darkness?"

"Yeah, yeah. I remember."

He seems to take this as a promise, which it clearly is not, and by the time I sneak out of the cabin later that night, Arlo is halfway across camp, asleep in his bunk. The girls are none the wiser also, too deep in their dreams to hear me leave. Viv returned home from the all-day excursion exhausted. I haven't even been able to update her yet, but I will, tomorrow. Right now, I need to return to Windsor. Whatever's going on lately—the way that place calls to me, the things I keep seeing that may or may not be real . . . I know deep in my gut that they'll keep happening until I confront them head-on.

I suppose Father Williams is right about one thing. We give power to the things we fear.

And I refuse to give Windsor Camp any more power over me.

———

Claiming that I wasn't scared was an easy declaration to make from the safety of Camp Durant's shoreline. Now, inside the belly of the deserted Windsor Camp, alone with dank moisture filling my lungs, it all feels different.

There is something foul about this place. Rotten.

Floorboards creak underfoot. Every hair on my arm

stands on edge. The scent of mildew and wet earth is overpowering, and I picture toxic spores infiltrating my sinuses, roots drilling between my ribs, weeds overtaking me. I attempt to ignore the image as I climb the stairs to the main level, then the second.

I move through the rooms I haven't explored yet. A master bedroom with a balcony that overlooks the water. A small study. The bedroom across from Avery Jane's. I don't know what I'm looking for, exactly, and even if I did, it seems unlikely I'd find anything of note here. Each room is in absolute disarray.

The bathroom between the two small bedrooms is the worst. The tiled floor is thick with dirt and grime. Tiny brown mushrooms cling to wood that borders the shower stall, erupting from the failing grout like curling fingernails.

I turn to face the mirror, clouded and cracked with age, and immediately have the urge to run. But I remember what Father Williams said—*We give power to the things we fear*—and I hold my reflection's gaze. In the glow of my phone's flashlight, my reflection stares back.

When I blink, she blinks.

When I tilt my head to the side, stretching my neck, my reflection does the same,

We give power to the things we fear.

But what if the thing to be feared is already inside me? Father Williams seemed afraid of it. He dropped my hand, asked me to leave.

There's that familiar noise behind me again, wet and

215

muted. Like water dripping from a shower faucet. A voice in my head tells me to run. Another tells me to look. Something wet touches the back of my neck.

I flinch, grabbing the edge of the sink in front of me. "I'm not afraid," I grit out, willing it to be true, forcing myself to not look away from the mirror.

My reflection ripples, and she's suddenly the girl I've seen before, her hair dripping with blood, her skull cracked open. I know, instantly, that the wetness on my neck is blood. My reflection is bleeding. I'm, bleeding. But none of it is real. It's all in my head. This has happened before, and it will continue to happen until I'm no longer afraid.

I watch in horror as my reflection's motions deviate from mine. Her arm raises slowly, toward me, as though she intends to reach through the mirror and grab me by the throat. But she extends her arm to the side, a blood-slicked finger pointing out the window.

"Look," she says. Her voice is mine, but not. It's deeper, more ragged. I finally scream and clamp my eyes shut. When I open them, the bloody girl is gone. My normal reflection is back, wide-eyed and panting.

But I hear her voice still echoing inside my skull.

Look, I can hear her urging.

I turn slowly, toward the window. I squint through the dust-caked glass.

Below, silhouetted in weak moonlight, is the cemetery. There is no police tape around it, as I'd have expected after the cops paid it a visit the other week. But there is a shovel, its blade gleaming like exposed bone, and a wheelbarrow, tipped upside down to keep it from filling with rain.

Look.

But I can't—not properly at least, not from this height.

I exit the bathroom, head down the stairs, and slip into the night. In the cemetery, the shallow grave I dug up with Viv is empty. But the smell of death remains. I grab the wheelbarrow by its smooth, worn handles and turn it over. The thing is old, most of its blue paint chipped away to reveal the gray metal underneath. I move my phone light over it, and there, along the edge—blood. A dried smear of it.

I step away, twist toward the house.

What do you know? I think, speaking to the mirror girl, to the darkness that prowls Windsor, to whatever strange force has infiltrated my mind.

Look.

And I see it finally. A narrow track in the dirt, leading away from the cemetery, weaving through the trees and heading downhill.

I follow it, stepping around saplings, marveling at how smaller brush is already broken and beaten flat. The wheelbarrow has been this way before.

The trail ends at the water. There's a buoy about fifty yards out, gently bobbing as it marks dangerous rocks for boaters. To my right, an old canoe leans against a tree. The shoreline curves sharply, disappearing behind a rocky outcropping. The wheelbarrow tracks stop here, beside the canoe.

Look, the voice tells me.

Eleanor. Look.

Moonlight bounces off the surface of the lake, making it gleam like ice. I'm close to whatever the house is trying to tell me, but I still can't see it. Because it's likely hidden around the rocky outcropping, accessible only by the canoe.

Unless, of course, there is nothing to see.

Unless all I'm following is a slow descent into madness.

Behind me, the house looms dark and angry. Ahead, the moon hangs high in the sky, a brilliant beacon above the pines where my cabin is nestled.

Do not let your fears lead you astray, Father Williams told me. *Do not walk toward the darkness.*

I return to my boat and paddle back to camp, leaving that darkness behind me, the nose of my kayak pointed toward a brilliant patch of water on the opposite shore.

For tonight, I choose the light.

CHAPTER
THIRTY

"I can come with you this afternoon," Viv says as we approach the mess hall. Usually I arrive here long before her, but I overslept, my dreams fitful and haunting. The plus side of this is that I've been able to update her about everything on the walk over—Father Williams, the talking reflection, the wheelbarrow tracks through the woods. "I've gotta do cabin inspection for the girls this morning, but then they have free time after lunch, and I can get away." She pauses, her eyes flicking toward the rear entrance to the kitchens, where Arlo waves a hand in greeting. "Please just don't go alone," Viv mutters quietly. "I don't like any of this."

"Okay. I won't," I assure her. "I'll wait for you."

I don't particularly like waiting, nor do I like how uptight my friends have become about things, but a few hours isn't going to make a difference, and there's a good chance I'll need an extra set of hands anyway. I keep thinking about that canoe, resting against the tree along Windsor's shoreline. How it almost appears to be waiting, how it needs to be paddled around the rocky outcropping.

Viv heads for the front entrance and I carry on toward the rear, where Arlo is smoking a joint. "What was that all about?" he asks, gaze drifting after Viv.

"Getting awfully bold with that, aren't you?" I nod at the joint.

"Dolores doesn't care," he says with a shrug, "and my mom took the day off. She's going into town with Goodwin for something."

"Right. Well, sorry I'm late. Are the dishes piling up?"

"Yeah. That's why I waited. I'm not doing them alone." A devilish smile.

I roll my eyes.

"So, what was that about?" he asks again. "With Viv."

I wonder how much he overheard. "Nothing, just making plans for later."

He snubs the joint out on the bottom of his shoe and pushes off the wall. "You're a terrible liar, Manhattan." He fishes a toothpick from his pocket. It takes the place of the joint, bouncing between his lips as he smiles at me.

"And you're a snoop."

Arlo pulls the door to the mess open, allowing the smell of eggs and bacon to assault us, along with the cacophony of clattering dishes, Dolores's barked orders, and sizzling food. "Guilty," he says, "but at least I can admit it."

I duck under his outstretched arm and into the kitchen.

———

I meet Viv by the boats after lunch. "What took you so long?" she says in greeting.

"You guys eat the food, I get to clean up the mess," I respond bluntly. "It's a crap-ton of dishes."

"Canoe?" She eyes the boat racks.

"Yeah."

We carry it to the shore and are just stepping in when a voice calls, "Room for one more?"

I glance over my shoulder and there's Arlo, approaching with a paddle propped on his shoulder.

"No, actually," I reply. "Canoes hold two."

"Oh, come on, we can make room," Viv says. "You can sit in the middle, Arlo."

I glare at her, but before I can even get out an argument, Arlo is climbing into the boat.

Viv scrambles into the bow seat. I give the canoe another hard shove, then hop into the back. There's no middle seat, so Arlo sits awkwardly on the floor, legs stretched long, arms resting on the yoke. His paddle is beside him, tucked in against the life jackets we're not wearing but are required to have on hand while boating.

"You're paddling on the way back," I tell him. "No free rides here."

"Happy to do my share, Manhattan."

Viv smiles at me over his head. "All right, *Manhattan*, lead the way."

I hold my paddle beneath the water for a moment, angling us. Windsor watches from across the lake. From this distance, the buoy is impossible to pick out from the glinting, choppy water, but I know roughly where we're headed.

I start paddling.

———

I don't know what I expected to find on the opposite side of the rocky outcropping, but it wasn't this.

"What are we looking for again?" Viv asks.

Windsor is hidden from view, swallowed by the craggy rocks we've just paddled around. The cove we've entered is completely ordinary. A quiet little pocket of water, protected from wind and waves, the edges bathed in shadow. A good fishing spot. The woods bordering it are dense and dark.

I thought for sure that the canoe and discarded wheelbarrow meant something was hidden around this way, something accessible only by boat, but there's nothing, not that I can see.

"It's fucking hot," Arlo complains. "Let's go for a swim."

"Where?" Viv asks.

"I might be wrong, but I believe we're on a lake."

"I'm not wearing a suit," I argue.

"Your loss, I guess," Arlo pulls his tee over his head, empties a few things from the pockets of his swim shorts, then dives over the side of the canoe. It rocks wildly in response. I grip the edges, trying to steady us, as he resurfaces a few feet away and rolls onto his back. "You guys coming in?"

"What are we supposed to do with the canoe—let it drift off?" I say.

"Tie it to a tree or something. Actually, wait." He dives beneath the surface and swims. Toward the canoe, then under in.

"If he tips us . . ." Viv grumbles.

"He wouldn't. His cell is sitting right there." I point to it on the bottom of the canoe, where it's nestled in his discarded tee shirt.

Arlo resurfaces on the other side of the canoe and climbs ashore. He shakes his hair out of his eyes, sending water flying, and my stomach does a stupid summersault. Not sure what that's about. "Throw the line over. I'll tie you to this tree." He points to a low branch that hangs out over the water.

Viv tosses the rope. Arlo catches it. His torso glistens in the sun, the muscles in his back moving as he secures us to the tree. I glance away. Viv laughs.

"What?" he asks from the shore.

"Nothing." Viv strips off her clothes in favor of the suit she's wearing underneath.

"You're ditching me?" I whisper.

"Swim in your underwear," she counters. "I don't care. And I don't think Arlo would mind either." Then she's gone, jumping over the side of the canoe with a splash.

She swears as she resurfaces. "Careful when you come in, Nell. I smashed my foot on a rock."

Arlo shields his eyes from the sun as he observes the rocky outcropping. It's steep, but he starts picking his way between trees and craggy growth until he reaches the summit. He walks to the edge, observing the water below. "You thinking what I'm thinking?" he calls to Viv.

She smiles devilishly. "Lemme see if it's deep enough." She swims till she's swallowed in the shadow cast by the outcropping, then takes a breath, and disappears below the surface.

"I can't see the bottom," she calls as she remerges. "I mean, I wouldn't dive in, but a jump is probably fine."

It's all the confirmation Arlo needs. He takes a few steps back, then runs to the edge of the natural diving platform, and jumps. As he falls, he arches backward, turning into a back flip, then splashes through the water feet first.

Viv coughs in the onslaught of waves. I watch from the boat.

We wait a beat, another, a third. He's not resurfacing.

"You said it was deep enough?" I call.

"Yeah, I think so." But Viv sounds uncertain. "Arlo?" she calls, twisting in a circle. She dips below the water for a second. Reappears. "Arlo?"

Nothing.

I stand up, the canoe wobbling aggressively. Yank off my tee shirt and shorts. I'm just about to jump in to help her, when he breaks into view, flinging his hair to the side again, sending water flying and laughing like a madman.

"That wasn't funny, Arlo," Viv yells.

"You scared us to death!" I shout from the canoe.

His laugh cuts off as his eyes find me, darting between my face and my sports bra. It offers more coverage than a normal swimsuit and yet I suddenly feel very exposed. "Manhattan, were you about to jump in and try to rescue me?"

"No, I was just hot."

He glances at Viv. "She's a terrible liar."

"I know," my traitor best friend says.

They both swim for the shore. I exit the canoe ungracefully and join them. The rocks along the water's edge are worn smooth, and slick with moss, the earth beyond carpeted in pine needles. Low branches scratch and claw at our wet bodies as we pick our way up the back of the outcropping. My feet are filthy by the time I reach the edge. Here, the rock is rugged and angry, scraping at our bare soles.

It's higher than it looks from the canoe.

"You're not scared, are you?" Viv teases as I hesitate.

I shoot her a look, then jump—out, into the air.

As I fall, time seems to pause. The sun beats down on my shoulders. The water winks and sparkles below. I'm suddenly ten again, a camper at Durant, unaware of my parents' relationship problems or the scandal that will one day engulf my family. My entire world is nothing but ignorance and joy. I don't have a single responsibility other than to enjoy the summer, to breathe in campfire smoke, to inhale the scent of pine needles, to swim until my fingers are waterlogged and pruned.

It was so fleeting, childhood. It was over before I realized it had even begun.

I hit the water and spread my limbs wide, not wanting to go too deep. I shoot to the surface just in time for Arlo and Viv to crash through beside me, showering me in water. Arlo dunks me when he resurfaces.

"You ass!" I shove water at him, but it's an empty threat.

He grabs my wrist, pulls me nearer. Beneath the water, his other hand grazes my stomach, a soft warmth in the cold lake. We're made slick by the water, impossibly smooth. I twist out of his grasp and get the up on him. Both hands on his shoulders, push him under. Then I flee, swimming for the shore before he can dunk me again.

I laugh all the way back up the rocks, ignoring the pain in the soles of my feet, because I can hear him chasing me now. I'm not sure if I want to be caught or not, but I can tell he's gaining.

He overtakes me at the summit, grabbing my hand like he did in the water. I don't fight him this time. A gentle tug, and we're chest to chest, lake water pooling at our feet. Droplets cling to his nose and lashes. I shiver despite the warmth in my stomach, the nearness of him.

His hands are in my hair, turning my face up toward his.

From far below us, still circling in the water, Viv shouts, "God, just kiss already!"

I could clobber her.

"Limited time offer," Arlo whispers with a smirk. "Going in three, two—"

I pull his face down to mine. His lips are impossibly soft and warm. He tastes like the lake and summer and a hint of spearmint gum. I'm somehow even closer to him now, crushed against his torso, my hands in his hair.

He pulls back first, rests his forehead against mine. A tiny bubble of a laugh escapes me.

"I've wanted to do that for a while," he admits.

The words make a heat curl up in my belly. I can't manage to say anything; I just smile. From below, Viv starts clapping. "Excellent performance. Bravo! Is it safe to come up now? I want to jump again." And Arlo shouts something in response—perhaps that yes, it's okay to come up—but I'm no longer listening. My eyes have latched onto something beyond his shoulder, down in the water. The buoy. White with a red stripe around the center, bobbing up and down. I can't look away. The lake is dark from this height, almost murky. Still, I can make out the shape of the rock that lurks just below the surface.

Pain drills through my temples. I cry out. Dropping to my knees.

"Nell, you okay?" Arlo is there suddenly, trying to help me up, but my skull is on fire. The space between my eyes thrums with pain.

I clamp them shut and see the bloody girl in the mirror.

The wheelbarrow crusted with blood.

The canoe along the shore.

Look.

I pull away from Arlo, stagger down the outcropping. Not the way I'd ascended earlier, but down the opposite side. Toward the wheelbarrow path and Windsor property.

"Nell?" he calls from behind me.

But all I can see is the buoy—a beacon, a flag, a marker for something hidden beneath the surface.

Heat blooms on my heel as I descend the rock, and I know I've cut it, but I don't pause. Branches smack and claw at my face. I lose my footing, sliding down the last bit of the steep terrain on my rump, until I come to an abrupt stop just paces away from the wheelbarrow track. It's a dark line marking the way.

I scramble to my feet, wade into the water. My feet sink into the mucky bottom. It's colder on this side, like ice. Rotten branches and driftwood snap beneath my feet. Decaying leaves squish between my toes.

I shudder and dive forward. Swim out to the buoy.

My pulse is like a fire in my veins. Everything hurts. I

know what I'm going to find. I want to see it and yet I don't. I'm terrified. And yet I have to look.

The darkness of the water below me.

The light here on the surface.

I know where Father Williams would tell me to stay, but I'm not scared, and I have to face it.

I'm not scared.

I repeat it to myself, as I take a deep breath, as I dive.

I use the chain of the buoy as my guide, following it down to the rock, just a few feet below the surface. The chain is anchored into the stone, but a second chain branches off from it, leading over the back edge of the rock, which drops off steeply. I follow it, down, down, into the murky depths.

As the water grows colder, my headache gets sharper.

Until suddenly, just below me: a foreign shape. Entangled in chains. A cinderblock holding it to the bottom of Corwin Lake.

My lungs are burning. My head is about to split from the pressure of my headache.

Look.

I know who it is even before I reach what remains of the body, before I grab the chain and yank, twisting my bloated corpse around to confirm it.

And there she is. Me.

The girl from the grave, the reflection in the mirror, only worse. Decayed beyond recognition. So much skin gone; what remains, now black and green. Clothes rippling like seaweed around her. She shimmers like a mirage, appearing alive and healthy to my eyes—as though I'm merely glancing in a mirror—before flashing back to this ungodly state.

A scream erupts from my mouth. Bubbles fill the space surrounding me.

When I break the surface of the lake, I'm still screaming.

CHAPTER
THIRTY-ONE

"Jesus Christ, just calm down," Arlo says.

I'm sitting on the shore, my knees pulled into my chest, shaking. I can't unsee it. Myself. In that state. I barely looked human.

"It's the body from the grave," I say, rocking back and forth. "The body we found." I look to Viv. Her mouth is frozen in a tiny O of shock, her face pale. She'd joined Arlo on this side of the outcropping when I broke the surface, helped him pull me, thrashing, from the lake.

"The same body?" she asks now, very slowly, the fear and disbelief creeping into her eyes.

I nod. "Yeah. It was real. We didn't imagine anything. It was real, and the body was moved, and it's a million times worse now."

"Oh, God," she murmurs. "Oh God."

"You guys can go talk to Goodwin again," Arlo says calmly. "It will be okay. I'll come with you."

"We can't fucking do that!" I erupt. "No one is going to believe us."

"You sure there's an actual body?" Viv glances at the buoy shuddering. "Should I check?"

"No. It's horrible, Viv. It's the worst thing I've ever seen."

She gapes at me.

"If it was so decayed, how can you even know it was you?" Alro asks.

"I just do. And there's no point saying anything because he covered it up," I go on. It's suddenly so clear. The way he came to the interrogation in Goodwin's office later than the cops. How his boots were muddy, his hair shockingly wet for a night of only spitting rain, the way his eyes went wide for just a split second when he saw me there—shocked, confused. How he sometimes seemed uncomfortable around me during our interactions— afraid, disgusted, confused—but played it off as best he could.

"Who covered it up?" Arlo asks, frowning.

"Donovan."

They both look at me in horror.

"Ashmore didn't even come to the cemetery. She called Donovan to tell him what Viv and I found, and *he* came. He said there was DNA evidence of my hair, of Viv's and my footprints, but no body. Because he lied, just like he did the other day when I ran into him at Bradley House. He's been lying all along. Covering his tracks." I glance at the buoy. "He moved the corpse. He sent it to the bottom of the lake and anchored it the buoy's cinderblock so that it can't resurface. And then he bought Windsor Camp so he could cover it all up, keep the truth hidden."

"But *why*?" Viv presses.

I have an idea, but it terrifies me, rips my heart in two. Which doesn't make sense, because how can you hate someone and still want them back at the same time?

"Dad's dead also. He's probably buried in the family plot." My gaze drifts up the hillside, toward Windsor. "If we dig again where we found me, we'll find him too. I don't know how it connects—how Donovan knows Dad —but he killed him, and I must have been with him when it happened. I got in the way. He killed us both."

"What the fuck are you talking about?" Arlo looks thoroughly bewildered.

"He's dead," I mutter. "They all think he's still missing, but he's dead. We both are."

"I thought he was just spotted down south?" Viv points out.

"Supposedly. But they still haven't found him. Donovan told me they recovered his duffel bag, but I bet he was lying."

"Slow down. Let's just take this one thing at a time," Arlo says, his hand falling on my shoulder. "You're right here, Nell. On the shore. With us. Just take a deep breath and try to calm—"

"Arlo," I say sharply.

"Nell, we're just trying to look at this rationally," Viv jumps in.

I glare at them. "I know it sounds impossible, but if you guys are my friends, you have to trust me on this." I turn to Viv. "You know what you saw that first night, in the family graveyard. We didn't imagine anything. He just made us think we did."

They're both slow to say anything. I can see the confliction on their features. What I'm proposing is impossible.

"Maybe someone *should* swim out there and look at the corpse."

"What? Fuck no," Arlo says. "I'm not getting in there with a dead body."

I grab my foot and turn it up to my face so I can inspect my heel. I cut it earlier, on the rock, but of course there's no blood now, no sign of injury. Just like with the pocketknife and my thigh. It most likely hurt because of traces of iron in the blade. Because I'm a ghost and ghosts don't like iron or salt, at last according to the forum discussions on *The Ghost Hunter's Haven.*

"Not just any dead body," I say. "Mine."

They exchange glances, incredulous.

"Please look. Please look so you can tell me I haven't lost my mind, that I'm not seeing things again."

This is the request that finally wins them over, because maybe it's all in my head. Maybe I've well and truly gone crazy.

"Can you go?" Viv asks Arlo quietly. "If it's really there—if it's what I saw in the grave—I don't want to see it again. Your word will be enough for me."

He sighs, shoulders sagging. Then, somewhat resigned, or perhaps even hoping to prove me wrong, he nods at Viv and wades into the water. When he reaches the buoy, he looks back at me sadly. He doesn't believe me, and that's broken something between us, but it doesn't matter. It was going to break anyway, because I'm not really here.

Arlo dips below the surface.

He's gone for five seconds, ten, twenty.

Then he shoots to the surface, swears tumbling from his lips, paddling frantically for the shore. He stumble-crawls out, bracing his hands against his thighs. Still hunched over, trying to catch his breath, he finally peers up at me. As lake water drips from his lashes he simply asks, "What *are* you?"

I'm dead. A ghost. Nothing but smoke and mirrors.

"It was her?" Viv says through her fingers.

Arlo nods. "It's her clothes. On the corpse. It's—"

He turns away and vomits. Viv begins pacing, looking like she also might be sick.

Arlo wipes at his mouth, lifts his gaze to mine. "Nell," he says softly. "What happened to you?"

I shake my head, willing the answer to come, but there's nothing. "I don't know. I was in New York. I left because the media frenzy was too much. Then I came here. I don't even have a blank period where things are fuzzy. There's a timeline with me leaving, traveling, and arriving here, and none of it accounts for a murder."

I recall how Donovan mentioned that he didn't see me on any public transit on the day I claimed to leave the city. Because maybe he'd already killed me by then. He was fishing for info, trying to see if I remembered what had happened. But I didn't—I couldn't—and I still can't.

She doesn't know anything, he'd said into his phone, that day at the Performing Arts Building. Is someone working with him? His wife, the lady behind NexusCapital? Maybe they lost all their money because of Dad and things got ugly when Donovan confronted him.

"Why can we see you?" Arlo asks. "Ghosts are supposed to be invisible, aren't they? Incorporeal?"

He's taking this exceptionally well. It *is* hard to believe.

"Maybe I'm only visible here, near the lake, because it's so close to where I was buried?" I offer.

"But you can even pick stuff up. Touch things. Can you walk through walls, too?"

"I don't know. I haven't tried." I try to make a joke of it, say it with a smile to lighten the mood. It doesn't help.

"I can't believe this. This isn't possible." Now Arlo's the one pacing up and down the shore, water droplets flying off him each time he turns.

"I'm sorry," Viv says, sitting beside me. "That I flipped on you. Said we imagined it." Her eyes flick momentarily up the hill, toward the cemetery. "I really did think we found a body—*your* body—at first. But then Donovan said there was nothing there and I started to think we both got confused, that the house was doing something to us."

"It was," I admit. "Or rather, *I* was. Everything I've been seeing and hearing? The light in the window, the voice calling my name, the reflections in the mirror. I think it was just me, reaching out to myself. Trying to show me the truth."

Never hungry.

Food that tastes like ash.

A chill I can't shake.

And all the strange visions and voices.

The signs have been there. They've been there all along. I've never been possessed; I've only been dead. All this time. Dead. The girl in the mirror is me, hair hanging before my eyes and obscuring my face so that I was unrecognizable. There's no Avery Jane. She's just a legend, a story, a rumor that has quieted over the years, even on the message boards I thought held answers. The only ghost is me.

I'm numb with the realization. I'll feel something eventually, I'm sure, but right now there's nothing.

"That night in Goodwin's office," I say, turning to Viv. "I cut my arm and it bled. That's the only thing that doesn't make sense."

"I don't remember blood. I thought Donovan got the blade away from you in time."

He'd bandaged my arm instantly, I realize, perhaps knowing I wouldn't bleed. He was a step ahead of me back then, already knowing what I was. What I am.

I look at my skin now. There is no scab, no new pink flesh. Almost as if the cut never happened. And even if it did . . . Did I see blood because Donovan was seeding doubts in my mind, causing me to question the truth? It's not hard to imagine. After all, I'd been seeing all sorts of things lately. I've seen blood that wasn't truly there.

"We're going to talk to Goodwin, right?" Arlo asks. He's finally stopped pacing but he looks no less flustered.

"No," I say quickly. "I need to talk to Ashmore directly, ensure that she doesn't involve Donovan. She can search the cemetery without him. When she finds my dad's body, everything will come to light."

"So we just . . . don't mention that your body is anchored in the lake?" Viv rubs her arms.

"Not yet. If I tell her I'm a ghost and I've found my own corpse, she's not going to believe me. We tried that once already, and I need her to trust me."

"So what *will* you tell her?" Arlo asks.

"I don't know. I'll figure something out. Let's go back. Unless you want to swim a bit more first." I look up at the rocky outcropping. How is possible that just moments earlier we were jumping into the water, oblivious and carefree?

"No," Arlo says at the same time Viv mutters, "I'm good."

The magic of the summer afternoon has shattered.

There may be no recovering it. Not today, or tomorrow, or any day that follows.

We retreat to the canoe and paddle back to camp in silence. Viv shoots me awkward grimaces. Arlo refuses to make eye contact.

Finally back on the shore, when the canoe is stored on the rack, I grab his hand. He doesn't flinch away, but he stares at my fingers a beat too long, as though he's picturing the bloated, decaying ones from the lake.

"I'm sorry," I say quietly, looking between Arlo and Viv, these two friends that I didn't expect to find to find this summer, the only two friends I seem to have in the world these days. "I didn't know. I'd have told you guys I knew, I swear it."

"Of course you would have," Viv says.

"Don't you dare apologize, Nell," Arlo adds firmly, giving my hand a squeeze. "You didn't do anything. Someone did the unspeakable to you. Someone . . ." He swallows hard, looks away. "You better hope Ashmore gets to the bottom of this, or I might murder Donovan myself."

"Don't get involved, Arlo, please. He's clearly dangerous."

Viv nods in agreement.

Arlo regards me for a moment, his eyes lingering along my hairline, where my skull should be cracked. His expression is so incredibly heavy; it makes something in my chest seize.

"I mean it, Arlo. Something bad could happen to you. But me? I've got nothing to lose."

"And I hate that for you," he says softly. "You deserved so much more."

It's only when I'm walking back to the cabin with Viv that I realize he's spoken about me in the past tense. Like I'm already gone.

CHAPTER
THIRTY-TWO

I call the sheriff's office that afternoon, from Goodwin's place. I ask her for privacy while I'm on the phone. She humors me, heading upstairs, but it's so silent in the cabin, I'm certain she's listening in as best she can. Maybe even with an ear to the floor.

I'm put on hold, and by the time Ashmore picks up, I've been waiting for almost ten minutes. I get straight to the point. "You have to search the cemetery at Windsor."

"We did that already," she responds with a sigh.

"I think we both know that's not true. Donovan searched the cemetery. You and Murkowski came to the camp and interrogated two teenagers as though they were wasting your time by reporting that they'd found a dead body."

She clears her throat. "Agent Donovan found nothing but your footprints and some hair at the site, Eleanor. You know this. We already went through it all the other week."

"Then where's the harm in checking again? You'll prove me wrong immediately."

"It's not that easy. The place is in the process of being purchased. I won't be able to do much without a search warrant."

"Then get one."

"I need good cause to file for one, and a seventeen-year-old camp counselor's request is not going to cut it."

Not a counselor, I think. *Just a dishwasher.*

"I was there the other day," I say instead. "There was a wheelbarrow by the cemetery. It had dried blood on it."

There's a lengthy pause. Muted chatter fills the background on her end.

"I think he moved the body, Sheriff. Not far. Just somewhere else in the plot."

"The body that looks like you?" she says doubtfully.

"My father's body. I think he's buried over there. I think that's why no one has found him."

"You claimed the body looked like you. And your father was just spotted in South Carolina."

"And has he been found yet?" I ask, ignoring the first part of her statement.

Silence.

"Right. So as long as he's still missing, it's just as possible he's already dead, buried in that plot. I think that's why Donovan purchased the place."

"He's the one buying it?"

"Sort of. It's happening through an LLC owned by his wife."

"And you know this . . . how?"

"Does it really matter how I'm managing to handle this better than actual law enforcement? Will you please just go look, Sheriff? I'm begging you."

It's quiet for a moment. I'm not sure she fully believes me, but I've piqued her interest. She's at least curious now, and perhaps a bit suspicious.

"I suppose it won't hurt to confirm that Donovan's initial assessment of the cemetery remains accurate," she says finally.

"Thank you. And please don't tell him you're looking into it."

"Of course not. We wouldn't want him to have a heads up and move bodies around *again*, would we?" I can hear the smile in her tone, practically see the patronizing expression on her face.

"No. We wouldn't," I respond evenly.

"Have a good afternoon, Ms. Bradley."

I hang up, uncertain if she has any real intention of checking the plot but praying she does just the same. It was one thing discovering my own body. Digging up my father's is something I don't think I can physically handle, not even in my current state.

I want—need—someone else to confirm it.

Even in death, I'm not strong enough to face him.

———

Sunday evening passes with an odd tension hanging over it.

Arlo doesn't necessarily treat me differently during the dinner rush, but he *looks* at me differently. Every time I catch his gaze, there's something foreign in his eyes, an expression I can't quite place. At times it borders on pity, but it's more complicated than that. There's sadness in his features, anger and confusion too.

At the evening bonfire, everyone is blissfully ignorant of my predicament. I wish I could muster their indifference. Instead, I feel undone. Like a spool of thread, unraveling. What is even tethering me to this place anymore? We're supposed to move on when we die, aren't we? At least that's what people say. Now, I don't know what to think.

I'm reminded of a sleepover party in middle school: me and Kylie and the Sorsare twins, who Kylie had recently decided we should add to our circle. We'd somehow ended up on the plush carpet of Kylie's bedroom floor, candles lit around us, hands held, her whispering to dead spirits to make contact with us. A seance. I can't remember if we were serious about the endeavor, or if it had started as a joke or a dare. I only know that I didn't buy into it then.

When you're dead, you're dead. You cease to exist. There's nothing more. I believed this my whole life, right up until this summer's strange turn of events.

A group of campers dissolves into laughter beside me. On the other side of the fire, Viv is smiling at something one of her girls is telling her. Jocelyn tosses her shiny dark hair over her shoulder. Gretta preens her nails.

It's all too much. The way their lives just carry on.

I stalk off, walking down to the beach where the smell of smoke can no longer reach me, and the coolness of the night tickles the back of my neck. I slip off my shoes and wade into the shallows, letting the water wash over my toes. I picture my actual body across the lake, the ungodly state of it. We're touching the same water, but we don't feel like the same entity. I am so separate from that version of myself that she seems like a stranger.

How can I be dead and not know how it happened? How can I remember my past but not the most traumatic, life-altering event that happened to me?

I watch Windsor for a while, waiting for it to whisper to me, or for the light to click on in the second-story window. It doesn't, and I doubt it will again. It told me what it needed to. All this time, I've only been trying to reach out to myself; those efforts became more violent, more visceral, more frightening after Viv and I first dug up the grave and came so very close to the truth. And now I have it.

It was never Avery Jane or the house itself or even a vengeful spirit. It was only me.

I wonder if Father Williams knew all long. If he told me to ignore the darkness—to walk *toward* the light— because he sensed I was a lost spirit in need of crossing over.

By the time I retire to the cabin, it's late.

"Sorry I couldn't get away," Viv whispers to me from the top bunk. "Two of my campers are fighting over the stupidest stuff. I mean, I know it feels big to them. Everything feels big in middle school."

Everything still feels big at seventeen. But doesn't it always? It's your life. Once you know how to deal with smaller problems, new and bigger ones always emerge.

"Don't worry about it," I assure her.

She rolls over onto her side, the mattress creaking above me. "What's going to happen now?"

"We wait, I guess. To hear from Ashmore." I tell her about my brief phone call, how I hope the sheriff will search the plot.

It's quiet for a long moment before Viv speaks again. "Do you think that's why you're here? To get justice for yourself and your father? Is that the closure you need?"

"I think so," I say. "Why else would I be hanging around?"

A shiver passes through me as I say the words. I'm hot and cold at once. Flighty. Clammy. My fingers shake. The room is too small. The air too thin. I take a deep breath and press a fist to my lips to keep them from trembling.

Do ghosts disappear once they learn what happened to them? Am I coming undone right now? What will it feel like to cease to exist? Will I even know it's happening? After all, I hadn't realized I'd died. What if I don't realize when this—whatever existence I'm currently experiencing—is also over? What if it all just . . . stops?

Without warning. Without a chance to make peace with anything.

I exhale slowly, attempt to calm my heartbeat.

Do I even have a heartbeat anymore? There's something inside me, still thumping, drumming, but it suddenly feels more like a countdown than a pulse. Like a clock about to cease ticking.

I'm a girl running on borrowed time.

"Viv?"

The only response is the shallow rhythm of her exhales. She's fallen asleep.

I lay there, restless, staring at the upper bunk.

The night encircles me like a blanket. Or perhaps I encircle the night.

I am the thing people fear, I realize. An impossibility. A horror. A feeling of dread on the back of one's neck.

I am the ghost in the dark, and I have nothing—and everything—to lose.

CHAPTER
THIRTY-THREE

"I feel like you're handling this really well," Viv says the next morning.

"How am I supposed to be handling it?"

"I don't know. You could be terrified, or in denial, or pitching a fit."

"I did kinda freak out yesterday. You guys had to drag me out of the water."

"Sure," she says. "But still. I feel like you've just kind of . . . accepted it."

I pull on a flannel. The morning air is cool and damp, sneaking into the cabin through the drafty wood. "I think I'm just glad to finally have an answer, an explanation for why I was seeing and hearing things."

She nods. "But you're not, like, scared?"

"Oh, I'm terrified. I have no clue how much time I have left. I want answers from Ashmore and to see Donovan in cuffs, but I'm also pretty certain that once those things happen, it will be the end of me, so it's hard to want to rush them." Jocelyn and Gretta begin stirring on the other side of the bunk and I drop my voice to a whisper. "Not much I can do about the timeline, though."

"When do you think you'll hear?"

"From Ashmore? This week probably." I pull on my sneakers and push open the screen door. "Gotta get to the kitchen. I'll catch you later, okay?"

"You know you could just . . . stop going, don't you?" Viv offers. "What can Goodwin do, fire you?"

"Yeah. But then I'll have to head home, and I'm worried I might not be visible anymore if I get too far from . . ." I think back to the buoy. "You know."

"You could stay at the lake house."

"Forever?"

She shrugs. "I guess."

It's a possibility. But as much as I'm terrified of my existence ending, staying at Corwin Lake for eternity doesn't sound very tempting either. What she's proposing . . . it's a haunting. She's suggesting that I haunt my childhood summer home.

"Aren't you going to be a senior this fall?" Jocelyn interjects. She's caught the tail end of our conversation upon exiting the bathroom.

"Yeah." I think of Mom, still back in the city, blissfully unaware that her only child is dead. I'm here at camp. Everyone thinks I'm alive and well, so I was never reported missing. It's only Dad who they can't find.

Dread swirls in my stomach. How am I supposed to

tell her? When Ashmore finds Dad's body and arrests Donovan and he confesses about mine too, is Mom going to learn about another tragedy from a stranger? Or on the news? Maybe I should call her and give her a heads up.

What would that conversation even sound like? *Hi, Mom. It's me. Your dead daughter. Yeah, you're speaking with a ghost. How are you?*

"So why would you stay at the lake after the summer?" Jocelyn presses. "That makes absolutely zero sense."

"Precisely." I duck out of the cabin before she can interrogate me any further.

———

I am a shell of myself, going through the motions. Drifting between the tree trunks. Wallowing around the camp.

I am, in the fullest extent of the word, a ghost.

No matter where I walk, I find myself turning toward Windsor Camp. Even if it's beyond the walls of the mess hall or hidden by a thick swath of pines, my body is angled toward it. Like a compass needle finding north.

As I await word from Ashmore, I carry out my duties, moving through each day in a trance, until I'm finally summoned to Goodwin's office on Thursday afternoon. The lunch rush is over, and Arlo and I have finally finished with the worst of the dishes. He grabs my elbow as I attempt to slip out.

"What's going on with you?"

I've been distant all week, answering his questions with short, clipped answers. Avoiding eye contact. It's hard enough with Viv, maintaining a friendship that I know is about to end, caring about someone—and letting them care about me in return—when I know I will disappear.

"Nothing."

"That's a blatant lie, Manhattan."

Against my better judgement, I look at him. His eyes are like anchors, pulling me deep into an ocean. "Please just tell me. Maybe I can help."

"How can you help, Arlo? I'm dead." I say this last bit softly, so no one else can hear.

His fingers trail down my arm, featherlight, settling on my wrist. He squeezes lightly, a reassuring pressure. "You know, I keep fearing that one of these times, you'll pass right through me. That I won't be able to touch you."

I shake my head. Look away. "Arlo, this isn't healthy. I'm not going to last. You know that right? Eventually, this will be over. I'm just not sure when."

"Is that why you've been like this? Holding me at a distance?"

Yes. But that seems cruel. So I simply say, "I'm not real, Arlo."

"Yes you are. You're real to me. You're real to everyone here at camp."

"But I won't last."

He shrugs. "Nothing does. Not people or places or

251

even stars. This whole planet will be gone someday. We're all just working with the time we have. Yours was incredible short, and that's completely unfair, but I don't think you should deny yourself friends in the final days because of it." His brown eyes gleam. His throat bobs. If he blinks, I worry I might have to watch a tear trail down his cheek, which is exactly why this entire thing is wrong. If he's sad about the mere possibility of this ending, why drag it out longer? Why fall any deeper into whatever this is? It will only make it that much more painful when it ends.

And it will.

It has to.

Unless you stay, a voice says in the back of my head. At the lake house, like Viv proposed. But what sort of life would that be? The camp is only bustling in the summer. It would be a lonely existence, and everyone I know will go on to do things. To college, to jobs. They'll live their lives. They'll age.

And I'll just be here. Ever the same. The ghost who haunts Corwin Lake.

I force a smile. "That's incredibly poetic."

"And I'm not even high," he says, laughing.

"Look, I have to go to Goodwin's office. Ashmore wants to talk to me."

"Will you tell her?" he asks. "About . . ." His eyes flick up and down my frame.

"If she says that she found Dad buried in the plot, yeah."

Only then will I tell her about the other body attached to the buoy, because only then do I stand a chance of her believing me.

He nods slowly. "Promise me you'll stop this though—the pushing me away. Unless you hate me or something."

"I don't hate you. Not at all."

"Then don't worry about me. I can handle it. This. Us."

"You're falling for a ghost, Arlo."

"I'm falling for Eleanor Bradley. This isn't that complicated."

But it is. It's perhaps the most complicated situation that could possibly exist. But I'm tired of arguing and Ashmore is waiting. I rest my cheek against his chest momentarily. His heartbeat thumps beneath my skin. I picture it there, between his ribs, pulsing with life, his blood warm, everything working as intended—the miraculous human machine.

"You're cold," he says.

But I don't feel cold, not in his arms at least. Not at this moment. "I'm sorry I've been weird. In my defense, I really have no experience being a ghost. I'm learning as I go."

"Just another reason to lean on others."

He touches my chin. I smile. Then I walk away, into the afternoon sun, toward Goodwin's office and whatever news awaits me there, uncertain if I want it to be the closure I need.

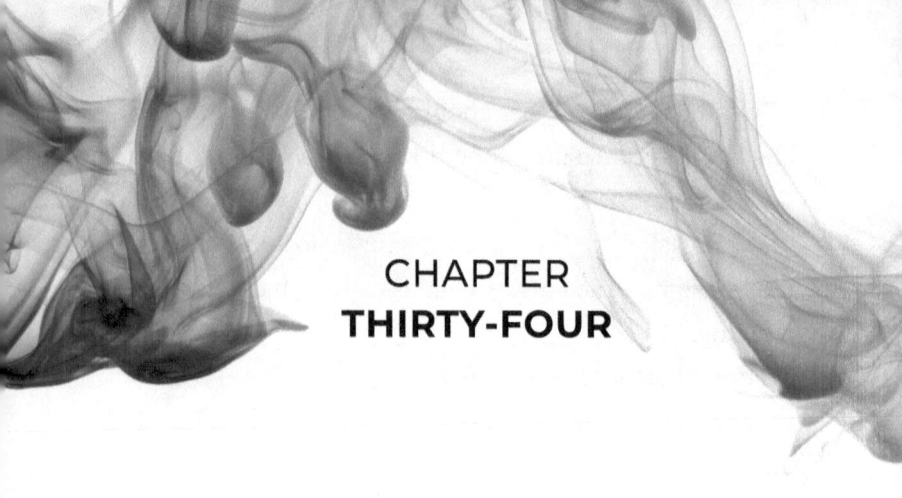

CHAPTER
THIRTY-FOUR

"An additional search of the Windsor property found nothing," Ashmore tells me.

"Nothing?" I echo, slack-jawed.

We're sitting in Goodwin's office. Well, Ashmore is sitting. I'm pacing in front of the fireplace while she watches me from the other side of Goodwin's desk, her fingers interlaced and resting atop an open-face planner. Goodwin is nowhere to be found—probably seeing to responsibilities somewhere else on the campus.

"We dug up the entire cemetery. There is nothing there except for the coffins of some very old Windsor relatives."

"You checked inside those coffins?"

"The coffins had not been tampered with." She leans back in Goodwin's chair and it creaks like a weathered dock. "Now would you like to tell me *why* you pushed me into digging up the cemetery?"

"I found something."

"Where?"

She won't believe me. Not when I'm standing right here.

I clamp my eyes shut. In the darkness behind my lids, I see lapping water. A bobbing buoy. A corpse tethered and decaying.

"In the lake," I say finally. "Along the edge of the property."

Ashmore's eyes narrow. "The now *private* property?"

"I . . . I didn't know it was private at the time."

"What did you find in the water, Eleanor?" She clicks her tongue against her teeth, exhales sharply. She's tired of me. Annoyed.

I open my mouth. Close it.

I don't know what card to play. If I tell her the truth, she will never believe me. I suppose I could lie. Just say I found a body in general. But the last time I reported a body things didn't go smoothly.

"Are you sure you searched the whole cemetery plot? My dad's buried there. He has to be!"

"If you're still protecting him . . ."

"Protecting him?" I erupt. "He's dead! How could I be protecting him?"

"Donovan said—"

"Donovan? You told me you wouldn't speak to him."

"Believe it or not, I do what I believe is best for my investigations, even if that means not following the advice of hysterical seventeen-year-olds."

"I am *not* hysterical," I screech, realizing far too late

that this is exactly how I sound. I stop pacing, put a hand on the mantel, count to three. "So what did you and Donovan discuss?" I ask as evenly as I can manage.

"That's a private manner."

I want to scream. Throw something. Start pacing again. It takes all my composure to simply smile and grit out, "So that's it?"

"Unless there's something else you want to tell us?"

Us. She means more than her department. She's working with Donovan now. I don't think she knows what he's actually done, what he's guilty of, but I can no longer trust her.

"No. I don't think so."

It's quiet for a moment while Ashmore regards me. Then she asks, eyes narrowed, "Why are you so convinced that your father is dead?"

"Because he would have shown up by now. The feds would have found him."

"They're working on it. Someone spotted him in South Carolina recently. Any day now, I bet they catch him."

"People don't just . . . disappear," I argue.

"Sure they do. It happens all the time. You should see the number of missing persons reports that cross my desk."

"And how many of those cases end with finding that person alive versus discovering a dead body?"

She blinks at me, then stands. The chair legs screech against the wood floor. "I'm done being lectured. Have a good afternoon, Miss Bradley."

I stare into the empty hearth as she leaves. I keep staring long after the door has clicked shut behind her.

I'll need to bring my body back on my own. I should have done this from the beginning. It was a mistake to involve Ashmore, to think she could solve things for me. But I was so convinced Dad's body was in that plot.

Now I see a more likely truth: When Donovan moved my body into the lake, he probably moved Dad's also. Maybe into the water, maybe somewhere else entirely. He'd almost been exposed, and he was quick to bury the evidence deeper.

I need to go back to the buoy and haul my own corpse into the sunlight. Right now. Ashmore won't be able to ignore me once she has proof.

I burst from Goodwin's office and freeze on the front stoop.

Donovan's car is parked beside Ashmore's cruiser. She's in her driver's seat and he's bent over, and arm resting on the edge of her open window, saying something I can't make out. She nods, then drives off.

"Eleanor." Donovan nods to me in greeting, a smile plastered across his face as he walks closer. "Ashmore was just telling me about a little digging expedition over at Windsor Camp. Apparently, she didn't even need a search warrant. She spoke with the new owner first and they graciously let her look around without protest."

He let her search the property?

"Oh," I say, feigning interest. "Who's the new owner?"

His smiles vanishes. "Eleanor, let's cut the bullshit.

Quit sticking your nose in places it doesn't belong. Let the grown-ups handle the investigation. Unless of course you know the whereabouts of your father and would like to come clean?"

He's much larger than me, and despite the fact that camp is filled with people, we are very much alone here by Goodwin's office. Then I remember that I'm dead. That he's already killed me once and there's nothing he can do to me now. *He* should be afraid of *me*.

"You killed my father," I snarl.

"What an accusation! You better have evidence to back up a claim like that."

"You killed him and that's why no one's found him."

"I did no such thing, Eleanor."

"You did, and that's why you're just sitting around in your car at Bradley House, twiddling your fingers until this all blows over and you can go back to your life. To the city and whatever you do at NexusCapital."

His eyes widen just slightly. Shocked, perhaps, to hear that I know about his connection to Windsor. He stifles the expression quickly. "I could make your life a living hell. You're no one. A kid, playing at detective. I'm a federal agent, for Christ's sake."

"How can you make my life hell when I'm already dead?"

"Dead?" He laughs. "Not this again. What are you going to do? Tell Ashmore you're a ghost? Get the media to report that I killed you when you're standing right here? You're delusional. You have absolutely no power. None! And if you stick with that story, you'll end up in a psych ward."

A few days ago, this line of reasoning may have worked on me. Heck, it worked the very first time he tried it, the night Viv and I first dug up my corpse. But I've seen the truth at the bottom of the lake now. I'm tempted to tell him I have proof, that I can drag it to the surface, but I know that if I bring this up, he'll only beat me to hiding the evidence again.

"Why?" I say instead. I sound meek and scared. "Why'd you do it?"

"I don't know what you're talking about. Go back to your cabin and stay out of things that don't concern you."

"Or what?"

"Or I'll find some reason to detain you, and if all these wild ghost theories happen to be true, I think I'll be able to detain you for quite a while." He flicks his jacket open like a cowboy sharpshooter, only it's not his gun he's trying to show me, but the cuffs that dangle from his belt.

I'm reminded of what I've read in the online forums, about ghosts and iron, and how the knife blade hurt me last week even when it did no real damage. Could metal cuffs on my wrists restrain me? What about the bars of a jail cell? Maybe I'm not as invincible as I thought. And maybe Donovan knows this.

"So what are you gonna do? Patrol Corwin Lake forever?" I ask.

"You either stay here, where everyone sees you're alive and well. Or you leave and you disappear." He scoffs. "Powerless, like I said."

I think back to our conversation in the Performing Arts Building, when he mentioned that none of the city cams caught me leaving New York. The tiny look of shock on his face when he stepped into Goodwin's office the night he first saw me.

I must only be visible when I'm here, near my burial place. Visible and so very cold. That chill not dissipating unless I put distance between myself and Windsor, as I did that day with Arlo, driving to see Father Williams. If I leave the lake, if I travel more than a few miles from the shoreline, I will become invisible to the human eye.

Donovan knows this, or at the very least suspects it. He put it together long before I me.

I still don't know how it connects. Did Dad steal all his money? Maybe Donovan confronted him after the story broke. Things could have gotten ugly—violent. Perhaps I was there too, in the way, a bit of collateral damage. It could have been over before Donovan even realized what he'd done, and now he's trying to save face. Burying the evidence before his life is as ruined as Dad's.

"Did you lose a lot?" I ask. "Because of my father?"

He's quiet a moment, eyes boring into me. Then, through gritted teeth, he utters, "Practically everything."

And there it is. The motive.

He hasn't stopped staring at me. He'd kill me again if he could. He just wants this to all go away.

I have friends who know the truth! I feel like shouting, but I worry admitting this puts them in danger. "My reflection changes in mirrors sometimes," I say instead. "Did you know that? Other people can see it. Maybe you *should* go ahead and arrest me. Maybe I need to sit in front of a two-way mirror with Ashmore."

He lunges forward and grabs my wrist so quickly I don't see it coming. It hurts, even though I know he can't truly harm me. At least not with his bare hands.

"You keep your mouth shut, Eleanor," he snarls, and I realize that while there may have been a time when my existence unsettled and disturbed him, he's not uncomfortable anymore. Now, he hates me. He wants me to know that I should fear him. "You keep your mouth shut, or your father will end up just like you."

I go bone still. The breath seems to leave my lungs. "Dad's alive?"

That sly smile spreads back across Donovan's face. "I have no clue where he is. I'm stationed here to watch his lake house, remember? Why, do *you* know where he might be? Can you help me find him?" He laughs and it sounds unhinged, like something from a movie. "Stop protecting him. He doesn't deserve it. And he sure didn't protect you." He shoves me, and I fall to the gravel path.

"Where is he?" I grit out, but he goes on laughing as he climbs into his car. "There's no way you'll get away with this!"

He rolls down the window. "Oh, honey," he says, the

condensation dripping from his lips as he starts the engine. "I already have."

Gravel flies as he peels out, hitting my skin like a thousand tiny razorblades.

CHAPTER
THIRTY-FIVE

am restless.

The irony is not lost on me. All ghosts are restless, are they not? Left to roam, wander, amble. Some purpose not yet complete.

And perhaps this is it. My anger with Dad has been misguided. He's done something horrible, yes, but he got away without having to pay for it. Justice could have been delivered during a trial. Maybe he'd have served time. Paid back damages. Made things right.

Instead he's vanished and that gets his victims nothing.

In fact, it's only made more victims.

Everyone who lost their money. Dad and me. Mom, who is alone in the truest sense of the word, not even aware she isn't mourning the right number of people.

If I didn't vanish when I discovered my body, this hasn't been about learning what happened to me. At least not exclusively. This is about something bigger. Revealing the truth. Seeing that Donovan gets his. Ashmore's been absolutely zero help; I'm going to have to clean this up myself.

On Friday night, while the girls are sleeping, I pace the paths outside the cabin. I'm barefoot, but the coolness of the pine needles beneath my feet barely registers. Eventually I slink down to the shore. I'm still connected to Windsor even if I no longer feel drawn there. I don't think that connection will truly fade, not until I cease to exist.

The sky is packed with dense clouds, and they flicker with lightning. Thunder rumbles in the distance.

Where is he—Dad? Is he actually alive, like Donovan implied, or did he only say that to distract and confuse me? It's just as likely Dad's dead like I feared. In the water near my corpse, tethered to another other rock. Or perhaps somewhere else on the Windsor's property, decaying in soil that Ashmore didn't unearth, or hidden in pieces beneath the house's floorboards. I think of Poe's "The Tell Tale Heart," which we read in English last year. The beating heart that the narrator heard even after the murder, slowly driving him insane.

A square of light suddenly illuminates—Windsor's window. It feels like ages since I've seen it, and I freeze. It doesn't make sense. The light was only ever me, calling to myself. Unless . . .

Something moves within the window frame. A figure, backlit by the light.

Donovan. It has to be.

I feel his eyes on me. Or near me, at least. I doubt I'm visible from his distance, not with such weak moonlight.

Then it dawns on me: he's looking toward the buoy. I can feel his eyes on *that* version of me. He's contemplating covering his tracks farther. If he moves me again, I'll lose the proof forever.

I need to retrieve my body before it's too late. Right now, maybe.

But the sky opens up, the rain coming down in sheets. Lightning cracks, brilliant fingers illuminating the dark. I'm soaked almost instantly.

The lake will be too rough. The visibility awful.

And being on the water during a storm is dangerous. Not for me, but for the living, which means Donovan won't try anything right now either. I have time.

Not much, but enough.

Tomorrow, then.

I walk back to the cabin, mud squishing between my toes.

––––––

"There is no way you'll be able to do it alone," Viv argues the next morning. "How are you going to lug it into a boat? Is it even . . . solid enough to *be* moved?" She shudders. "Besides, it's still storming."

Much to my disappointment, this is true. I woke to the sound of rain hammering on the cabin's roof. Outside, the tree limbs rock and sway, creaking in the wind.

"I can't waste any more time," I insist.

"This is supposed to transition to lighter rain by lunch and be over by midnight." She jerks her head toward the roof. "Come on the hike to Notch's Point with me, and I'll help you tomorrow."

"It's too rainy for the lake, but not too rainy to hike?"

She shrugs. "You know camp rules. A little rain doesn't stop much except water activities. Plus, I won't be able to get out of this. Pine Knot hasn't done Notch's Point yet and the girls are looking forward to it."

"Fine," I say. "*Fine.* But if it's still raining tomorrow, we go anyway. No backing out."

"Deal," she agrees.

I head to the mess, where I tell Arlo I'm ducking out for the afternoon to hike with Viv. He takes this exceedingly well. Mostly, I think he's just happy I have plans to go somewhere other than Windsor. I don't tell him those plans still exist, just for later in the day. The less he knows, the better. I already know how he'll feel about it, but nothing is going to change my mind.

———

The storm has dwindled to spitting rain by the time we reach the summit.

The Pine Knot girls are giddy and secretive, whispering in small huddles, their heads pressed together, arms slung over one another's shoulders. I remember the energy of this type of friendship. The girls' joy and innocence makes me melancholy.

I will never be that young again.

I will never be any older, either.

These girls will go on to do so many things. Maybe their friendships will hold through the years. It's just as likely that they will break and disband. Nothing lasts forever and middle school has a way of changing people.

As Viv herds them into position for a group photo, I move to the very edge of the outlook, where it's rumored that you can get a bar or two of service on a good day. The rocks drop off quickly, revealing an angry, steep incline of boulders and shrubs. Ahead, Corwin Lake stretches to the south, its shape an angry slash that carves through the jagged landscape like a very fat and crooked snake. The surface is rough beneath the rain, like pebbled asphalt.

I extend my phone and wait.

It takes a moment, but then a bar flickers into view.

I contemplate what to do with it. Do I text Mom? Tell her to get in touch with the family lawyer, or the press, or . . . someone? It all seems impossible to explain over text and I know the service isn't strong enough to hold a full phone call. I should wait until I've retrieved my body. I can take a photo, secure the proof on my phone. Then I could reach out to any number of individuals. Even Ashmore wouldn't be able to ignore that kind of photographic evidence.

My phone pings, and I frown. I have a text from Viv's phone.

I open it, noting that my text to her from several days ago—*The owner of this phone wants it back. Text me so we can meet up*—has been marked as delivered. I'd initially tried to send it from the Performing Arts Building, the night I went back for Donovan's Zippo lighter. It must have gone through after all. Maybe after I locked my phone.

Whatever the case, there's a response to it now, four earth-shattering sentences encased in a gray talk bubble.

> El, is this really you? I'm so sorry about everything. Come to Windsor Camp as soon as you're able. We need to talk.

I read the text again, certain I've hallucinated. But there it is.

My hand trembles. My mouth is dry.

I show the message to Viv while her girls eat a snack. "It's a trap," she says.

"What do you mean?"

"Donovan bought the place, right? He probably found my phone and is now trying to lure you there."

"I don't think so. No one calls me El except my dad. How could Donovan know about that nickname?"

Viv frowns, a crease appearing between her eyes. "I don't know. It just feels wrong."

"Donovan insisted Dad was still alive. I thought he was just messing with me, but . . . maybe my dad's at

Windsor. Maybe he found your phone after that night with Davie."

"And has been hiding there ever since?"

My eyes widen. "Donovan threatened to hurt Dad if I spoke up. Maybe my dad's not hiding. Maybe he's been held captive this whole time—by Donovan!"

"Then why wouldn't he have used my cell to call nine-one-one?"

"Because he's wanted for fraud and embezzling!"

"Sure, but wouldn't dealing with that be better than staying captive with the guy who killed his daughter and will likely kill him, too? Something doesn't add up."

"Viv, did you bring sunscreen?" one of the campers calls.

"What do you need sunscreen for? It's still misting," Viv responds.

"You can still burn when it's cloudy," the girl whines.

Viv tosses a tube of sunscreen to the girl and turns back to me. "Let's just get your body and go to the sheriff. Ignore that text. *Please.*"

I nod in agreement. But as she moves to help her campers gather their trash and ready for the descent, I shoot off a quick text.

Prove it's you. Sundays at . . .

The progress bar hangs for a moment, then the message goes through.

"Ready girls?" Viv calls.

269

A tiny chorus of *yeses* chimes back. I kneel and fiddle with my shoelace. Viv leads the way, the girls following her like a line of small ducklings. I stand, hold out the phone, wait.

The group disappears from view, swallowed up by the trees.

I count to ten.

Check again.

I've just stuffed the phone in my back pocket, resigned to run after them without an answer, when it chimes.

Bethesda Fountain.

It's him.

My father is most definitely alive.

CHAPTER
THIRTY-SIX

can't wait any longer.

As the evening activities wind down and the storm weakens to spitting rain, I slip away. The campers and staff drift toward their cabins and I drift toward the shore, a shadow that no one seems to notice, not even Viv.

I wonder if I'm fading, if I'm not quite as visible anymore.

The end feels very close, like a visceral presence hanging over me.

I take a kayak.

The lake is quiet. My cheeks are cold.

I shiver and suddenly the house looms before me. I can barely recall the paddle across the lake, the hike up the trail.

I stand before the partially boarded up slider door. Somewhere behind me, my body swims in its watery grave. I could retrieve it, do the smart thing as Viv suggested. But somewhere ahead of me, hiding in the shadows of Windsor Camp, are answers. Answers that I can get before she realizes I haven't returned to the cabin with the others.

Energy thrums in my core, fills my chest. It's now or never.

I take a step forward and gasp. Heat laces my leg, a pain so sharp and hot I stagger backward, grabbing at my shin.

A line of salt curves around the threshold of the door, like a circular welcome mat.

He asked me to come but put out salt to repel me.

Viv's warning that the text is a trap echoes in my mind, but I push it away. I'm close. So close. I can feel it.

And besides, what do I have to fear? I am the ghost in the dark, the thing of nightmares. I cannot be killed. The only thing to be feared here is *me*.

After all, that's why this salt was spread. He's scared. Even after everything—the texts, the request that I visit—he's scared. A daughter is a powerful thing.

I step aside, examine the worn, rotting siding of Windsor Camp. I touch it and feel the wood grain beneath my fingers. I press and it presses back, protesting me.

But I'm not here, not really. Some version of me is, but the one with mass waits below the surface of the lake. That body is real, but this one, that I inhabit . . . I need to let go of it. I should be incorporeal. I *am* incorporeal.

I nudge at the wall again. This time not as a girl but as a ghost, as an entity that challenges the very idea of reality.

My hand passes through the wood. Like water through a sieve, light through a window, it just happens. It feels like an exhale, like air meeting air.

I take a step forward and the rest of my body follows. Through the wall. I'm inside now.

The shadows seem to pull away from me, retreating into corners of the room. Something skitters to my right. A dried leaf or startled mouse, perhaps. I have no concern for it tonight.

I glance at the ceiling, toward the bedrooms overhead. I think I could rise straight through the floors now, if I wanted, close my eyes and will it to be. My confidence in this new skill is concerning. Why can I do this suddenly? And so easily?

I'm nearing the end. I'm coming undone.

Not much longer now.

I shove the thought aside and move to the stairs. If I do tasks literally, as though I'm still alive, maybe I can keep this corporeal form a bit longer.

I climb to the first floor. Drift down the hall, running my fingertips over the stained wallpaper.

Here are the next set of stairs, unfurling before me. I ascend again, silent. Soft light leaks from beneath Avery Jane's bedroom door. *His* door?

I step up to it, put a hand to the wood grain. Beyond, I hear the bedsprings groaning, the sound of metal on metal—a fork or spoon scraping the last bites of food from a tin can, perhaps.

I push the door open. It swings inward, squeaking on its hinges.

He leaps from the bed. My first impression is of a wild animal. His spooked eyes, the fight or flight instinct lurking there. A beard covers his usually clean-shaven jaw. His hair hangs into his eyes and curls behind his ears. He's wearing sweatpants and a plain white tee-shirt. He doesn't look particularly dirty—the lake would make a fine bathtub—but he's a far cry from the man I remember, who was always polished and preened and professional.

"Eleanor?" he whispers.

"Hi, Dad."

He blinks, at a loss for words. "I can't believe it," he said finally. "I thought it was a joke, a trick. This isn't possible. This is . . ." He looks at the can of beans he'd been eating, sets them aside. "Why are you here?"

"You told me to come." I take a step nearer and he cringes like I've burned him.

"Yes, but . . ." He puts a hand to his brow, shielding his eyes from me. "You're dead, you're not real—this isn't real. You're *dead*."

Did he watch it happen? Did Donovan take him here after—hold him for some reason? It dawns on me that he doesn't look like a prisoner. There are no cuffs or chains, no ropes or ties. Is *he* dead too—another ghost haunting Corwin Lake? But no, he's eating, something I haven't willingly done since I lost my life.

"Did you see it?" I tilt my head. "What happened to me?"

He twists, looking frantically about the room. At the bed, the sleeping bag on the floor—anything but me. He considers the window a moment, as though he might be able to escape through it. Then he runs.

I brace for contact, but it doesn't come. Instead, he passes straight through me and into the hallway.

It's like being sliced open with a knife.

Everything goes white, a cold so piercing it burns. I'm losing my physical presence in this world and that would terrify me if it wasn't for the colors exploding behind my eyes. Colors that merge into shapes.

I can see it, suddenly: his office building. I'm standing outside it.

I'm wearing the outfit from the grave, my hood pulled up to ward off a heavy rain. My cell is clenched in one hand, a text from Kylie still echoing in my mind. She said he was guilty of it all, that all the stories on TV are true. Her family has lost everything.

It's impossible to believe. But why would she lie to me?

Backpack straps digs at my shoulders, weighted with all my camp gear. My duffel feels like an anchor slowing me down. I'm getting out of the city, away from this scandal and its imploding mayhem as soon as possible, but I want to talk to him first. He won't be here, I know he won't, and yet I feel compelled to check.

I storm through the lobby, finding it odd that the security guard usually stationed there is missing. I hit the elevator's call button, ride it up, up, up, a sick sensation deepening in my stomach. Then I'm stepping out onto his floor, moving down the hall, passing an empty receptionist desk, potted plants, abandoned cubicles. The lights are off, everyone sent home for the day.

I'm disappointed, even when I knew it was unlikely he'd be here. Still, I can't seem to turn around.

I run down the hall and into his corner office.

Two glass walls provide a spectacular view of the city below. It glistens and sparkles in the rain. A third wall holds bookshelves, and the fourth—the one with the doorway I've just burst through—is home to a Southwestern-style tapestry that hangs behind chairs for clients. In front of the chairs is a glass coffee table with lines so modern, it looks like something out of a futuristic sci-fi movie, its corners razor-sharp. His gym duffel rests on the ground beside it. And a few paces beyond this table, sitting at a desk that faces the doorway, is my father.

Impossible. The feds said they checked here, and surely they wouldn't quit watching the building, but here he is, sitting at the computer, his hair disheveled and brow sweaty, clicking frantically at the mouse. "Eleanor," he says, barely looking up to greet me. "You shouldn't be here."

"*I* shouldn't be here?! What the fuck, Dad?"

"Language," he warns.

I storm to his desk, where I thrust my cell in his face. Kylie's text is still pulled up. "Is this true? Is it all true?"

He swallows, glances back at the computer.

"Jesus, Dad. What is wrong with you? How could you do this?!"

"Do *not* discipline me like you're the parent."

"Oh, yeah, 'cus you've always been so good at that role. So active and involved and—" I pause, catching sight of his computer screen. A progress bar ticks steadily to the right. As it grows, a number—*files*, it says—becomes smaller. I notice the wastebasket, filled with external hard drives, smashed and shattered. I spot a hammer on his desk.

"Are you destroying evidence?"

"No." He says it with the type of confidence only a man who's gotten away with everything could. It's an obvious lie, but he speaks it like fact. He expects me to buy it.

"Yes, you are. I can see the broken hard drives." I wave a hand at the garbage. "I can see the files getting deleted right now." I lean in, grappling for the mouse.

"Eleanor!" he warns.

I claw the device from his fingers, gain control. "Eleanor, stop it!"

His fingers are digging into my opposite arm, but I have the cursor over the *cancel* button now.

"I said *stop!*"

He yanks, hard, and I'm thrown backward—away from the computer, away from the desk, toward the coffee table with its ice-pick edges. I stagger, try to keep my footing, but gravity takes me. As I fall, I see only the

277

ceiling and an explosion of white. Pain floods through my body, then becomes sharp at the side of my head.

"Oh, God," he says. He's standing over me, looking down. "Eleanor, are you okay? El, say something."

I try, but I can't seem to figure out how to use my mouth. Darkness creeps in from the corner of my vision. Wetness trickles down over my ear, my neck, into my lashes.

He's kneeling beside me now, lip trembling. "Oh my God." He looks around the room. "I'm fucked. It's all over now."

Darkness overtakes me.

———

I gasp, coming back to myself. He's fleeing down the stairs, the clomp of his shoes echoing through Windsor.

I went to confront him.

He pushed me away from the computer.

I hit my head and then . . . He cleaned the office and wrapped my body in the tapestry from the wall and fled that night. Viv saw him as he passed through Glens Falls. He made it here, to Corwin Lake, where he buried me in a shallow grave. He isn't being held here; he's lying low. I sensed him the very first night I came here—that crack of twigs in the woods as our group snuck into the estate. Viv and I even heard him when we returned for her phone. We thought it was Avery Jane moving through the house, but it was him. Slinking. Hiding. Waiting. For what, I don't know. But I was wrong about how it happened. I did get in the way—*his* way. *He* did it.

My jaw tightens.

Ice spreads over my limbs.

I exhale hard and descend straight through the floor and into the sitting room, cutting off his escape.

"Fuck!" he yelps, skidding to a stop before me.

"I remember now," I tell him. "I remember everything."

He glances right, then left. It's a long way down the stairs and out the basement French doors. It's not quite as long through the ballroom and out the boarded-up front of Windsor Camp, but he'd have to go through me to get there, and I'm ready this time. Ready to be solid if I need to. Ready to melt into vapor if it benefits me best.

"Do you know Mom was waiting for you when I left? Standing there at the window, hoping you'd come home."

He looks at his feet. His limbs are shaking.

"You couldn't just ruin all your investor's lives, you also had to steal mine and ruin hers, too."

He refuses to make eye contact.

"LOOK AT ME!" I scream, and the room shudders in response. The windows rattle. The mirror flexes. The items atop the mantel jitter like an earthquake has struck.

He raises his face slowly, eyes coming up to meet mine. He is nothing like how I remember. I'm not a nuisance to him anymore, a thing he has to placate and entertain before getting back to his real life. I'm something he can't bear to witness. He is terrified of me.

We give power to the things we fear.

I catch myself in the mirror on the wall behind him. I look the way I did when it happened, and somehow, I know he sees this version of me too. Not just in the mirrored glass, but standing right before him. Blood covers half my face and mats my hair. A gash near my temple glistens with wetness, the flesh bright and soft.

"This isn't possible. This is . . ." He gasps, trembling. "What are you?"

"It's me, Dad. Nell. The daughter you always avoided, the ghost you know so well."

He's shaking his head like he still doesn't buy it. "Please. It was an accident. Just go away."

"I'm not going anywhere."

"W-what do you want?"

"What do you think I want?"

"Revenge? You want to kill me because I killed you?"

I actually laugh. It echoes through the house and comes bouncing back to me. I sound deranged and wild, like a ghost who indeed wants revenge. But even after everything, it's not that. I don't want revenge with my own hands. This isn't about blood and violence and two wrongs making a right. I almost wish it was. Because that would be easier.

What I want is a reason. What I want is his regret.

What I want is to know that he loved me, even just a little, after everything.

"Were you sorry?" I hear myself asking. "When it happened, did you think about how much you loved me and how terrible it was, or did you just immediately start planning how to save your own ass?"

He opens his mouth, closes it. "El, you don't understand."

I have always hated that nickname. No one ever called me it but him, and perhaps that's why it sounds like rot and decay coming from his mouth.

"It's complicated," he goes on.

"It shouldn't be! It's not a hard question."

"You don't know what it's like. To be in my shoes, to—"

"Most people don't know what it's like, Dad. Because most people are decent. Most people aren't even a fraction as awful as you. Do you get that?"

He scoffs lightly, even smiles a little. I've made a mistake. My only edge was his fear of me and my veneer is cracking. He's seeing the hurt child now. My confusion and anger make me vulnerable. They make me weak.

I can feel that horrific vision of me—the blood and the gash—fading. I am back to just Nell. A small, scared girl. That's all he sees.

"I'm leaving here soon," he says. "It was just a matter of time, of gathering the right documents."

Identification documents. So he can slip away as a new person, let Duncan Bradley die, leave this inconvenient nightmare he created behind.

"They haven't been delivered yet. Because of you. He said you put everything at risk and we needed to clean things up first."

"Who did?"

Dad scoffs to himself, ignoring my question. "I thought he was kidding. I didn't believe him when he said he'd seen you."

And suddenly it clicks.

I thought it was a joke, a trick. That's what Dad had said when I first entered the bedroom. I'd thought he was talking about my text to him, from my phone, but he was talking about someone else. A friend who's been helping him since the scandal broke.

The stakeout at Bradley House, the interrogations, the purchase of this property. It was all a cover, a way to buy Dad time. To buy them both time.

A flashlight clicks on and there he is, stepping from a shadowy corner and into view. Agent Cormac Donovan.

I told you to stop playing detective," he snarls.

"Easy, Mac," my father says. I follow his gaze and see the gun in Donovan's hand.

"What? Like I can actually hurt her?" he throws back. "No, you already took care of that."

"I didn't take care of anything. It was an accident!"

"An accident that's fucked everything. I'm not going down with you, Duncan. This was perfectly clean until it somehow turned into a paranormal horror movie."

"It wouldn't have turned into anything if you'd just let me turn myself in when it happened. This was your idea—covering it up, getting rid of the body, coming north until you could get me new papers. Papers that you're now holding hostage because of . . . *this*." He waves a hand at me.

"You were there?" I say dumbly, staring at Donovan. It

still doesn't add up. He's helping Dad—he's *been* helping him—but why?

"Of course I was there. Who do you think told the lobby security guard to take a break? Who do you think cleared out the office so we could trash the evidence? Who do you think wiped down the damn room and got rid of the coffee table? And even after all that, you're *still* jeopardizing everything!"

He fires his weapon. The bullet rips through me, in my chest and out the back. There must not be iron in the bullet because there's no real pain, only a brief slice of coldness. In that instant, the colors burst before my eyes again.

I'm on the floor of dad's office, the pain in my head now unbearable. My vision is tunneling, but there's something there in the corner. Another figure. Shadowy. Unfocused. Stepping nearer.

"You're not fucked," the figure says. "We'll get rid of her."

"Get rid off—?! Mac. I-I . . . I can't do this. This is El. Maybe if we call an ambulance she'll be okay. She has a pulse still. She—"

Donovan strikes him across the face. "I trusted you, Duncan. I covered for you. I had eyes looking elsewhere for months, even when you started to get sloppy. And now you've gone and gotten yourself caught, and it's going to come out that I helped you."

Dad's crying now. I can feel his hand on my shoulder.

He's begging me to hang on. He's telling me it will be all right.

Donovan yanks him to his feet. "I can make this all go away. I can clean it up so that when it's over, you're a new person, living in a new country, and no one knows about our involvement. I'll wire you half the money when it's over."

El, he's saying. I feel wetness on my face. I'm not sure if it's my own blood or his tears or both. Everything hurts. Everything is blurry too, like I'm looking through a fogged window. *El, please hang on.* My vision swims.

"Duncan, she's gone. Do you want me to clean this up, or do you want us to both rot in prison for the rest of our lives?"

Dad must answer because Donovan says, "Okay. Good. Here's what you do." Something rough and scratchy comes down over me. The Southwestern tapestry from the wall. This close to my face, I can make out the detailed pattern even though my vision is failing. "My car is parked on the corner. Drive to Albany and leave it at the bus stop. Wear the spare clothes in my trunk, keep a hat on, and hitchhike north, to the lake." I'm jostled, lifted. I've moved beyond pain now to coldness. It's everywhere, spreading down my limbs, threatening to drown me. I feel stiff, brittle. I can't move, but they move me. "Go to Windsor Camp. Bury her there. I'll retrieve my car tomorrow and meet you at the estate."

"But how will—"

"I'll get myself put on the case. Stake out your

summer home or something. Can you do this, Duncan? Can you do this exactly as I said?"

Dad's response is emotionless, numb. "Yes."

"Good."

There's the sound of a zipper—Dad's duffel closing—and my world becomes darkness.

———

The bullet lodges in the wall behind me.

I stare at Cormac Donovan, fury threatening to overtake me.

"What is that?" Dad murmurs. "Do you feel that?"

The entire house thrums with energy—my energy, I realize. Dust flutters down from the ceiling. Frames and mirrors and crucifixes rattle on the walls. Plates and china chatter on the shelves.

Did you lose a lot? I'd asked him.

Practically everything.

I'd thought he'd meant his life savings. That Dad had stolen all his money like every other client. But he'd meant his life. His reputation. He's freedom.

He'd been in on it from the beginning. Dad's partner. The mastermind. The soulless monster who wrapped a still-alive girl in a blanket, stuffed her in a duffel bag, and ordered her buried in a shallow grave.

"I might have lived," I hear myself say. My voice sounds strange, distorted. Like it's happening at two different pitches. I sound like a person possessed.

"No," Donovan replies bluntly. "You'd have been dead by the time an ambulance arrived and then we'd both have been in cuffs." He glances toward Dad, who has his face buried in his hands. I think he's crying again.

No wonder he looks like shit. He'd wanted better for me. If Donovan hadn't been present, this all might have ended differently. Instead, it unfolded as Donovan had orchestrated. Dad came north. Donovan "staked out" Bradley House. He bought Windsor Camp through his wife's company. He kept the local cops looking the other way when Viv and I found my body and he updated Dad every step of the way. "She doesn't know anything," he'd said in that phone call from the Performing Arts Building. I'd thought he was updating a colleague and at one point, maybe his wife. More likely, he was calling Viv's phone to reach Dad, leaving a voicemail assuring him that I didn't remember what had happened to me, that they were still in the clear as long as they could figure out how to get rid of a ghost.

"Did you send the text?" I glare at Donovan. "Did you lure me here?"

"No. Your dad sent that. I only learned about it later, so I put the salt lines out. I didn't want you distracting him. He nearly threw everything away for you that afternoon in his office. I was worried your ghost would dredge up those same feelings of duty and responsibility."

Something flickers in my chest, a small spark of pride and relief that maybe, somewhere, deep down, he really did—does—love me. That the father in him is bigger than the monster. Maybe. Just maybe.

"Little good that salt did me." Donovan tilts his head to the side. "How long have you been able to move through walls?"

"It's a recent development."

"Maybe it means you're passing on. You've learned what happened to you. Maybe you can make peace with it now and stop haunting us, let us get on with our lives."

"You killed me."

"No, Daddy dearest did that."

"I'm so sorry, El. Really. It was an accident." He's blubbering, his cheeks covered in tears, his hands clenched over his heart. "I wanted to call an ambulance. I've replayed it in my head every day since it happened. I can't sleep. I hate myself. I'm sorry. I'm so sorry."

He looks so pathetic, so broken, that I have to glance away. "He hurt me, but you murdered me," I say to Donovan. "You sealed my fate."

"You were already dying. I did nothing that wasn't going to happen on its own. Now tell me, Eleanor. What can we do to put this behind us? How do we strike a deal so everyone can get on with living?"

"Living?!" I roar. "*Living*? I'm a ghost! I'm dead because of *you*. If you think I'm going to work with you, cooperate somehow, you are out of your mind!"

He sighs loudly. As though I'm being dramatic. "I really hoped it wouldn't come to this. I feel a little bad, truly. It would be easier if you'd just pass on. But now I have to keep you here."

"Keep me?"

He walks toward the fireplace, where he picks up a wrought-iron poker. He points it at me, smirking down the length of it as though it's a sword.

"This place has always been rumored to be haunted. I think it's high time I gave it a proper ghost."

I know what's coming before he moves. He's going to skewer me with the poker, anchor me to a wall or floor, trap me here for eternity on an iron pike.

But before I can move, before he even begins to strike, there's a loud creak in the doorway. We all turn in unison.

It's Viv, holding Arlo's phone in her outstretched hand, filming the entire altercation.

CHAPTER
THIRTY-EIGHT

She tucks the phone behind her back, but everyone has seen. The tension in the room shifts. Donovan lowers the poker but raises his gun.

"What are you doing here?" I hiss at Viv.

"I followed you. I waited at the beach but then I heard a gunshot. I came to check on you." Her eyes are wide with urgency. "Quite the conversation I walked into."

"I recognize you," Dad says slowly. "You were with that group of kids that came snooping one weekend. And then you were back the following night, too. I saw you with El, but I thought I was imagining her, that my brain was torturing me."

"And yet you didn't see them the night they dug up the grave, did you?" Donovan growls, turning on his partner.

"No, I didn't." But Dad's throat bobs as he swallows the lie. His eyes slide to me and there's something mournful there. Regret. He saw us that night. He let us dig, almost as though he wanted my body to be found.

"Eleanor. You have to believe me. It was an accident. You're my girl, my only child." He chokes down another sob. "I'm so sorry."

It's sincere. I've watched him lie and avoid and mislead enough times to know that what he's saying tonight is honest. It doesn't make me hate him any less, but it confirms what I suspected. He just wanted it to be over. He wanted my body to be found and for the truth to come out. He wanted some semblance of justice, even if it meant being punished for his crimes.

He just hadn't anticipated Donovan covering things up yet again. Or on me being a ghost.

He could have left, turned himself in, but then my text came through and he realized the ghost he'd seen those nights was real. That he might be able to see me again, attempt to apologize. He stayed for that reason.

And I came to him, walking right into Donovan's trap.

"Come on, Nell," Viv says now, motioning for me. "It's time to go."

"Oh, I don't think so," Donovan says. The poker lays forgotten at his feet. It's no longer his weapon of choice, because I am no longer the worst threat in the house. His gun is aimed keenly at Viv. "You're not going anywhere."

Dad says, "Put the gun down, Mac."

"You're the one who IDed Mr. Bradley in Glens Falls," Donovan continues. "Recognized his duffel. Called in the tip."

Viv doesn't deny it.

The air in the house has shifted. The mugginess of the damp evening seems to have vanished, replaced with something tangy and sharp. We are toeing the edge of a ravine and I cannot see the bottom.

"Toss that phone over," Donovan says.

She holds it closer to her chest.

Donovan cocks the weapon. "Toss the phone over or you're dead in three, two—"

Viv obeys. Donovan kicks the cell toward my father. "Destroy that." Dad hesitates for a beat too long, and Donovan brings his own boot down on it, crushing it beneath his heel.

"All right. It's broken. We're going now." I move to join Viv.

"No one is going anywhere."

"I don't know anything," Viv says quickly. "I have no clue what happened between you three and I didn't hear anything as I came in."

"Like I believe you'll stick to that story once you get back to camp." Donovan trains the gun on her. "I've come too far—covered my tracks too well—for it to fall apart now."

"Mac," Dad says helplessly.

"Turn around," he orders Viv. "Face the wall."

She complies, her eyes finding mine just briefly as she turns.

"Mac, I mean it. She's just a kid."

"We already killed one." He presses the barrel to the back of her head. "What's one more?"

I think, *there is no way he'll go through with it*, even when I know he will. He's already covered up my death, hidden the facts, aided my father in robbing hundreds of their retirement. He will rot in prison for the rest of his life if it gets out and that is motivation enough for him to do whatever is necessary to avoid that outcome.

"Nell?" Viv says shakily.

His finger reaches for the trigger.

And I dive. Barreling into him as the gun fires, knocking his arm just enough to alter the shot. The bullet lodges into the wall. "Run!"

"Don't let her leave!" Donovan shouts.

Even after everything, Dad must block the exist, because I hear Viv's feet disappear deeper into the house, pounding up the stairs.

I try to keep Donovan pinned in place, but he's solid, heavy. He grunts beneath me. Something cold and sharp slices across my neck. He's got a knife, pulled from a pocket or boot. The blade must have just enough iron in it for me to feel it.

But it's not enough to slow me.

I grab his head, lift it toward me, slam it into the floor. He howls, screams for help. Something grabs my hair—

Dad—and pulls me back. Donovan staggers to his feet, runs for the wall. I lunge after him, breaking free.

Donovan thrusts a silver object in my direction, brandishing it like a shield. A crucifix, pulled from the wall. Now right-side-up, my eyes burn. I clutch at my face, shrieking.

He sprints through the living room, then up the stairs, chasing after Viv and growling like an animal.

I blink away tears, my eyes still stinging. Dad's just standing there, shell-shocked, eyes rooted on me. The crucifix and gun are gone, but Donovan left the knife. I stoop and pick it up, careful to only touch the plastic handle.

"Agent Donovan?" I call out in a singsong voice as I head for the stairs. His footsteps lurch to a pause. "I know you're up there." Another few steps, moving down the hallway.

I pinpoint his position as best I can and then rush up the stairs like a gale of wind. My feet barely touch the steps. I'm carried by a force larger than myself—by a lifetime of anger, betrayal, the pain of all the things I've lost and will never become.

I corner him in the hall. He holds the crucifix out, but I know how it affects me now. I avert my eyes, focusing on his feet. He curses and throws it aside, brandishing a baseball bat. I don't know where he got it and I don't have the time to guess. I dive at him with the knife. He swings.

His weapon connects with me as a solid force. Pain

explodes through my body. I land on my back and, for a moment, I can't breathe. He steps over me and I realize it's not a bat at all. It's the wrought-iron poker from downstairs. He looks down on me like I'm a bug, an infestation he needs to squash. He raises the poker overhead.

"Mac, no!" Dad yells.

He's racing up the stairs, eyes wide, and his arrival distracts me. I don't have time to sink through the floor, to vanish. Donovan brings the poker down, straight through my middle and into the floor, anchoring me there like a body on a pike.

Icy heat courses through me. I'm on fire.

I'm making a noise that doesn't sound human.

Donovan smiles down on me. "Enjoy haunting Windsor," he sneers. The he draws the gun from his holster and disappears down the hall, after Viv.

I scream on the floorboards. Writhe. I grab the poker with both hands and try to lift it free. My hands smoke like they're burning. I let go, panting, tears streaming down my face.

I'm dead already.

How can I feel more pain?

The poker lurches upright and I gasp. For a moment, I think I've propelled it from my body, but then my father bends over me and offers me a hand. He's pulled the poker free. He helps me up, puts a finger to his lips to signal silence, and slinks after Donovan.

I dart after him.

"Please," I can hear Viv begging. She's in what used to be Avery Jane's room, the room my father has been hiding in. "Please, don't."

I enter in time to see her cowering on the floor, scrambling backward like a crab, toward the window, Donovan advancing on her with the gun aimed and Dad running after Donovan with the poker raised.

Dad swings. The poker connects with Donovan's back and the gun goes off. Viv shrieks, a mangled sound that gets lost in Donovan's roar. He turns and, without hesitation, fires a bullet into my father's chest.

It happens so quickly. The noise. The way Dad falls, striking his head on the doorframe and then slumping to the floor at my feet. His eyes lock on mine. "I'm sorry," he grunts out.

"I know," I say, and in that moment, I believe him.

He smiles. And then another gunshot splits the night.

"I should have done this weeks ago, when things first went sideways," Donovan snarls. He puts a third bullet in him for good measure.

Dad's head lolls to the side and the light leaves his eyes.

I keep staring at the body.

For the smallest moment, the world fades away. It's just me and Dad, his vacant eyes looking through me, and everything we fought about seems distant and small. I'd wished him out of my life a hundred times earlier the summer, when the scandal first broke. I wanted him gone, but now it feels wrong. Not like this. Not at Donovan's hands.

"You want something done right," Donovan grumbles, "you have to do it yourself."

He turns on Viv.

She's whimpering, her breathing labored.

I look at the poker beside Dad's body, the dark shape of it.

We give power to the things we fear.

I can still feel its touch, the way it burned me from the inside out. Did I give it this power, simply by fearing it? I don't want to fear anymore. Not objects or answers or even the monsters that walk among us.

I have nothing to lose—quite literally. Donovan's taken it all, and he won't take it from Viv, too.

I grab the poker and shove to my feet. My body responds to the iron in a distant way. It's uncomfortable to hold, but not painful. Annoying, more than anything, like an itch you can't scratch.

I swing the poker as my father did, striking Donovan in the back. He falls to his knees, cursing. Then turns the gun on me and fires.

The bullet does nothing.

No flashbacks.

No forgotten memories.

I strike with the poker again, this time bringing it down on his forearm. The bone snaps audibly and he roars, dropping the gun to cradle his mangled arm to his chest. His eyes skirt for the door—an escape. I jerk my head and the door blows shut with the motion, slamming. Dust motes rain from the ceiling. He fumbles blindly for the gun, as if it can stop me now, as if anything can. I kick it beneath the dresser. He grabs the nearest thing he can find—the can of beans Dad had been eating earlier—and throws it at me.

I let out a scream—part growl, part fury—and the mirror above the dresser shatters. The windowpane shatters too. Shards fly, zipping across the room is if on an invisible wire. They slice at his arm and back. He ducks his head to protect from the glass.

When the shards plink and chime to a standstill, he puts his hand to the floor, pushes upright, until he's half standing with his good arm braced against this thigh, the broken one dangling uselessly by his knee. His expression is wild—like a cornered animal, ready to claw and spit and bite to break free. Feral. Rabid. Terrified. His steely eyes glow like embers.

He pants, teeth bared. "You bi—"

I swing the poker, striking the side of his head. Blood sprays from his mouth. He staggers backward, arms pinwheeling, legs tangling with Viv, who still lays hunched beneath the lone window, now broken and open to the night. Donovan's hip hits the ledge and time seems to slow. I can pinpoint the exact moment that gravity will take him.

I blink and I've crossed the room, grabbed a fistful of his shirt in my hand. He lurches to a standstill, torso completely out the window, toes barely grazing the floor. He weighs nothing to me. He *is* nothing.

"Thank you," he gasps out.

"For what?"

Panic flickers across his face. "You wouldn't."

"You know, I think I might. After all, you were the one who said I should quit playing detective."

"No, please. Eleanor, we can talk about this. We can—"

I let him fall.

CHAPTER
THIRTY-NINE

His scream seems to echo long after the earth accepts him, after he stops moving, after I've ducked back inside and knelt beside Viv.

"Let's go," I say, offering her an arm.

But her head lolls against the wall as she tries to look up at me.

"Viv?"

That's when I see it. Her shirt is dark and wet, blood having soaked through. I bend closer, trying to find the bullet wound. It's somewhere near her shoulder, but it's too dark to see properly and there's far too much blood.

"Did you tell anyone you were coming here?"

"Arlo," she manages through shallow breathes.

Of course. She'd been recording on his phone.

Phone.

I whirl and drop to my knees beside Dad's body,

rifling through his pockets until I find Viv's phone—the one Dad had been using this summer. It has no service.

"Shit," I mutter. *Shit, shit, shit.*

But Dad had received my text on this phone. And he'd sent me a response. How could he have done that if there's never service anywhere on this lake—

I shoot to my feet.

"Don't . . ." Viv manages, sensing my intentions. "Don't leave." She reaches one hand for me, fingers curling. But I can't stay. Every moment is precious.

"I'm going to get you help," I tell her. "Hang in there. Just a few more minutes."

And then I'm sinking through the floor, dropping like an anchor, her phone still clutched in my fist. In the basement, I run for the boarded-up French doors, blowing through them in a gust of wind. I pause only once, to look at Donovan. His body lays still, limbs bent at wrong angles, his head is turned away from me, toward the graveyard where he unearthed my body, flung it into a wheelbarrow, and relocated me to a watery grave.

The trees blur as I race down the path. My feet fly through roots and rocks. I cannot be tripped. I cannot be slowed. I wonder, distantly, if I might be flying.

On the boys' beach, I race down one of the docks. Arlo is at the end, pacing.

His eyes go wide when he sees me. "What happened? I heard gunshots."

I hold the phone out an arm's length away. The screen

illuminates, a square of light in the dark. The battery is almost dead. There's still no signal.

"Nell, what happened?"

This is where everyone said there was service, that something about the boys' beach and the angle of the surrounding mountains and hillsides allowed for it. I turn in circles, desperate, praying. And then—

A single bar.

I make the call, fingers trembling.

"Nine-one-one," the operator says. "What's your emergency?"

"My friend's been shot. At the old Windsor Camp on Corwin Lake."

"Nine-one-one," the woman repeats. "What's your emergency?"

"My friend has been shot!" I shout.

"Hello? Is anyone there?"

"Yes. I'm here. We need an ambulance."

"Hello?"

She can't hear me. Something is wrong with the service. It's too weak.

"Nine-one-one," the woman repeats yet again. "Do you have an emergency?"

Arlo lifts the phone from my hand. "Hello. Can you hear us?"

"Yes, I can hear you. Go ahead."

I tell him what to say, practically tripping over my words. He repeats it all into the phone.

"My friend's been shot by Cormac Donovan at

Windsor Camp on Corwin Lake," he tells the operator. "Donovan also killed Duncan Bradley and his daughter, Eleanor. Her body is anchored to a buoy off the shore of the property. Duncan's is in an upstairs bedroom. That's where my friend is now."

There's a brief pause. He gives Viv's name, age, my best guess at the location of her bullet wound. "A unit and ambulance is en-route," the woman says. "Are you at the house as well?"

"No, I'm at Camp Durant for Boys. On one of their docks along the shore. It's a short walk from the estate."

"Are you injured?"

"No."

"Okay. Please stay on the line with me until an officer arrives."

"Sure, of course." He turns around. "Nell?"

"Yeah?"

But he looks right through me, then spins, searching. "Nell, where'd you go?"

"I'm right here." I grab his arm and suddenly his eyes lock with mine.

"Shit, that scared me."

"What?"

"You were gone for a sec. I couldn't see you."

My stomach knots. There wasn't a service issue with the phone. The woman couldn't hear me because this is the beginning of the end. She couldn't hear my voice. And now Arlo couldn't see me for a moment. I'm coming undone.

In the distance, sirens disrupt the quiet. They're mangled and distorted by the time they reach our ears, a warbled bird song. They get fainter. It will be a few minutes before they grow louder again. The road around the lake is curved and winding.

I glance at the footpath that leads into the woods, back to Viv.

"I have to go," I say. "I have to be with Viv, make sure she's okay."

He frowns, lowers the phone from his ear. "Will I see you again? Or will you . . . ?" His eyes search mine.

"I don't know. I wish I could give you an answer, but I've never done this before." It's an attempt at humor, but he doesn't smile.

"I hope I see you again. But I also hope you get whatever you need, even if that means leaving. Does that make sense?"

"So much. And thank you, Arlo."

I tell him what to say when the cops arrive, a story that will make sense and explain his presence here tonight. I'll give Viv the same instructions—*if* I get back to her in time.

I turn toward the dirt path and Arlo grabs my arm, tugging gently to bring my body against his. His lips brush mine. Just once. Soft. Already filled with longing.

It's a parting kiss. I think we both know this is the end of us—of me.

"I don't mind if you haunt me," he whispers.

I smile against his mouth. "I have to go now."

"I know."

I back away, noticing how his eyes don't properly track me. "Goodbye, Arlo."

He jerks toward my voice, looks at me, though I know he's only staring at an empty patch of air. "Bye, Nell."

I run, faster than before, as though I've grown lighter now that eyes can't find me.

I'm halfway up the footpath when I hear cruisers approaching. Red and blue lights flash through the trees, casting Windsor the shade of blood and bruises.

CHAPTER
FORTY

slink toward the driveway.

An ambulance is parked there, its back doors open. A cruiser, lights flashing but siren now silenced, waits beside it. I can hear the rattle of a stretcher being opened inside the house. Shouts to check for a pulse.

"Found Donovan!" someone yells from the back of the house. "You locate the girl's body yet?"

"No." The voice belongs to Ashmore. "The diver is suiting up."

While everyone is preoccupied, I duck into the ambulance and wait. A few moments later, medics pile in, loading the stretcher, and closing the doors behind them. They don't so much as blink at my presence. Viv is on the stretcher between them, her brow caked in sweat, her skin far too pale.

I reach for her hand, give her fingers a quick squeeze.

She starts, jerking against her restraints, eyes flying open to find me. "Nell?"

She can see me. The ambulance begins to move, bouncing down the unpaved dirt driveway.

"Shh," I say, putting a finger to my lips. I don't want to draw attention to my presence. But the medics don't seem able to see or hear me. It must be because of my history with Viv. Or perhaps because she is so near to death herself.

"Nell!" she grapples for me, hand flailing.

"Her blood pressure is dropping," one of the medics warns. "Is that IV in yet?"

"Working on it."

The vehicle rocks as we turn onto the main road.

"Hang in there, sweetie," the first medic says. "You're gonna be okay."

Viv's head jostles back and forth from the sway of the ambulance, but she keeps her eyes rooted on me. "Nell," she murmurs a final time, and then passes out.

————

I don't leave her side. Not when they wheel her into the hospital. Not when they fish out the bullet or give her a blood transfusion or stitch up the wound. Not even when they move her to a room to recover at three in the morning.

The cops and feds are in the hall, arguing with the doctors about when they can talk to Viv, when her door bursts open and a middle-aged woman with a dark bob and Viv's eyes rushes the bed.

"Vivian. Oh God, Viv." She bursts into tears and gathers Viv's hands in hers, kissing the back of her knuckles, sobbing.

Poor Viv startles out of her sleep. "I'm okay, Mom. I'm fine," she says groggily.

"What happened? I mean, they told me some. But Duncan Bradley? And an FBI agent? How . . . Why?" She clutches a tissue to her chest and looks at her daughter. "Actually, you don't have to explain anything right now. I'll . . . I'm going to . . . Oh God, I'm so glad you're okay."

"I'm fine, really." Viv pats the back of her mom's hand in a parental sort of way. I can make out the shape of the IV inserted above her knuckles. "You look tired, Mom. You should go get a coffee or something."

Her mom shakes her head aggressively. "No, no. I couldn't leave you."

"I'm not going anywhere. I'm too exhausted to even stand. Go get a coffee and then we can talk."

The woman licks her lips, swallows. "Okay. A coffee. But then I'm coming right back and not leaving your side for the next fifty years."

"Oh, joy," Viv teases.

Her mother rises from the chair, looking back multiple times before she slips into the hall. Viv turns toward the window and finds me standing there. She's not on death's doorstep anymore, but she can still see me.

It should make me happy, but instead I feel a tinge of

sadness. I want her to *keep* seeing me. I don't want to disappear even though I need to.

Wants and needs are quite different, I realize. I smile to myself. I've gotten quite philosophical on the threshold of the afterlife.

"You're a little fuzzy," Viv says by way of greeting. "Your edges are glowing."

I can't see it myself, but it doesn't surprise me. My eyes drift to her freshly bandaged shoulder. "Does it hurt?"

"Can't feel anything right now, but it will probably be brutal once the drugs wear off." She worries a thumb against her opposite palm. "Where'd you go? When you left Windsor?"

"The boys' beach. There's a bit of service there, remember? Arlo helped me make the nine-one-one call using your phone."

"Helped?"

I tell her how the operator couldn't hear me. How I disappeared for Arlo and then rode in the ambulance invisible to the medics. "It's almost over now. I can feel it."

"Well, what are you doing wasting your last few minutes at a hospital?"

"I had to make sure you'd be okay. And also, your story needs to match Arlo's." I sit on the edge of her bed. "They're going to have questions. About why you guys were there. About what happened. Here's what you need to say."

The story isn't complicated. It's simple, very close to the truth, and doesn't exonerate my friends from trespassing on private property, and that's why I think it will work. I tell her everything I told Arlo, everything she should repeat when the feds come questioning.

That they saw me sneaking from camp and they followed in their own boat. That they trailed me to the house, where they discovered a confrontation between me, Agent Donovan, and my father. Arlo got the confession on video—but Donovan caught them and destroyed the cell phone.

Donovan wouldn't let them leave, not once they knew the truth. A fight broke out. Viv was shot. Donovan killed my father. Arlo managed to get hold of a poker, which he used to strike Donovan, causing him to fall through the window.

Arlo then retrieved Viv's phone from my father's pant pocket—the very phone my dad had been holding since Viv misplaced it earlier in the summer. Arlo ran to the beach and called for help.

That's it.

"It's not perfect," I admit. "You'll still probably get in trouble for leaving camp and sneaking onto private property. But it gets the right info out. And if they check your phone records, they'll see any calls or texts my dad made. It makes things right."

"It gives Arlo all the credit for everything you did."

I roll my eyes. "It's not about credit."

"But what about how *you* fit into this story? We

followed you to the beach? We saw you confronting your dad and Donovan. And then what—you just disappeared?"

"Yep. I got my closure."

Viv frowns a moment. "You think they'll believe that?"

"Once Ashmore pulls my body from the lake, they'll have to. There are dozens of people who saw me at camp this summer. Goodwin, Dolores, you and Arlo, Jocelyn and Gretta, all the other staff and campers. It sounds impossible, but with that many witnesses, they'll have no choice but to accept it."

"I guess. And the text you sent your dad from your phone? How will we explain that?"

"No explaining necessary. I sent it. That's it."

"They're not going to buy this."

"They might. Donovan and my dad are dead. I bet they'll just be happy to wrap the case and file it away."

The quiet hangs between us, interrupted only by the passing of nurses out in the halls. It's as if we are standing on the ridge of a towering cliff. Any minute now, the door will open and Viv's mom will return—or the authorities will spill in.

"How'd you have your phone this whole summer?" Viv asks. "If they killed you in the office building . . . and then the blanket and the duffel and that shallow grave . . ."

It's a piece of the puzzle I don't have a clear answer

for. There was no vision to explain it. But I have an idea of what happened.

Donovan said there was no footage of me leaving the city, and I don't think he was lying. I was in the duffel. Viv spotted me in Glens Falls without even realizing it; she recognized only Dad and his bag.

I remember hitchhiking to Bradley House that night. Part of this could be a shadow memory because Dad had hitchhiked his way north. But I think I hitchhiked the final way on my own, from Windsor Camp on one side of the lake to Bradley House on the other. I think my ghost stepped from that shallow grave, grabbed my phone and gear, and walked toward the road with my thumb out while Dad shoveled dirt over my corpse.

Why don't you give me your phone, Donovan had said that day in the Performing Arts Building. Not because he wanted to confirm my location but because he and Dad had realized my phone and backpack were missing. He was, yet again, looking to collect evidence and cover his tracks.

"You're leaving soon, aren't you?" Viv asks. Her voice cracks on the words.

"I think so."

"Are you scared?"

"Not really. Anxious is a better way to describe it. Unsettled."

"Not resting." She smiles sadly. "Not at peace."

"Yeah. Something like that."

She reaches for me, hooks one finger around my

pointer. "You were better than him always, Eleanor Bradley. You didn't deserve what happened to you."

"I know."

"Sure," she agrees. "But I still wanted to say it."

"Thanks."

"I'm gonna miss you," she adds.

"Yeah," I say, tears pooling in my eyes. "I'm gonna miss you, too."

———

I stay with her through the questioning and interrogation, the lawyers and the cops. She's groggy, tired, not fully there. I whisper reminders in her ear as she needs them, keeping the story straight so that it matches Arlo's. When the authorities finally leave, the sun is coming up. Viv falls into a deep slumber. Her mom dozes on the couch beside her.

I linger at the window a moment, watching morning light spill over the hospital's parking lot. I close my eyes. Wait.

But nothing takes me.

Not yet, I realize.

Not here.

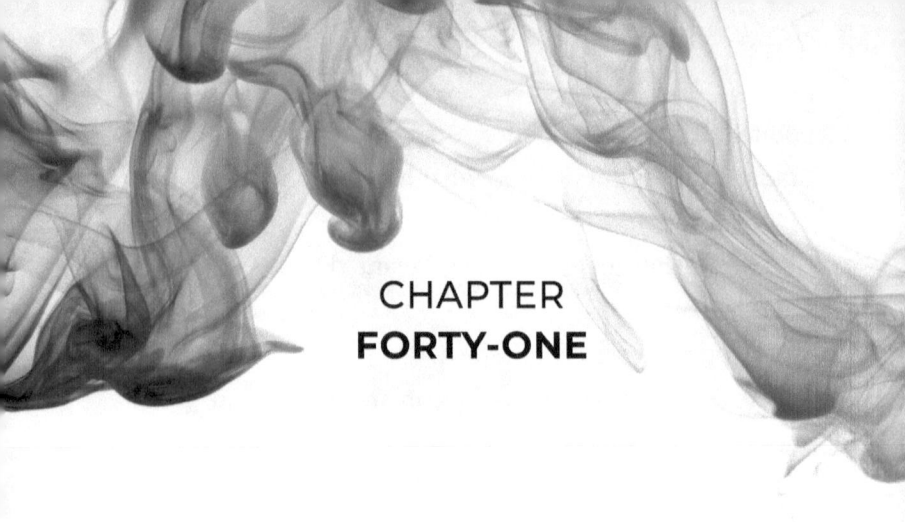

CHAPTER
FORTY-ONE

hurry from the room, tailing the officers until I find Ashmore in deep conversation with the feds. They instruct her to return to Camp Durant and update Goodwin on the state of things. She nods solemnly. This is my ride back.

I follow her to her cruiser, drift through a door, and settle into the passenger seat.

She doesn't notice me.

Her dispatch radio cackles—something about a domestic dispute in a nearby town—while her cell rings. She fastens her seatbelt and answers the call on speaker. "Ashmore."

"They've got the girl's body. What's left of it, at least. It's being transported now." It's Murkowski. "Autopsy should come later today, but even given the state of decay, early guess is it will match the teens' story. Looked like a nasty wound. She'd been dead for some time. Definitely several weeks."

"God, what a mess. That poor girl," Ashmore's eyes lift to her sun visor, where a 4x6 photo is pinned. It shows her in street clothes, an arm slung around a girl that appears to be maybe nine or ten. It could be her own daughter, a niece, a neighbor. The relationship doesn't matter. I know what she's thinking.

"What does this mean, Jenn?" Murkowski goes on. "When we interrogated her in Goodwin's office . . . was that not her?"

"It was her. Some version of her, at least."

"You believe in ghosts?"

"I didn't. Not until today."

A quiet holds between them for a moment. Murkowski breaks it first. "Also, the screen of Arlo's phone was badly cracked, but we're thinking we may still be able to get the video off it. Time will tell. And even if not, we've got enough here to wrap things up."

"Thanks. I'll be back soon. Gotta swing by the camp first and speak with Goodwin."

"Better use the rear entrance when you get back here," Murkowski warns. "The media is already arriving."

Ashmore sighs. "Okay. Talk soon." She ends the call.

She sits there for a while, just staring out the windshield. Finally she puts the car in drive.

We turn onto the camp road, passing beneath the *Camp Durant for Girls* archway for what I know will be my final time.

I expect to be struck by the unfairness of it all—my mother now a childless widow, friendships I just began to form cut short, my life and all the possibilities that may have stretched before me, slipping through my fingers like sand. But instead, I find myself grateful—for this extra time I was given. For the chance to unveil a truth, to save a friend, to make things as right as possible. Not everyone gets that opportunity.

The cruiser's tires crunch over the gravel path. When we stop in front of Goodwin's, I don't attempt to use the door. I know I won't be able to open it anymore. The mere thought of pulling the handle sounds exhausting. But I want Ashmore to know I'm here. I want to thank her for the ride.

I reach for the dispatch radio. When my hand nears it, it crackles and hisses. Ashmore stills, stares at it. I make it produce feedback again.

"Eleanor?" Ashmore looks at my seat, her eyes never quite finding me. I touch the rearview mirror, making light wink off the glass.

She gasps, then stares at the passenger seat. "I'm sorry I didn't believe you. I'm so sorry."

"It's okay. It's all right now."

She can't hear me, but she smiles slightly, and I feel like she understands, that the message was received.

"Will you tell my mom I love her? That I say bye?"

She moves to exit the car, then pauses, looks back in my general direction. "I'm going to call your mom," she announces. "Right from Goodwin's office. I want her to hear it from a person before she sees it on the news."

I make the rearview mirror wink again, communicating my thanks. Then I pass through the door and into the morning heat.

It's the first day of August. It's warm, sticky. I'm not cold for the first time in ages.

Ashmore steps onto Goodwin's stoop and knocks on the door. I turn around and look over the camp. The worn paths and the sentinel pines and the buildings that rest beneath them like faithful, slumbering pets. Coming up one of the paths and heading toward the mess hall, is Arlo.

He pauses when he spots Ashmore's cruiser, the toothpick pinched between his lips sagging slightly. His eyes don't find me, not even when I step into view around the side of the car.

I consider rushing to him, trying to touch him. Would he see me then? Would he feel my presence? But it will only make leaving harder, so I simply wave.

He senses it—something intangible. His lips spread into a smile. And he raises a hand in response, knowing I'm near even when he can't see me.

I wonder if he'll always feel me at this place, among these pines, beside the water.

I hope so.

It's a nice place to be remembered.

He starts walking, off toward the mess. And I walk too, in the opposite direction, down to the shore. For the very last time.

———

The lake is pristine in the morning—a plane of deep cerulean that stretches away from the eye, the trees on the opposite bank reaching toward the heavens while a reflected set extend back across the water. A mirror image. Two worlds colliding on an edge so thin, you almost can't discern where they meet.

I drift trancelike toward the water. I'm being called again, pulled by an invisible thread. The sand is cold and rough beneath my toes. I'm barefoot, I realize, though I don't remember taking off my shoes. I'm wearing clothes I never brought to camp—a plain white sundress.

The water grazes my toes and I gasp—not in shock, but surprise. It's warm. Like bathwater. I walk a little farther, water creeping over my shins, my knees, then soaking the hem of my dress. Ripples spread out around my legs, causing the fabric to dance. I'm reminded of the plastic bag I mistook for a dress several days ago. I feel it with overwhelming certainty: every oddity I encountered this summer—every tug that drew me toward the shore, the house, the *truth*—was my own doing. I was guiding myself, healing myself, showing myself the way.

As the water crests my waist, I look up toward Windsor. Its dark silhouette is a scar against the forest. I find the window, vacant and empty. If I willed it to illuminate, I almost think it might. But I don't care to try. The water is so warm, so pleasant, and the half of me not in it feels cold.

I take another step, a few more. My dress billows, gathering about my torso. I shove it down with my hands, but it's defiant. I dive headfirst into the water and swim until I tire. When I surface, I'm nearly in the middle of the lake, Windsor ahead of me, the camp behind.

I lay back, turn my face to the sun. I close my eyes.

It's dark behind my lids.

The water supports me. I am balancing on another edge, here on the surface of the lake—a space between realms. My body thrums with energy, but my mind is still.

We give power to the things we fear.

But I'm not afraid anymore, not even of the unknown.

I float until the breeze quiets, the sensation of water vanishes, the world itself dissolves.

I float until I'm lighter than air—nothing and everything at once.

And then . . .

Then . . .

I open my eyes to the light.

ACKNOWLEDGMENTS

I first started playing with the idea that would become *In the Dead of the Night* in 2012. It often got put on the back burner so that I could focus on other contracted projects, and I didn't finish a first draft until 2020, during the early months of the pandemic. Over the next few years, I revised, polished, and *finally* managed to bring the story to readers via serialization on my Substack in early 2024. Fast forward another few more months, and it's finally book-shaped at long last.

If you've read this far, I owe you a very special thanks. Yes, *you*. You are the most crucial ingredient. Without readers, a story is just words on a page.

This book had a unique-for-me road to publication (this is my first self-published full length novel!), and many friends and colleagues helped me get to this moment. In no particular order, many thanks to: Susan Dennard, Jodi Meadows, Sara Crowe, Michelle Wolfson, Erica Sussman, Jenn Rush, Beth Revis, Kyla Linde, Kayla Olson, Sara Raasch, Julie Dao, and Laura Bernier. I'm so grateful for your early reads, editorial feedback, copyediting, cheerleading, general support, and/or shared knowledge regarding indie publishing.

Additional thanks to the paying tier of my Substack: Subscribers Abby Murphy, Adam Silvera, Anna Leighton, Bill Blume, Caroline Fowler Davis, Chelcie, Cherokee Collier, Cheryl Binnie, Delaney, Elisa, Hannah Martian, Hannah Teachout, Jennifer Rush, Jessica Spotswood, JM Laine, Joanna DaCosta, Karyn M, Kate Leahy, Kate McGovern, Kathlene Brown, Lauren Fie, Leigh, Liz Griffin, Maisie, Mari Lancaster, Megan Gold, Mel, Morgan Adams, Nicole Mathew, Rachel Jenkins, Rebecca, Rebecca Obrock, Sarah Lamagna, Savannah Foley, Siobhan, Susan Dennard, Theresa, and Whitney Chewston. Your support made this project possible.

Last and certainly not least, all the love and thanks to my family. You guys are the best.

ALSO BY ERIN BOWMAN

THE TAKEN TRILOGY

Taken

Frozen

Forged

Stolen (companion e-novella)

WESTERNS

Vengeance Road

Retribution Rails

Kate & Jesse (companion novella)

THE CONTAGION DUOLOGY

Contagion

Immunity

STANDALONE NOVELS

The Girl and the Witch's Garden

Dustborn

Photo by Carey Hough

Erin Bowman is the critically acclaimed author of numerous books for children and teens, including the Taken Trilogy, *Vengeance Road*, *Retribution Rails*, the Edgar Award-nominated Contagion duology, *The Girl and the Witch's Garden*, and *Dustborn*. Her books have been published in numerous foreign territories. A web designer turned author, Erin has always been invested in telling stories—both visually and with words. Erin lives in New Hampshire with her husband and children.

Visit her online at embowman.com and subscribe to her newsletter for bookish news and updates.

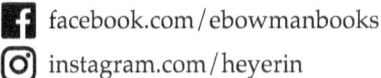

facebook.com/ebowmanbooks
instagram.com/heyerin